incommunicado

incommunicado

Randall Platt

Sky Pony Press
New York

Sky Pony Press books may be purchased in bulk at special discounts for sales promotion, corporate gifts, fund-raising, or educational purposes. Special editions can also be created to specifications. For details, contact the Special Sales Department, Sky Pony Press, 307 West 36th Street, 11th Floor, New York, NY 10018 or info@skyhorsepublishing.com.

Sky Pony® is a registered trademark of Skyhorse Publishing, Inc.®, a Delaware corporation.

Visit our website at www.skyponypress.com.

10 9 8 7 6 5 4 3 2 1

Library of Congress Cataloging-in-Publication Data is available on file.

ISBN: 978-1-62914-646-1
Ebook ISBN: 978-1-63220-210-9

Cover design by Rain Saukas
Cover photograph credit Thinkstock

Printed in the United States of America

For my agent, Andy Ross, who
never stopped believing
in this story.

incommunicado

CHAPTER 1

"Oh look! There's my dress!" Aggie squealed loud enough to be heard all the way to Astoria, let alone acrost our small school cafeteria. She snickered with some other girls and everyone looked at me as I made my miserable way to the farthest table.

I was nine and in the fourth grade when I finally figured out the true meaning of "enough is enough." So, it's not as though I wasn't ready for it. This girl, Aggie Steen, centerpiece of the sixth grade girls' table, had been saying "oh look, there's my dress!" all day—first on the walk to school, then in the girls' can, then echoing in the halls, and now in the cafeteria.

I set down my tray, went over to Aggie, and stood in front of her.

"I loved that dress," she cooed to her pals, "when I was in third grade!"

I stood my ground and stared at her, cool as I could be, and then I started to unbutton the dress. First the pasty-pearly type buttons at the lacy neck and going right down to the frayed belt at the waist, and then unzipping the sticky zipper. Well, things were getting pretty quiet at the Queen Bee table. In fact, by the time I stepped out of the dress, all eyes were on me, including Mrs. Adams's, the principal.

But, criminently, I had to do it!

"Here! You can have the dress back! It smells like a hog trough!" I wadded up the dress and tossed it on Aggie's hot lunch, the belt whapping her in the face.

Her milk spilled and she screamed and jumped up and called me something pretty awful. And there stands me, in my cheesy cotton slip, scarred, knobby knees, hairy legs, skinny arms and all.

I returned to my table, took my lunch, and walked toward Mrs. Adams. Even her face was blank, her eyes and mouth both wide open. It was quiet as death in the cafeteria.

"How many days?" I asked Mrs. Adams, getting it over with before she got her senses back.

"Three," she mumbled. "I'll send over your homework assignments."

But that day I learned two lessons, and they didn't have anything to do with homework assignments. Number one:

the only thing worst than being the poorest kid in town is being the poorest kid in the poorest town. Number two: never wear anything to school your mother buys at a church rummage sale. In a town like ours, someone's bound to recognize it.

That was in the fall of 1938, more than three years ago, and I can still hear the laughter after I left that cafeteria and walked down the hall to my classroom, where I grabbed my coat—also second-hand—and rode my bike home. I can still feel the sting of the rain on my steaming face.

I think the whole town of Sea Park, Oregon, population 542, is still laughing about it.

Today, I'm a twelve-year-old seventh grader stuck smack-dab between being that skinny, dress-less girl and a half-grown "lady-in-waitin.'" That's what my oh-so-Southern mother calls it. That's me—a lady-in-waitin'—and I don't even know what I'm waitin' for. Mom does, though. She also calls this change-over thing pooooo-berty. Yes, that's what she called it when I got the facts of life lecture—pooooo-berty. Sounds more like what you'd name a dang lap dog. Anyway, pooooo-berty and me are on a first-name basis. The curse, pimples, greasy hair, these bumpy chesty things and all. So far, twelve is a raw deal.

I fight it sometimes, this whole pooooo-berty thing. Sometimes I can't wait to grow up, and sometimes I just want to stay a kid. And that back and forth tug-of-war is kind of the reason I am where I am now—sitting in Sheriff

Hillary Dutton's office with my older brother, Rex, staring down at the complaint form.

• • •

"I don't care if you did it or not. I don't care if Martians landed and painted those lion statues' eyeballs. I don't care if Franklin Roosevelt and his dog Fala did it. You are now officially the one responsible," the sheriff says to Rex, pointing her cigarette lighter shaped like a tiny pistol at him.

You can tell she's said that line more than once. This is what it means: now, whenever anything goes wrong in Sea Park, no matter who does what, my brother, Rex Alan Stokes, will be blamed for it. Here's why: Sheriff Hillary Dutton picks a high school boy to officially take the blame for any prank or joke or vandalism the kids in town do. She calls the position Town Hood. She says since she's the only cop around, she just doesn't have time to deal with us kids and the stuff we do to kill the boredom or impress each other and the tourists. Just about every boy has to take a turn at being Town Hood.

Being Town Hood is sort of like being drafted, only you don't get a uniform, a gun, and a ticket out of town. Town Hood is half Public Enemy Number One and half town janitor. The Town Hood will make sure all the other kids toe the line so he doesn't take the rap for anything. I might be the only one, but I think it's a Badge of Honor, and I sure want to wear it. Being the first-ever girl Town

Hood has been my first-ever goal in life. I love being a first-ever—like I was the first-ever girl to take off her dress in a school cafeteria.

"Hey, I painted those lions' eyeballs crost-eyed! Make me Town Hood!" I pipe up.

The sheriff looks at me and says, "I guess you might have a crack at being our first girl Town Hood someday. But not today."

"What about Billy McCormick? Just last week he snuck into the Majestic Theater and lifted a box of Milk Duds," Rex says.

"How do you know?" she asks, lighting another cigarette and swishing away the smoke.

"I was standing right next to him when he did it."

"Well, as of now, it's your fault. You know how this works, Rex. As the T. H., you're officially to blame for any delinquent behavior. Make sure all the boys get wind of this. Some boys send around a memo," Sheriff Hillary says. "Jerry Adams even took out an ad in the Sea Park Sentinel."

Then she turns to me and says, "And you, missy. You of all people need to straighten up and fly right."

If I got two bits for every time someone has told me that, I could buy those stupid lion statues and paint them yellow with little pink polka dots.

"But this whole Town Hood thing is Draconian," Rex says. "About the most uncivilized thing I've ever heard of. And I'll bet it's unconstitutional. I know it's unethical! Even England did away with whipping boys centuries ago!"

That's Rex all over. I never understand half of what he says, like he swallowed a dictionary. But Rex can go on and on about his political opinions, which he has on everything, and pretty soon my own eyes go crost just like those lion statues.

"Get yourself a soap box and head over to the park, son," Sheriff Hillary says, shuffling some papers around on her desk.

"And," Rex goes on, "guilt by association is not guilt. It's association, and nothing more."

"What are you, a lawyer?" she asks, giving him a look of disgust.

"No, but I will be someday. And then I'm coming back here and suing everyone!" he barks.

"Fine. Until then, Clarence Darrow, you'll have to settle for Town Hood."

"Aw, come on, Sheriff Hillary. I'm too busy with my senior year to babysit all those other kids. Give a guy a break."

She makes like she's playing an invisible violin.

Rex points a finger at her and says, "You know what you are? You're an autocrat. No, a fascist! No, a dictator! That's what you are! A regular Hitler!"

She looks up at him and there's something kind of sad in her face. "No, son, I'm just a small-town cop filling in until her husband's hitch is up."

See, her husband, Sheriff Norm Dutton, joined the Navy over a year ago, the summer of 1940, and Hillary stepped in since his uniform fit her and she had a gun and knew how to use it and all. Temporary or not, she keeps a tight rule over the town, and I think this Town Hood thing is one reason why.

She tells us to get out and warns the new Town Hood to make sure I repaint the eyeballs of those two lion statues so they look normal and not like constipated clowns. I thought crossing the lions' eyeballs was funny, and heck, kids have done that every year since those stupid lions were put there. Same thing with that black jockey statue standing in front of Mayor Schmidtke's house. That poor iron jockey looks pretty darn confused standing where he is, on a pedestal in a town where the blackest person anyone has ever seen is leathery ol' Babs Bishop after a summer on the beach, soaked in her own personal concoction of baby oil and iodine. And the closest thing to a racehorse we have is an eighteen-year-old beach nag named Florence.

Look, you don't go putting up any statues in a town like Sea Park and not expect kids to express themselves with a little paint. Then again, if I hadn't been so bored and looking for a way to express myself and some ol' biddy Lioness butinski lady hadn't caught me red-handed, then my brother probably wouldn't suddenly be wearing the badge of Town Hood.

The badge I deserve.

CHAPTER 2

Now about Rex and me. Guess you could say we've pretty much been on our own for a long time. Fact is, I can't remember much about our father except just noise. Rex remembers more, being older. He remembers getting clobbered and yelled at and bullied. Rex told me one night these men in uniform came—cops, I guess—and all of a sudden, *poof!*, our old man just wasn't there anymore. Ever.

If Mom's had enough to drink and you really bug her about it, she'll let a few clues slip: that bum, what a rat, ruint us all, "I loved that jerk!" After a few years, I stopped asking about him, and I think we all just forgot there ever was a father, jerk or no.

Anyway, since we were "gettin' on" as Mom called it, we could do for ourselves. But since Rex is seventeen and I am twelve, that's twenty-nine years betwixt us and yes, we can pretty much do for ourselves.

When Mom is out to sea cooking or on a binge, me and Rex work to keep the forty Stay and Play housekeeping beach cabins neat and tidy, but it seems like I am always the one who gets stuck cleaning the toilets after the tourists leave. We don't own the cabins; we just clean them. We get to live in two of the cabins, though, connected with a plywood kind of hallway. We also get all the food we can pilfer since Mr. Kaye, the owner, has this fancy restaurant next door, the Look-Sea Lounge. And there's the Kozy Korner Kafe under the lounge, so at least we get what Mom calls hots and cots—food and a place to live.

Mr. Kaye. I like him a lot. He sort of just stepped in when our old man stepped out. Just like I don't remember when my father was there, I don't remember when Mr. Kaye wasn't there. I guess if it weren't for him, we'd been out on our butts.

I figure Tommy Kaye owns most of Sea Park. At least, that's what everyone says. The cabins, the restaurant, the café, and the bowling alley that turns into a dance floor for some pretty big bands he brings in from Portland and Seattle. He also owns the Feed and Seed where I help out sometimes. I love it there. Something makes me feel good about feeding animals and making things grow. Just the smell of the Feed and Seed makes me all warm and settled inside.

Mr. Kaye also owns acres and acres of land up behind Sea Park—mostly forests and pastures. Mr. Kaye says Sea Park has a big future and that someday the world will sit up and take notice of our little tourist town.

I used to hope that Mr. Kaye would pop the question to ol' Malice Alice—oh, that's what Rex and me call Mom sometimes, but never to her face and only when she deserves it, which is pretty much every Saturday night. Rex told me I was an idiot for even thinking about Mom marrying Mr. Kaye. "Look at him and look at her. Figure it out," I remember him telling me. I guess he was right. Mom's something of a handful . . . okay, make that a beach floozy, and Mr. Kaye is quiet and refined and smart. They say opposites attract but that's in science, not in Sea Park.

When you're the daughter of Malice Alice Stokes you don't have much of a chance at anything here in Sea Park. As far as I figure, the highlight of her life was being appointed Miss Good-Time Charley of 1937 at Edna Glick's Inn and Out. Oh, she can dig clams faster than anyone I know. And oh yes, there's that billboard outside of town that she claims she posed for. Okay, I can see as how she *might* have been pretty on her own, you know, without all that makeup and henna hair rinse and girdles that pull her in on the bottom and then jut her back out on top.

But Rex . . . he's our saving grace. Rex is smart enough for all three of us Stokes! With a brother like Rex, you just have some hope things'll be okay.

Alright, I've put this off long enough. I've been saving this part up because I don't want you to judge me on account of my name. Ready? I am RubyOpalPearl Stokes. Don't ask me where my folks got all those names from. Could have been names from my ol' man's little black book of old girlfriends for all I know. I can barely stand to say my names, let alone write them. So don't ever call me RubyOpalPearl or Ruby or Opal or Pearl. I will just ignore you.

Call me Jewels, or don't bother calling me anything at all.

CHAPTER 3

"Hey, Stokes," Eldon Johnson says, pulling Rex around by his jacket. "If it ain't the new Town Hood and his sister, the Town Clown. Guess I'll go steal me a car."

See, that's the problem with being Town Hood. Depending on what the other kids think of you, *you* could end up in more trouble on account of *them* than if *you* did the hooding yourself. If they like you, that's a whole other kettle of fish: you're sitting pretty and they'll keep you clean. Didn't sound like Eldon was going to let anyone sit pretty, though.

Eldon Johnson is cute, I'll give him that. I had a crush on him for maybe about six seconds when I was ten. If anyone deserves to be Permanent Town Hood, though, it's Eldon.

Not even looking at him, Rex says, "Make sure you're smart enough to steal one with gas in it."

"Me stealing a car lands the Town Hood in jail, I figure. What a sweet deal," Eldon says.

"Take a long joy ride off a short pier," Rex tells him. We're in Wingard's Five And Dime getting model paint for the lions' eyeballs. I pretend to be watching Mrs. Wingard balance on a ladder putting up Christmas garlands, but I'm listening.

You need to know something else about my brother: he doesn't fight. Anyone. Ever. He won't even fight me, and believe you me, I've chalked up first blood on him many times. He doesn't go for violence. I think we have our old man to thank for that. Usually dogs that get kicked around will turn mean, so you'd think Rex would put up his dukes once in a while. But I don't think he's ever even made a duke, let alone put one up.

Don't get me wrong, Rex is no coward. He's just smart. He told me once that fighting might be an answer, but not a solution. He thinks there's better ways. Maybe that's why he took a trophy in State Debate last year up at Astoria High. I don't know what they were debating about. I think I'd just rather fight and get the whole discussion over with.

"Like I say," Eldon says with a smuggish smile, taking a balsa wood airplane and slipping it into his jacket pocket, "you're the golden boy now. Maybe you'll grow a set of nuts."

He turns and, pretty as you please, walks right out of the store.

I look at Rex. "Does that mean what I think it means?"

"Cou-rrrrage," Rex says, making like the Cowardly Lion.

"You're not afraid of anything! Besides, you can clobber him. He's a jerk."

"Yeah, but nothing makes him madder than when someone won't fight him." Rex grins down at me and adds, "I win as long as he's mad."

"Well, I think you should knock his block off. If Mrs. Wingard misses that balsa plane and she's seen us here at the model counter, then . . ."

"Quit yapping, Jewels, and pay for that paint. Leave an extra nickel on the counter."

"Why?"

"Just do it," Rex says, heading toward the door. I don't know if that's his first official duty as Town Hood or if it's because the Wingards have six kids, one of them with polio and, like us, need every nickel they can get their mitts on. But that's Rex for you.

We leave the store and bump into ol' Frank McAloon, just tying his horse to the bumper of a car. "Hi buckeroos," he says. He calls all kids buckeroos. You just have to get used to it. "Say, where's your ol' lady been? Haven't seen her around lately."

"Cooking. She got a job on the *Tinker II* out of Warrenton," I say, patting the velvety nose of Florence, his broken down beach nag. Frank and his twin brother, Leo, are okay. Old as God and if you ever wondered if twins grow old looking alike, well, they do. Both are old soldiers from

The Great War. Here's a hint: don't *ever* ask them about that or you'll be stuck listening to them for hours. You know how old folks can be talky about that stuff.

In the distance, the bells of St. Bart's church start ringing. It's noon on a Sunday, so I don't think too much about it. But Frank and Rex look toward the steeple, then back at each other.

Then, "Frank! Frank!" Leo McAloon hollers out from the back alley. The hooves of his galloping horse throw up soft clumps of sandy dirt as he gets closer. "Frank!"

Leo sits a horse pretty good for an old man, I'll give him that. He pulls up to a stop. Jeez, Leo looks like he's ready to explode and his horse doesn't look much better.

"Leo!" Frank says, grabbing the horse's bridle. "What's the matter?"

"Come on! Over to Edna's! She's got that new radio! Come on! Mount up!"

"Why? What's happening?"

"Not sure. Sheriff Hillary just drove down Pacific and said everyone's to get to a radio on the double! Come on! Mount up! Edna's Inn and Out!"

Edna's Inn and Out is what they call a roadhouse. It's a restaurant and a bar just north of the city limits. She has dancing there sometimes. That hoochy coochy stuff. It's where the locals all go to get away from the tourists. It's where ol' Malice Alice has a bar stool with her butt imprinted in it.

Frank and Leo gallop off, their identical jackets flapping in the wind.

"Wonder what that's all about," I mumble. A few more cars screech north and south. Some people come out to look toward the church steeple, then to the sky, then to the north, then go back inside.

Both Rex and me look skyward. Just gray, and a gentle gray at that. Not even much of a wind. Emergencies on the coast usually have something to do with either the weather or the ocean but all seems calm and quiet. "I don't know," Rex says, yanking his bike out of the rack on the sidewalk. "Come on."

I pull my bike out, too, and have to peddle fast to catch up with Rex as we dodge cars along Highway 101.

Edna's is crowded and steamy and noisy. Her joint always smells of burning driftwood, stale cigarette smoke, overcooked coffee, and cheap cologne, and I like every whiff of it. Actually, Edna herself smells like her roadhouse, and I like her, too.

Kids aren't supposed to be in a bar like this, but no one in Sea Park ever cares just as long as we don't drink. Most kids drink out on the logging trails or, heck, pick any sand dune between the old air strip in Warrenton and the abandoned dairy barns in Tillamook or any empty clam digger shack or summer cottage. There's lots of drinking going on in Sea Park on any day, and right here, right now, everyone has a drink in their hand. I don't think it's even legal to drink in Oregon on a Sunday. Figures. Kids get run in for painting lion statue eyeballs but drinking laws hide under the table right along with the drunks. Sometimes I think we have our own set of laws here in Sea Park.

No one notices me and Rex when we enter. There's Edna, sitting on top of the bar, leaning into her new mahogany radio and fussing with the dials. She's short and dumpy and I always think she looks like a little kid with her rolled up dungarees and saddle shoes. Mom says being short makes Edna mad as all-get-out and maybe that's why nobody ever messes with Edna Glick.

"Shut up! I can't hear!" she yells. People hush some and Edna adds through the static, "Here! I got Portland!"

The man on the radio fades in and out, and it's like the whole room inhales and leans toward the radio. Folks closest to the radio tell everyone to shut up. They all cram in closer, but I back away toward the fireplace and wait for someone to tell me what the heck is going on. Something's up, that's for dang sure.

Rex breaks loose of the crowd and grabs me by the arm. "Come on. Let's go."

Once outside and away from the noise, I pull away from his grip. "What's happening, Rex?"

"Planes from Japan bombed our navy fleet somewhere in Hawaii."

I look at him, wondering if I heard right. "What'd they want to do a thing like that for?"

"For kicks, you dope! How the heck should I know? Come on. We better go home."

"But what's going to happen?"

"I guess we're at war."

"I thought the Germans were the ones making war," I say, pulling my bike out of the bushes. Sure, we kids have been taught all about Hitler and the war in Europe. Even about the Germans bombing England, which I think would be exciting and sure as heck break up the boredom. But that's a whole world away. Means nothing to me here in Sea Park where the most exciting thing to happen in months was Corliss Ainsley breaking a tooth trying to crunch open a crab leg, making her lisp even lispier.

Rex looks out over the Pacific Ocean and says, "Wonder where Mom is."

"Why? Isn't Hawaii a million miles away?"

"Folks in there said the Japanese are going to invade us here."

"Here? In Sea Park?"

Suddenly people start to pour out of Edna's, running to their cars, hustling off down the street, honking, swerving. The McAloon twins mount their horses and take off like they're Paul Revere and John Wayne riding side by side. Rex and I look at each other. This is all just crazy.

But it's also new and different and, okay, maybe a little exciting. Like the spirit in the air on Decoration Day, which is the start of our tourist season and everyone knows there'll be cash in pockets again after a long winter of living on credit and good looks. Like the spark you can feel on the Fourth of July when the town is filled with excited, paying strangers and when the parade is lining up and when the fireworks display is being set up out on the spit. Like the first day of school when you're sort of happy, sort of scared, about maybe meeting a new best friend. Crazy, but exciting.

We bike home. No Mom. Not only that, the radio's out. And we can't get a line to even make a phone call. Okay, now crazy's becoming scary. Our four-party line is nothing but spit and static.

"Maybe Malice Alice didn't pay Ma Bell again," I say.

"No, everyone and their dog is making a phone call right now."

I make some boloney sandwiches. Rex says he's going to his own cabin to do homework. I swear, Adolph Hitler could be helping himself to a sandwich out of our fridge and Rex would still go do his homework.

Not me. I pull a quilt around my shoulders, sit, and stare at the clock, wondering what this Pearl Harbor thing means.

And yes, I'm worried about Mom. Out there. On the ocean.

CHAPTER 4

"School's canceled," Rex says early the next morning, hanging up the earpiece on our wall phone.

"Why?" I ask, looking outside into the darkness. "You mean because of that Japan attack?"

"I guess." He peeks into our mother's small room next to mine.

"She's not there. I already checked," I say.

He pads into the kitchen, well, not *into* the kitchen because the cabin me and Malice Alice share is just a room with half a couch, one table, three chairs, one mousetrap, a two-burner gas stove, and a small old refrigerator that wheezes like a McAloon beach nag. So if you're in the cabin, you're also in the kitchen.

Rex stands in front of the open refrigerator. "Anything to eat around here?"

"Are we worried?"

"Yeah, about starving to death," he says, opening a cupboard and pulling out a box of Post Toasties. He puts the box to his mouth and taps out the last few flakes, then tosses the box in the sink.

"No, I mean worried about Mom, Hawaii, well . . . about anything."

"Look, don't worry, Jewels. Mom said they'd be out fishing for at least five days."

We switch on the radio and wait for it to warm up. Nothing. Not even any static to give you hope of finding a song or a game show. Sometimes on clear nights we can pick up stations real far away. We even heard a Chinese man talking all the way from San Francisco once! I loved that. Made me realize there really *was* a whole world out there and, for a little while, I had eavesdropped on it, my ear glued to the speaker. Who cared what he was talking about?

"Great. No food. No radio. No school. No Mom," Rex says, heading back through the plywood hallway to his cabin. I follow him.

"You going back to bed?"

"Nah, think I'll bike over to the docks and talk to the harbormaster. See if the *Tinker* has called in or anything."

"What should I do, Rex?" I ask, sounding like a scaredy eight-year-old staying home alone for the first time.

"Go get us something to eat. I'm hungry."

"Should I lock the doors?"

"Yeah, right. Lock the doors. That'll keep the Japs out." He puts on the old pea coat our dad left and it darn near fits him now. Gives me some hope I might grow a few inches yet and sort of stretch all this pooooo-berty into a tall, slim body. So far, I look more like Edna the Fireplug than Alice, who's skinny as a cat tail.

Rex reads my face as he's leaving. "Look, Jewels. There's probably going to be a ton of rumors flying regarding all this war stuff. Let's just wait and see what it's all about. Go next door and see what Arley's cooking up for breakfast. I'll be back in an hour."

I follow him outside. He pulls his bike out from under the eaves, hops on, and calls out, "Pancakes! Bring back pancakes!"

Just the mention of the word *pancake* makes my stomach growl. I close the cabin door and go to my room to dress. My closet is just a cubby in the wall with a curtain as a door. I pull on the lightbulb cord and stand looking. No school, huh? Well, at least that's a good thing. I don't have to iron anything or flip a coin to see which of my four dresses to wear.

I pull on corduroy dungarees and an old sweatshirt. I try to keep my saddle Oxfords just for school. Those poor shoes have more coats of white paint on them than those lions' eyeballs. Maybe I'll get a new pair for Christmas since Mom's working some. But for now, I step into the big rubber boots I wear for clamming and mucking around at low tide. Besides, Mom isn't here to tell me in her gooey Southern accent "you're grown up now, Jewels honey, and you need to start dressin' like a young lady all the time and not just when you have to."

Mom was born in Alabama, and she thinks that gives her a right to talk like Scarlett O'Hara, even though she's as "Pacific Ocean" as I am. Of course, I can tell what sort of mood she's in by how much accent she uses. She thinks it's charming. I think it's stupid. But that's Malice Alice for you.

There's a wooden plank path that runs from the cabin to the south side of the Look-Sea Lounge and Kozy Korner Kafe. I know my way blindfolded but still don't like going through these pathways in the chilly darkness. There's only a tinge of light on the eastern horizon.

Well, this is odd. The café is still dark, too. I look around town. Hardly any lights are on anywhere—just a few streetlights shimmering in the breeze. Where's Arley? He's usually already opened, got things fired up, started the bacon, the oatmeal, and the pancake batter so by the time Corliss stumbles in, everything is ready for the regulars.

I try the door. Locked. I know where the key is and I look around to make sure no one's looking. I pull the brick away, feel for the key, and unlock the door.

"Arley? Corliss? Anybody?"

I switch on a light and peek into the kitchen. "Anybody here?" Nope. No one anywhere. Well, maybe they are up in the Look-Sea Lounge. So it's down the back hall, through the door, up the stairs, and then down another hall and into the kitchen of the Lounge. And it's dark and empty, too. I grope for the light switch, wondering where the heck all this sudden courage is coming from.

"Hey! Arley? Corliss?"

The kitchen is large and bright and shiny. I look into the dining room through the diamond-shaped windows of the padded swinging doors. Totally dark. I slip inside and then hear something weird.

Wonk wonk wonk.

Now I'm scared.

"Hello?" I whisper into the darkness. I know the bar is somewhere ahead.

Wonk wonk wonk.

"Who's there?" I whisper again. *Lord, what am I doing here?*

Wonk wonk wonk.

I feel the leather edge of the bar, bump into a barstool, go inside where I feel my way along the counter until I find one of the refrigerator doors, and open it, giving me just enough light.

Wonk wonk wonk. There, on the floor, is the wonker. A dog's tail—the tip *tap-tap-tapping.*

I recognize that long, pointy tail, which is attached to Mr. Kaye's bloodhound. "Hero! What are you doing here, boy?" I love dogs, and Hero and me are old pals.

"How'd you get yourself stuck up here?" Now his tail is *wonking* the counter and there on the floor is a man. It's Mr. Kaye.

"Mr. Kaye? Mr. Kaye! Are you all right? Please don't be dead, Mr. Kaye," I'm thinking out loud. *What do I do? Who do I call?*

Then I get a whiff—it's some kind of liquor. Yep. There's a bottle of booze laying on its side, empty, on the floor next to Mr. Kaye.

"Mr. Kaye, it's me, Jewels. Come on. Here, sit up." Hey, I'm the daughter of Malice Alice Stokes. I got plenty of experience in this department, believe you me. But not with Mr. Kaye. I've never once seen him drunk, let alone in-a-heap-passed-out drunk.

He sort of moans and Hero looks at me as if to say, "Thank Dog you're here!"

"Come on here, sit up." I get Mr. Kaye to sit and lean against the bar. His shaky fingers find his head and he touches a huge bruised bump there.

"Mr. Kaye," I say, crouching down to look in his eyes, "should I get Doc Ellis?"

"I . . . don't know . . ."

If he's like my mother coming down off a binge, he'll be nothing but anvil headaches and foggy memories and reeking breath and regrets and apologies and all.

I help him to his feet. He sways as he runs his hand over his face, blinking like he has to figure out where he is.

"I'm okay," he says, sounding anything but.

I get him to a table. The sun's coming up and there's finally some light in the restaurant—the kind of sunlight that comes in tinges of bright pink and makes you remember the "red sky at morning, sailors take warning" saying.

Finally, his eyes meet mine, sitting acrost the table.

"Hi, Jewels," he says, but not sheepish-like, like my mother talks when she knows I've found her drunk. "I'm . . . I'm sorry . . . I'm so . . . sorry . . ."

And like with Mom, I say, "Don't worry. I'll make some coffee."

He lowers his head and just nods.

"I don't know where Corliss and Arley are. It's weird out there. It's like the whole town is . . ."

He looks up, and we lock eyes, and I think I've figured out what it is he's sorry for.

You see, Tommy Kaye is Japanese.

CHAPTER 5

I slip off toward the kitchen to make the coffee. I can tell Hero isn't sure if he should follow me or stay with Mr. Kaye, but I tap my leg and he follows. He's probably as hungry as I am.

I check the dumbwaiter. Hmm, no milk, no bakery delivery, which means no one's at the registration desk downstairs, either. I find some biscuits in the pantry and make a tray for Mr. Kaye. Hero catches the two I toss to him, and I also polish off two biscuits. I've been drinking coffee for a few years now and help myself to the first cup. Mom let us kids drink coffee a few years back. Mrs. Johnson, Sea Park's official Know-It-All-ski, said we shouldn't because it'll stunt our growth, but both Rex and I know we get to drink coffee because it's cheaper than milk.

Mr. Kaye is standing in front of the huge picture windows that look out over the beach and the boiling gray of the Pacific. He has a drink in his hand. Hero *clip clip clips* acrost the shiny dance floor and sits next to him. Mr. Kaye's other hand goes to his dog's head and it's sort of a nice picture, them like that, silhouetted with the ocean as a backdrop.

"Mr. Kaye?" I whisper. "Here's some coffee and biscuits. Maybe you ought to . . ."

I come closer and see what he and Hero are looking at. Down on the beach are two men on horseback. Finally! Business per usual! The McAloons have a few customers! Then I see it *is* the McAloons down there. But they aren't wearing their usual old cowboy hats and moth-eaten chaps. They're wearing those helmets that look sort of like upside-down pie plates. You know, like those that old soldiers wear marching in an Armistice Day parade. They pause now and then to raise binoculars to their eyes as they gaze toward the horizon.

"What are the looking for?" I ask.

Mr. Kaye takes a drink. "The enemy."

I look out over the ocean. "All the way from Japan?"

Then the McAloons turn their binoculars up toward us. Mr. Kaye says, "Or maybe already here." He raises his glass to them, downs the liquid, and says to me, "Where's that coffee?"

I wave down to the McAloons like I always do when they ride past. They don't wave back. Guess they don't see me.

Mr. Kaye settles into a booth and tries to pour some coffee from the pot with a shaking hand. I've seen my mother's hand shake that same way a million times.

"Want me to pour it?"

He leans back and runs his hands over his eyes and mutters, "Sure." Hero edges in under the table and puts his head on Mr. Kaye's lap. Mr. Kaye's hand goes from his own head to his dog's and Hero thunks his tail in thanks. Like he's talking to Hero, he says, "I can't believe they did it."

"Who did what?"

"My idiot cousins. I can't believe they . . . oh, God. I can't believe they did it."

"You mean that bombing thing?" I ask.

He finally looks over at me. "Nothing will ever be the same, Jewels."

"How come?"

"War changes everything." He smiles a little and adds, "I'm the enemy now."

I don't get it. I've known Mr. Kaye all my life. He has a whole wall of certificates and awards and licenses and newspaper articles and college degrees. Everything but the Good Housekeeping Seal of Approval and he probably even has one of those somewhere. He knows just about everything and he's a real stickler for good English and is always correcting me. Not only that, he's a philan-something—you know, people who use their money to help just about anyone who ever needs it. How can Mr. Kaye be anyone's enemy?

But it scares me the way he looks at me and it's a lot more than the booze in his eyes. Alls I think of is to change the subject. "Mom's out fishing. Wisht she'd get home. Getting stormy out there." I nod my head toward the ocean.

He looks out at the ocean, his eyes as far away as Egypt, and he just nods his head.

"Rex went to the harbormaster to see if they've called in."

I can tell he sees I'm a little scared now and he touches my hand. "Jewels, I've known your mother a good long time and she always finds her way back home." I'm not feeling all that much better, but he's right. She always gets herself back home, even if it's me or Rex hauling her in a tourist handcart.

Mr. Kaye finishes his coffee. "Say, aren't you supposed to be in school?"

"Canceled. No one's coming in to work, either. It's like the whole darn town is canceled. If you want, I can go start up the café. I've done it a few times. Remember last summer when Corliss was sick and Malice Alice was . . ."

Mr. Kaye looks at me. His thick black hair is streaked with pure white and it all sticks out screwy. I've never seen him look so, what's Mom call it, discombobulated? "Please don't call her that. She's your mother, for crissake. Show her some respect."

Well, I've heard him call her a lot worst over the years, but I don't want to argue with someone who's coming off a bender and whose cousins might just have bombed Pearl Harbor, wherever the heck that is.

CHAPTER 6

"What do you think you're doing?" Rex asks, finding me in the café kitchen and up to my elbows in pancake batter. I'm not very good at fractions so instead of cutting the recipe by eighths, I'm making up the whole batch and figure we'll be eating pancakes till the cows, or Mom, come home.

"You said you wanted pancakes."

"Yeah, but to eat, not to shingle the roof with," he says, pouring a cup of coffee.

"What did you find out? Has the *Tinker* called in or anything?"

"They said there's an air wave blackout. No transmissions coming or going."

"Why? You mean because of . . ." I tick my head toward the west like I was having a hard time saying Japs or bombing or Pearl Harbor or even war.

"I guess. Look, don't worry. Captain Jenkins probably just followed a good run and they went out farther than planned. He knows what he's doing. I crewed for him for the last two summers and he's no dummy. Flip those things. They're about to take off," he says, pointing to the bubbling circles of batter on the grill.

He sits down and inhales a stack of pancakes, heaped with real butter and oozing with maple syrup—all stuff you'll never find around our meager kitchen. Then, like I'd done earlier, he sort of picks his head up, looks around, noticing the quiet everywhere. "It's weird out there. Hardly anyone out. You'd think a bomb went off."

We look at each other. I crack a smile. So does he. I feel sort of bad about it, though. "Did you get the radio to work?" he asks, wiping the smirk off his face.

"No, I've been here. Arley and Corliss never came to work. Hey, there's a radio behind the counter. We should try it." I pull it onto the counter and switch it on, then eat another pancake while it warms up. When the static gets louder, I start to hone in on the most reliable station. Good ol' KOIN in Portland, 960 on the dial. Even on cloudy days we can usually pick up KOIN in Sea Park.

Finally, the static starts to form words. Some man is talking. I turn the volume way up. Rex comes over to the radio and we're head to head, leaning in toward the speaker.

We must be on the tail end of the speech because alls I hear is a radio man saying, "To repeat, Governor Sprague has called on all Oregonians to remain calm. Following dictates from Washington, he has ordered all persons of Japanese descent to stay in their homes for their own safety. This ends this emergency broadcast. Further broadcasts will be intermittent as more details are released." The static takes over again.

"Look, a customer," I say, pointing to a car careening into the parking lot.

"That's just Sadie Moran," Rex says. "Newspapers."

"Wow. She's early."

Normally Sadie takes her own sweet time delivering the newspapers from Portland and even a few times stops off for a drink or two along the route. And other days, she never even bothers delivering at all. But it's like she is on a mission this morning. She barely slows down, tosses out a bundle of papers, then storms out of the parking lot, tail-spinning and going like sixty.

Rex brings in the bundle and we don't even have to cut off the twine. The words WAR WITH JAPAN! are printed so big you can read them from clear acrost the Columbia River.

Rex pulls out a copy and pages through. I'm hoping he's going for the comics, but nope, not ol' Rex. Straight to the editorials.

"Uh oh," he says as he reads.

"What?"

He points out the words, also in great big print: NEVER TRUST A JAP.

"So?"

"In case you hadn't noticed, Tommy Kaye is Japanese," Rex says, pointing upstairs.

"No, he's an American. He only *looks* Japanese," I say as though I've just solved that whole problem.

"Have you seen him today?"

"Yeah. He's up in his apartment, sleeping it off."

"He knows?" Rex taps the paper.

"He says his cousins did it. Funny, he's never talked about having any family."

"You dope," Rex says, giving me *that look*. "Not his relatives. His . . . you know, his . . . um . . ."

"His what, Rex?"

"His . . . *cousins*," he says, pronouncing the word louder and with a different pitch, like that changes its meaning. "His *race*."

All of a sudden, I don't like any of this. Between our mother being somewhere out on a stormy ocean, the whole town hiding itself, no radio, no phone, giant letters written in a newspaper, and Mr. Kaye being, well, of the Japanese *race* and all, I'm a little weak-kneed. I look at my brother and ask, "You going to tell me when to be scared?"

"Look, I'm heading over to city hall. See what folks are saying." He smiles at me and that makes me feel a little better. “You may as well clean up and close up. Nobody’s going anywhere today.”

He puts on his pea coat and cap and heads back out into the rainy morning.

Nope, no siree. I’m definitely not liking any of this.

CHAPTER 7

I use the newspaper to wrap a stack of pancakes and head back to our cabins. If Mom got home, she'd just head straight to bed. But no one's here. I put the pancakes in the oven then go back to the café to clean up, and well, see if maybe Mr. Kaye might call down for something. And I wait. Finally, I turn the radio back on and listen to the broadcast of President Roosevelt asking Congress for a war and they say sure, you betcha. Probably don't even ask for a show of hands.

I don't know what I think. I'll bet if Rex was a senator or something, he'd stand up and turn the other cheek. And they'd probably kick him out of there on both cheeks.

Arley and Corliss finally show up at the café together in the same car, which they hardly ever do because they clash like orange and red. She's looking a little too gooey-eyed for my liking.

"I already did the pancake batter," I announce to Arley.

"Too bad. Throw it out."

"Don't you . . . ?" I follow him into the little office where he's putting his belongings into a duffle bag.

He holds up four or five old aprons and says, "These here are mine, Jewels. I ain't taking anything that ain't mine."

"But where you going, Arley? Get a better job?" I ask.

"Yeah, the U-S-of-A army, if they'll take me," he says, now going through some utensils. "These here are mine, too."

"But Arley . . ." He's into the cash box now and counting out money.

He shows me a handful of bills and says, "And this here is what's owing to me. No more, no less. You write it down, Jewels. Fourteen dollars and sixty-three cents."

"But Arley, you just quitting?"

Corliss is behind me and says, "Yesth, he'sth quitting. And me, too."

I turn to face her. Corliss is nice sometimes. Sometimes she's a piss-ant, whatever that is. I just like the sound of saying it and not getting a dirty look for it because I guess there really are such things as piss-ants. Folks make fun of her lisp, but I don't. Besides, she's gotten pretty darn good at avoiding words with esses. You got to give her that.

There's a honk from a truck out front. I look out the window and there must be three heads in the cab and some other men hunkering down under a tarp in the bed. The horn honks again. Arley has his duffle and his cash and is putting on his slicker.

"Well, babe, I guess this is it," he says, pulling Corliss to him. He plants a great big smackeroo on her lips, right here in front of God, me, a truck full of soon-to-be soldiers, and Hero the dog. Anyway, she gives Arley a great big smackeroo right back on the lips and says, "Kill one for me!"

The truck speeds off as fast as it had sped in, and I'm standing with my mouth wide open. Corliss says, "And what are you gawking at? My man'sth goin' off to war!"

"Your *man*? You hate Arley! You're always screaming at him and calling him names!"

Corliss is no looker, especially now with her chipped front tooth, so I guess I get it when she smiles sort of dreamy-like, waving at the truck, holding one of Arley's dirty aprons to her chest and cooing, "Nah, I *love* a man in uniform."

"I get Arley quitting, Corliss. But why are you quitting? Think the army will take you?" I ask.

"Don't be thilly, Jewelsth. Tell Tommy I quit. And if you know what'sth good for you, you, Rex, and your mother will quit him, too."

"Quit? Why?"

"Why? It'sth as plain as the chipped tooth in my mouth!" She pulls the skin back on her temples, giving her slanty eyes, and adds, "Here'sth a hint!"

"You mean, just because . . ."

"I can't work for a Jap! Anyway, I have war work to do, now. We all do! Even your muuu-ther."

I'm used to the way folks in town refer to my mother as my "muuu-ther." I don't know why, but Rex says don't let it get under my skin. Anyway, Corliss wraps her muffler around her like a flying ace and just walks away, off to find her some war work, I guess.

• • •

It's late Tuesday, our second day of official war. I guess they'll have to call it something other than the Great War because that name's already taken. Anyway, there's still no word from our mother or the *Tinker II*. Rex says they had to turn off the navigation lights up on the Columbia River because, get this, they thought the Japs were going to just row right up the river and take over Portland, then all of Oregon, then the entire country, and then the world and meet Hitler somewhere in the middle. Oh yeah, we declared war on Germany and Italy, too, and they all declared war on us and England and France and Canada and gosh, I figure just about everyone has tossed their hats into the war ring by now. Everyone except me and Rex and maybe Hero.

Anyway, Rex says probably what's happened is the *Tinker II* had to put in somewhere north, maybe even Gray's Harbor. Also, there's this big storm going on with high tides, so they could have even gone south and are safe and sitting it out down in Tillamook Bay. All sorts of things happen at sea. Rex says all we can do is wait. We can't use a short wave, and the radio isn't working anyway, and now we have to start putting blackout cloth or tar paper over all the windows. Cars can't drive with headlights on either. I don't get it. How can everything change so fast? No more streetlights, no more porch lights, and don't even think about Christmas lights! I'm telling you, the whole world is turning black.

Mr. Kaye stays in his apartment and alls I can do is put food out for him and take Hero out for a walk and a ball-toss a few times a day. When I come calling, I wait for Hero to come lumbering down the hallway from Mr. Kaye's apartment. At least I know Mr. Kaye is up and about. But he's keeping his own company and I'm getting worried all over again.

I've been handed bolts of blackout cloth from a load that came in from Portland. Don't ask me. Maybe they make the stuff and keep it around just waiting for a war. Sadie Moran told me to get to work on all the Stay and Play windows. Heck, let's see, forty cabins, five windows, and two doors in each. Can't even figure that out in my head. *Bet the war is over by the time I finish,* I think as I walk up to Mr. Kaye's apartment.

"Mr. Kaye?"

The door opens but it has the chain on it.

"What?"

"We need to tack this cloth to all the windows. What about those big windows in the Look-Sea Lounge? Do you want Rex to get a ladder and blackout those windows?"

"What for?"

"Uh, well, you know. The no-lights-at-night rules."

"No business, no lights, no problem!" Mr. Kaye snaps. I figure he's been drinking.

The door closes, the chain comes undone, the door reopens, and he says, kinder, the way he usually speaks to me, "I'm sorry, Jewels. But the windows are so big. There won't be enough cloth and . . . I might be closing soon anyway."

"What?" I ask. Okay, I admit it. My first thought is what about Rex and me and Mom? Where will we go and what will we do if Tommy Kaye closes up?

He smiles down at me and says, "I'm thinking I need a change of scenery."

"You going to enlist? Arley did and so has half the town. Seven more men left yesterday. Just like that!" I snap my fingers. "Up and quit and going to go fight the dirty Jap . . ." I let the word just sort of slip away into that place where words you wisht you'd never said go. "You're really not very . . . Japanese," I add, not that I know much more about Japan than geisha girls, chopsticks, and bonsai trees, which Mr. Kaye is crazy in love with and has everywhere.

The papers are filled with *lots* of reasons why the Japanese are the enemy and most of it is pretty darn angry. I mean, we all know Hitler and the Nazis are evil, but, well, Tommy Kaye's our friend and our employer and our maybe-someday-to-be stepfather.

"Can I get you anything?" I ask, feeling pretty helpless. "Coffee?" I let my eyes drift over to his liquor cabinet.

"Yes, you can get Corliss in. I'm getting tired of your pancakes."

I hate to tell him what she said about quitting because he was a, *you* know, so I dress it up some and say, "Oh, she's too busy since she's doing 'war work,' as she calls it."

"War work? Are they rolling bandages already?" he mumbles. "Well, she won't be too busy come payday. Same with Virg Johnson at the Feed and Seed."

"And Barry at the bowling alley," I add. "Everyone's doing the war. But when Malice Al—um—Mom gets back, she'll take over the kitchen."

"Still no word?"

"No. But other fishing boats aren't back in yet, either. No one's heard nothing."

He shoots me a look. So I re-say, "No one's heard *anything*. Folks think all the boats probably took shelter someplace."

"Look," he says, "I'll fix myself something down in the kitchen. I used to be a pretty good cook."

"I already did the windows down in the café. You have to just make sure the lights don't bleed out or the McAloon boys will shoot first and ask questions later. I thought they were going to call J. Edgar Hoover on me when I left the light on in the café. What do they think, I'm signaling to the . . ." and there it is again, that word. Japs.

Tommy puts his arm on my shoulder. "*The Japs*. It's okay, Jewels. The *Japs* are my enemy, too."

I don't know what to say, so I just spurt out, "I'll bring you the paper when it gets here. Sadie can't drive during the dark, so everything's late coming from Portland and Astoria. I figure that's why no one's delivering and why there's no customers and who wants to go to the beach now—and the cruddy weather, and it's almost Christmas."

He smiles and says, "Yes, you're right. That's why."

I'm no dummy, and I think we both know what's happening here. No one's around because Tommy Kaye is the enemy.

I take Hero's collar and let him lead me down the hallway for his run on the beach.

We both need it.

CHAPTER 8

Roosevelt just proclaimed Sunday, December 7, 1941, as a date that will live in infamy. When I ask where infamy is, Rex throws his dictionary at me and says, "Look it up, you dope! Jeez, Jewels, if you'd read something besides those stupid movie magazines and comic books, you might know a thing or two!"

But as much as things changed that Sunday, everything for me ever since the attack is going ka-blooey. That's comic-book-talk for upside down, inside out, and Wrong Way Corrigan thrown in as a bonus.

It's even stormier today—Wednesday. Still no word about the *Tinker*, her crew, Mom, or anything. We got word that a freighter ran aground up on Clatsop Spit—

that's about ten miles north and at the mouth of the Columbia River. Any ship running aground is big news so it spreads throughout town pretty fast through our local gossip network, the *Sand Dune Telegraph*. Word is that this freighter was on its way to Hawaii when it got orders to turn back, which it did, but without the navigation lights back up the river . . . *whamooo*!, which is comic-book-talk for they ran aground. Flotsam and jetsam started flowing out everywhere.

So I'm thinking if a big freighter can run aground, what can happen to a cruddy, old, leaky forty-foot fishing boat named the *Tinker II*?

I'm glad to be at Edna's Inn and Out right now so I don't have to think about anything. Edna's been checking in on Rex and me and invited us to come over for lunch. Rex stayed at home. He's the captain of the debate team and you better believe they're getting lots of stuff to debate this week.

Edna fixes me a hamburger, saying, "Might as well enjoy 'em while I can get 'em because we'll all be eatin' horse meat so's our fightin' boys can eat beef."

I sort of just point to the end of the bar where the McAloon twins are sitting. I whisper, "Don't say 'horse meat' around those McAloons."

"They're so busy rattlin' their swords and writin' editorials, a bomb could go off in here and they'd just think someone sneezed," Edna says.

"What swords?" I ask, sort of leaning back to see one.

"Sword-*rattlin'*, Jewels. That means workin' up more war than you need. Yak, yak, yak. The drunker they get, the louder they rattle them swords!"

"Oh," I say, cramming down my burger. It's been a long time since anyone's fixed me a hot meal and man, I sure am sick of pancakes, so I tell Edna how good the burger is, horse meat or no.

Pretty soon the McAloon boys' sword-rattling and glass-clanking grows louder and they're laughing and patting each other on their backs. Finally, Frank dismounts his bar stool and says, "Hey, everybody! We got it! Listen to this!"

Leo joins Frank on the fireplace hearth so they are sort of on a stage. Two tipsy, identical twins. They even sway identical. It's sort of funny.

Frank holds the paper, they both pop their spectacles on their noses, then Leo says, "A-one, a-two, a-three!" And on "a-three," to the tune of the "Battle Hymn Republic" they sing:

> Mine eyes have seen the glory
> Of the squashing of the Japs!
> Never more they'll bomb us
> While the navy's taking naps!
> We'll murderlate, decapitate, and
> Rub 'em off the maps!
> Our truth goes marching on!

Folks think that's pretty dang funny and it earns them applause and a round of beers. I turn to Edna, who is not laughing. I wipe the grin off my face.

"What's wrong?"

"I don't like this," she says, looking hard at the McAloons.

"Why? Everyone else did."

"Hey! Let's go serenade Tommy Kaye!" someone says.

She looks at me and says, "That's why." Then, to the crowd she hollers, "I'll blackball any man here who does and this is the only waterin' hole in town!"

That shuts 'em up.

Edna lights a cigarette and says to me, "I tell you, I think we'd all be a lot safer around here if they just let those two old coots re-up. Let them go kill the enemy. Probably end up cleanin' stables and givin' mules enemas like they did in The Great War."

"I thought they were heroes," I say.

"They were heroes like I was Miss America."

I'm just about ready to ask for another chocolate shake when the door blows open. But the person coming in gets all caught up in the blackout curtain cloth. Alls I hear is a muffled, "Merry Ch . . . oh, Christ! What the heck's all this?" The cloth comes down and falls to the floor.

There, in the doorway, she stands, soaking wet, looking like a half-drowned I-don't-know-what. In one hand she holds a live, but half-drowned, upside-down turkey, and in the other she holds a small, but decorated, Christmas tree, also half-drowned. The pockets of her coat bulge with ribbons bleeding color and soggy Christmas wrapping and crushed boxes.

"Merrrrrrrrrry Chriiiiiiiistmas!" she sings out, holding up her gifts. "I bring to y'all the bounty of our own most gracious provider, King Neptune!"

Now you know why Rex and me call her Malice Alice.

CHAPTER 9

"Close the door!" someone barks.

Frank and Leo rush to rehang the blackout cloth, cussing and telling each other what they're doing wrong. Edna stands in front of Mom, hands on hips. "Where in blazes have you been?" she says, sounding more like a mother than a best friend. "Look at you!"

Mom stands taller, puffs out her uneven falsies, and says down to Edna, "I have been incommunicado, not that it's any of *your* business." Incommunicado is Mom's way of saying a bender. Spree. On a toot. Out of sight, out of mind. You ought to see how Mom wraps her lipstick-stained lips around the word as she says it again, "In-comm-u-ni-ca-do."

"Yeah, you look like you've been incommunicadoin', all right!" Edna snaps. "Someday you'll go there and not come back."

"Let her go back!" someone calls out.

"Drop dead!" Mom hollers back.

"Everyone just shut up or get out!" Edna sure has a set of lungs on her.

Mom finally notices me sitting at the bar and there's that goofy, hi-schweety-miss-me-love-me? grin on her blotchy face. "Jewels! Honey, this here's a bar. Edna, what're you doin' lettin' her in here? She's just eleven!"

"Twelve," I say, knowing times like this it won't even sink in.

Then, the turkey makes a garbled gobble and Mom holds it up again. "It took some doin', but I got him! And look!" She plops down the tree and it leaves a circle of sand, water, needles, and tinsel on the floor. "Already decorated! Oh, and presents! Look, all y'all!" She holds up a pair of thick knitted socks. "Presents. Think these'll fit Rex?" She dangles the socks up in front of my face. "And there's lots more where these come from! All up and down the beach! I tell y'all, it's a Christmas miracle!"

"Gimme that thing!" Edna seizes the turkey and tosses it out the door. She turns Mom around and plops her down on the end bar stool.

The crowd just stares in amazement. I'm humiliated. Mom looks around and says, "Why's everyone so glum? Somebody die?"

"Yeah, a couple shiploads of men, that's all!" Frank says.

She turns on her stool to face the room. "What happened? Where?"

"What rock have you been under?" Leo asks.

"Pearl Harbor?" Frank prompts. "On Sunday? The Japs bombed Pearl Harbor!"

"That roadhouse down in Depoe Bay? Why would anyone want to bomb a dump like that?"

"Someone draw her a picture!"

I take her arm and get her to look at me. "Mom, we're at war with Japan. How come everyone in the world knows it but you?"

Her face goes blank and believe you me, her face can go from happy and bright and let's-have-another! to stone-cold sober and I-don't-get-it in an instant. "Huh?" she asks.

"Mom, where have you *been*?" I ask with gritted teeth and lowered voice. I can feel my cheeks burn and the chocolate shake in my stomach rumbles.

"Fishing!" she snaps as though it's *my* fault she is so confused. "Captain Jenkins headed us west to outrun the storm, but the darn radio went dead. Then what? That must have been about Tuesday. Then all the coast navigation lights went out . . ." Then, seeing she has everyone's attention, she adds, "Anyone know what idiot did that?"

"Mom. Then what?"

"Oh, the seas! Up and down and up and down. We were all pukin' our poor guts out. Got across the Columbia bar but near tore apart the engine. So we drift! What a week! You don't know how scary things are when you think you're one place and turns out you're in another. Without radio or lights or navigation. Well, anyway, we found some backwater log boom and tied up."

Now I'm feeling like crud for being mad at Mom. She was in danger a lot more than we were.

"So, you know those *Tinker II* boys. Out comes the bottle and the singin' and I make us some fried fish. Jenkins gets us running again and we come back to Warrenton. I got in my car, started home, but lordy, I was tired and . . ."

"Drunk!" someone added.

"Dry up!" Mom goes on. "Well, I remembered this old clam-digger shack off Beach Drive and I just passed out, I mean, rested there. Think I slept for a whole day. It was that dang turkey woke me up. You know, there's just something out of sorts about a turkey gobblin' here on the coast. I walk outside and all this stuff is scattered on the beach. So I gather it up, come here, and alls I get is yelled at."

Then Frank jumps in with, "You mean to tell us you don't know *anything* that's been going on?"

"No. What happened?"

Frank, Leo, and a few others give her the rundown speckled with plenty of their own two-cent, sword-rattling opinions. No one knows much, but everyone knows the *Mauna Ala* went aground on the spit.

"And those socks and that tree, that turkey," Edna says, "all those Christmasy things were on their way to the boys in Pearl Harbor. If there *are* any boys left in Pearl Harbor. You can't keep those, Alice. You just can't."

Mom looks at the soggy homemade socks on the counter. "But I found 'em. You know the laws of salvage. My car's full of this stuff. I was plannin', well, Christmas for everyone . . ."

There's a card pinned to the socks and the ink is pretty runny, but I can make out the words and read aloud: "Merry Christmas to our wonderful son, Joey! I didn't know you'd be in sunny Hawaii when I knitted these woolies. Ha Ha! Your real present awaits you here at home. Can't wait till you get your leave and can visit us here in snowy Kansas! Don't get sunburned! You know your fair skin! Love, Mom and Dad."

Edna takes the card, her eyes large with tears. The room has gone silent. I'm thinking these hand-knit stocks are the first real, touchable thing that makes us all realize and really *feel* what this war means. All the Joeys in Hawaii who won't get their socks and their trees and their turkey dinners—and what all their deaths have brought us into.

"If you don't mind," Leo says, running his sleeve under his nose and taking the socks, "I think me n' Frank'd like to keep these."

Then ol' Malice Alice says, "Aren't you boys a bit old to hang Christmas stockings?" She looks around like she's expecting laughter, but her grin quickly vanishes.

"No, you fool," Leo says, handing one sock to his brother.

"As a reminder," Frank finishes for him.

Alls Mom says is a weak little "oh." Guess it's all finally sinking in. *Way to go, Mom*. I'm a living, breathing pile of embarrassment. Maybe even shame. Boy, do I understand infamy now!

That pretty much breaks up the crowd. The tree gets tossed into the fire where it hisses and pops and curls all into itself until only the strands of tinsel are left.

One by one, Mom tosses the rest of her Christmas salvage into the fire and she stands watching it all burn. "We'll stop by the dump on our way home," she says to me. "Get rid of all the stuff I found. You drive, Jewels, honey. Mom's tired."

I grab the moldy old cushions from the back of our rusty Dodge and set them so's I can reach the pedals, and I drive us to the dump.

I think this is the hardest thing we've ever had to do—us always being a scrape and a pull away from living in a dump ourselves—but we toss all the food, the presents, and the trees she'd salvaged. Mom finally turns to me. She's still in her fishing gear, looking like a half-slickered fisherman and half-worn mermaid missing all her scales. Tall, thin, and even sort of statue-like.

She puts her arm around me and says, "Well, come on, Jewels, honey. Let's us get on with this dang war."

CHAPTER 10

Mom's yawning and already dropping layers of clothes halfway into her bedroom. She's in bed and sound asleep before I've even lit the stove to make some coffee. I look in on her and mutter, "Welcome home, Mom."

Rex is out and you know how fast a kid gets bored without a radio or a telephone or a new magazine so I go next door thinking maybe Hero needs a walk. And I figure Mr. Kaye will want to know that Mom got back from her incommunicado pretty much in one piece.

Everything is as dark and dreary as February. So much for Christmas. Normally, Mr. Kaye would have the café and the restaurant all lit up in dancing, bright lights for the holidays. The café door is unlocked and I go right in, making my way up to Mr. Kaye's apartment.

I knock on his door. No answer, not even Hero's tail wonking on something, hoping for his walk. I knock again. Nothing. I turn the door knob and it opens.

"Mr. Kaye? It's me, Jewels. Mr. Kaye?" I wonder if maybe he did leave like he said he might. But there's a light on in what he calls his library and I creep toward the doorway. "Mr. Kaye? You here?"

I take a long, close look at the three midget bonsai trees Mr. Kaye has been working on. It's what he calls his "sanity and serenity." He has these little trees all over his apartment, the Look-Sea Lounge, and the greenhouse up at the Feed and Seed. He says he's going to make a whole garden of them for tourists someday. Sort of a tree museum. Here's a hint: don't touch them unless you want to get your hand slapped and an earful of swear words. Bonsai are for grace and beauty and something else that I forget, but definitely *not* for touching.

Okay, I admit it. I can be a snoop. I don't think I've even been in Mr. Kaye's library before. There're books, of course. Lots and lots. There's a photograph in a tortoise shell frame on a table and I look closely at it. It's of a young couple. The man is in a military uniform, only the officer kind. You know, the hat and braid and trimmings. The woman is Japanese, but not dressed like one. I mean, she's sporting American clothes, looking pretty elegant, too. Her black hair is in a short bob like those uppity jazz women used to wear. The little boy standing between them is in a little sailor outfit like they used to dress boys in in the olden days. I look closer. Is it?

"Jewels?"

I whip around, embarrassed to be caught holding the picture frame. My face goes redder than my first name. Mr. Kaye spots the photograph.

"Is this you?" I ask, figuring I'm already caught dead to rights.

"Yes."

"Who are these people?"

He takes the photo and smiles down at it. "Major and Mrs. Calvin Kaye. My parents."

I look at the man in the picture and say, "You sure don't look like your dad."

"Actually, I don't look much like my mother, either. I was adopted, Jewels. They adopted me when my father was with the US Embassy in Japan. I was four years old."

Man, you could have squashed me with a feather. The things you learn about people you think you know when you just come right out and ask. I don't think I've ever known anyone whose folks weren't both white. I don't think I've even met anyone who was even adopted.

Like he could read my mind, he says, "Wasn't easy, growing up in a mixed family. My mother spoke perfect English but made sure I continued to speak perfect Japanese. I think it's really the only Japanese thing about me." His eyes landed on a bonsai sitting on a marble pedestal. "Well, maybe my love for bonsai, too. How's that for irony?"

He sees my face and realizes I've got no idea what he's talking about.

"Mom got back okay," I say, changing the subject.

He smiles. I see he's finally shaved and combed his hair, and he smells of some nice men's cologne. "Good," he says. "Where was she?"

"Just about everywhere. Then Warrenton. She just had to wait things out," I say.

"She alright?"

"Yeah. Tired. Maybe a little hungover," I say, keeping my eyes and voice low.

"That's our Alice. Where is she now? I could sure use her help. Got a note that Virgil Johnson quit today. Didn't even have the guts to tell me to my face. So I don't have anyone to run the feed store. Not that there is much to run."

Kaye's Feed and Seed is just east of town, sort of out of sight and out of mind.

"But folks don't stop feeding their chickens and cows just because of a war, do they?" I say.

"No deliveries. Able men are enlisting. Doesn't matter," he says. "Doesn't matter. Payroll is going to be hard to meet now." He turns away and sits next to the closest bonsai. "But it would be good if Alice could see if maybe she can . . . I don't know. See what she can do."

"I'll go wake her up."

"No, no. Let her sleep. We'll talk tomorrow. Have you been by the bowling alley?"

I hate to tell him but I do. "Sign on the door says 'closed.' I heard Billy McCormick's dad said he can't work there anymore."

"God, what did I ever do to deserve this?" he whispers down to the photo I'm still holding.

I've never heard Mr. Kaye talk this way. I mean, he's a businessman. And smart. Now he just seems sort of . . . lost. Well, I guess we all are in our first week of infamy.

"Where's Hero?" I ask, noticing he isn't on the end of the leash Mr. Kaye has draped over his shoulder.

"You know him, once he gets his nose to the ground . . . he'll be back. He always finds his way back." Then he turns and smiles at me. "Like your mother."

"Did the governor say your dog has to stay inside, too?" I ask, thinking I'm being funny.

"Only Jap dogs. Like the Johnson's pug. Nothing's more American than a good old reliable bloodhound. Even if his name *is* Hero."

"Well, he's heroic, isn't he?" I ask.

"Well, don't tell anyone, but it's H-*I*-R-O on his papers. As in Hirohito. The emperor of Japan. Never mind. He's just good old Hero to us, okay, Jewels?"

"Well, I'll go find him," I say, taking the leash from Mr. Kaye. "Hero, not that emperor guy."

He gets it, smiles, and tells me to get lost.

Which I do. More and more, I'm happy to get lost. Everything is getting too crazy. Sometimes I wisht I had my own incommunicado place to dive into and not have to hear, see, or feel any of this war stuff.

CHAPTER 11

I head toward the beach because, if I were Hero, that's where I'd head. There's a moon hanging up there somewhere, but it sure is dark out. But that wasn't the ocean I just heard. It's laughing. Boys' laughing. I hold my breath to hear better. Eldon Johnson's husky voice rings out from between two beach shanties. I creep closer.

"Grab him!"

It's Eldon all right. I duck into the shadows and try to get a better look. And there's Eldon's security blanket, Bully Hallstrom. They make a fine pair—make that a fine gang. Wonder what those two creeps are up to.

In a high-pitched voice, I hear, "Come here, poochie, poochie, pooch. Got a nice big steak for you full of Vitamin P."

Did I hear Vitamin P?

I peep around the corner and see Eldon open some butcher paper and in it is a big glob of something dark and bloody. I hear Hero's bloodhound howl. Something's very wrong here.

"Hurry up, I can't hold him! Give him the poison!" Bully says.

Poison!

Just as Eldon drops the meat, I rush forward and scream, "Stop it!" I grab the meat and hold it up high. I'm short and Hero's long and he can almost jump up to it. "Down, Hero!" I scream, hating to give him my knee. Then to the boys, I scream, "What're you creeps doing?"

"Get lost, Jewels!" Eldon says. "This is none of your business!"

Hero's jumping for the meat, almost knocking me down. I hold the package even higher and scream, "No! Down! No!"

"Get out of here, Jewels. I mean it!" Eldon tries to grab for the meat and so does Hero. Eldon gets it and tosses it to the ground. Hero goes straight for it and I just manage to pull on this collar with both hands before he snatches it up.

"Hero! No! No!" I scream and pull and Hero is almost on the meat when another pair of hands grab Hero's collar. I quickly click on his leash and haul him back with all my weight.

"Rex! They're trying to poison Hero!" I yell. Rex takes the leash and stands between me and the boys. I scoop the meat off the ground and hold it up. "It's got poison in it!" I wrap the meat back in the butcher paper.

"Throw it away," Rex says.

"No, it's evidence! I'm getting Sheriff Hillary!" I tell him. Then to Eldon, "You're not getting away with this! I should give this to *your* mother's prize pug!"

"Throw it away, Jewels," Rex orders again. "There's a can right over there."

I do it fast, making sure the lid is on good and tight, then go back to my brother as our new Town Hood faces Bully and Eldon.

"Why would you want to poison that dog?" Rex asks.

Eldon points toward Hero. "You know whose dog that is!"

"Meaning?"

"He's a Jap, that's what!"

"He is not!" I yell. I've never been in a fist fight, but there's a first time for everything and I'm ready. Me and Rex. Shoulder to shoulder, just like in the movies.

But it doesn't go that way. Rex hollers, "Jewels, take that dog home! Go on! Get home!"

You'd think it was *me* doing something bad the way he screams at me.

"You come, too. Mom's home," I say.

"Oh, so the Town Bimbo's back from work, huh?" Eldon says, laughing with Bully. "Hey, the whole family's got a title! Town Hood, Town Clown, and Town Bimbo!"

The insult goes right over Rex's head.

"Did you hear what he called Mom?" I demand, coming at Eldon with two fists.

"Jewels, get out of here!" Rex yanks me back.

I try to kick Eldon's shin, but Rex pulls me back again. "I said, get home!" he hollers.

I feel my heart banging against my chest. I don't know who I'm madder at—these hoods for trying to poison Hero, my brother for screaming at me, or myself for running away from them all.

Hero gallumps behind me. I run up the back stairs of the Stay and Play and let him find his own way down to Mr. Kaye's apartment, thinking there's no way Jewels Stokes is going to run away from a fight! So I turn-tail it and run back to help Rex.

But there is no fight. I stand frozen and watch Bully and Eldon beat the living daylights out of Rex, who's curled up on the ground, never lifting a fist. It's horrible. I see the kicks and the punches; I hear the laughter; I see Rex's horrible face. I burst out of the shadows and start screaming.

"Stop it! Stop it!" I scoop up gravel and throw it at them while I kick and scream and pull and slug. Until finally they stop, back up, and then Eldon gives Rex one last kick to his side, folding him in half again.

Eldon stands there, his face red and his eyes narrow. He points first at me, then at the Stay and Play, then he points down to Rex and screams, "I oughta kill you, you

Jap-loving coward!" Then, he and Bully both run off, vanishing into the distance.

And there it is again. My own private infamy. I help Rex up, blood gushing from his nose and mouth.

"Why didn't you fight back? You just took it!"

He sways as he tries to catch his breath. "I'm smarter than those two jerks. I wouldn't lower myself to their level."

"Well, they sure lowered you! What was your plan? *Debate* them?"

"Just shut up about it! Got that, Jewels?" He bends over, holds his stomach, and pukes out some blood. "This isn't your fight, so you just shut up about it!"

"What fight? That wasn't a fight. That was a massacre."

"I said, shut up!" he screams at me. I feel little splatters of spit and blood hit my face. He picks up his cap and limps off toward the beach.

The war is only four days old and already I'm sick of it.

CHAPTER 12

I get up early the next morning. I'm not sure I even slept at all, between Mom's snoring and the memory of everything that happened the night before. My first thought is Rex. I go to his room, ignoring the Do Not Disturb sign, and knock.

No answer. I knock a bit harder. Cripes, he might be dead. I open the door and whisper, "Hey, Rex. How you doing?"

"Go away."

Of course I don't. I go over to his bed and pull on the overhead light. A pillow goes over his head. "Kill the light, creep!"

I tug at the pillow and he groans as he tries to hold it in place. "Don't, Jewels. Don't . . ."

I catch a glimpse. "Rex! Look at you!"

"I know," he whispers, his arm covering his eyes.

"Has Mom seen you yet?"

"She just stuck her head in the door. She didn't see my face. And she's not going to, got it?"

"She'll go haywire. Let me see."

Slowly, his arm comes away from his head. Oh, Lord! He has a black eye and there's blood where the white part should be. There's a bandage on his forehead and his jaw has a huge bruise on it.

"How bad's that cut? Need stitches?"

"Nah, but it took half the night to get it to stop bleeding."

"You should have woke me up. I would have helped."

He makes an effort to sit, but he grabs his sides and winces with shaky breaths. "Jewels, bring me that old canvas belt in my closet. This one isn't doing it."

"Doing what?"

He gingerly raises his shirt and shows me the leather belt he has hitched around his chest. "What's that for?" I ask.

"I think I have a few broken ribs. It kills to breathe. We learned the belt trick in first aid at school. Got to bind 'em."

"No, I'm getting Mom," I say.

He grabs my robe and pulls me back. "No you aren't, Jewels! Mom's not going to know how bad I got beat up."

"Well, one look at that face and she's going to get suspicious."

"Just a black eye and small cut," he says.

"Oh yeah? You look like you went through a meat-grinder!"

"Shut up about it! I'll be fine."

"But broken ribs, Rex!"

"I just need to wrap them. There's nothing you can do for broken ribs. I know, get me that stretchy bandage Mom got when she sprained her ankle last year. That'll help, and I can cinch it with a belt."

I help him to his bathroom. We fill the sink with warm water and I help him clean off the dried blood. Looking at him in the mirror, I say, "Guess that's why Carla broke your date." Why am I always the one spilling the bad news? "She called this morning."

He just looks down into the basin of soapy water and blood and says, "The whole town must know by now." He sort of laughs and then grabs his side in pain. "Some Town Hood I turned out to be. Town Coward is more like it. I don't care what they call me."

"Me either," I say. But I think I do.

Like he reads my thought, he says, "But you will, Jewels."

• • •

I head to the café to cook up the last of the pancake batter I made earlier that week and pack up some ice for Rex. As I cross the parking lot, I get a feeling something is different, though nothing looks out of place. I look around before unlocking the café door. But the memory of Eldon and Bully laughing as they ran off, leaving Rex in a heap, is alls I can see in my head.

But then I turn and there it is. In blood-red, dripping paint acrost the front of the Kozy Korner Kafe are the words: KILL THE JAPS!

I look up at the second and third stories of the building to the large windows of the Look-Sea Lounge and Mr. Kaye's apartment. One, two, three panes of glass are broken. I look around me. The town is still quiet, almost dead.

Then I hear car tires on gravel.

Sheriff Hillary drives into the parking lot. She gets out, looks at the paint, the broken windows, then at me. "I got a call from Bea Johnson there's been a little vandalism." She looks up at the building.

"She'd know," I say.

Sheriff Hillary ignores me and asks, "How's your brother?"

"You know?"

"Of course I know. It's all over town he got the living crap beat out of him."

"They could have killed him, you know," I say.

"Boys'll be boys," she states. "I've always made it a policy never to interfere with these teen rivalries. They'll iron it out."

"They'll iron *him* out!" I shout. That gets me a "watch it, missy" glare.

She points to the red paint. "Who did this?"

"You know who!"

"Don't you raise your voice to me, young lady!" She lights a cigarette with a shaky lighter. Then she tones it down some. "Look, Jewels," she begins, looking at the ocean, not the building, not at me, "Rex is Town Hood. He better learn to defend himself." Then she adds, "Why do you think I chose him?"

"To turn him into something he isn't?" I holler. "Rex was right! You *are* all those things he called you! A Hitler-facist-whatever-else he said!"

"A man has to learn to defend himself. This is no time to be a coward."

Hearing Sheriff Hillary call Rex a coward makes me want to burst inside. I want to knock her down. She takes my arm and says sternly, the cigarette bobbing as she talks, "Jewels, you just listen to me. We're at war. We all have bigger problems than this!"

"You take it back! Rex is not a coward!" I holler, pulling myself away.

"Doesn't matter, girl. Once people think you are, you have to prove them wrong. That's just the way the world works."

She tosses down her cigarette so she can hold me, both hands on my shoulders, and she looks at me straight on. I can tell . . . there's something different. Her eyes. Red, puffy, angry, maybe even scared.

"Men are dying every day because of cowards," she says. "Jap cowards!" She lets go of me, picks up her cigarette, puffs it back to life, and just stares to the west. "Maybe even my own Norman."

When she turns back around, I see tears in her eyes but she runs her sleeve over her face. She says, "Look, Rex is Town Hood. Beat up or not, his job is to clean all this." She looks up at the broken windows. "Tommy'll have to fix those himself. He's got the money. Where is he anyway?"

"I don't know. Upstairs, I guess."

"He better be. He knows the orders," she snaps, crushing out her cigarette with her husband's perfect-fitting Wellington boot.

"What orders?"

"Governor Sprague's. All Japs need to stay inside. It's for their own safety." She points to the building. "As you can see, folks are a little upset right now."

"Mr. Kaye didn't do anything. He's an American. Just like you and me."

She looks hard at me. "It's like being a coward—once people *think* you're the enemy, there's no changing their minds."

"But he's *not* the enemy." I'm trying to control my voice.

"Doesn't matter. He looks like he is."

"So does Mayor Schmidtke," I say. "In fact, he even *sounds* like the enemy. Being German and all. I mean, aren't we at war with them, too?"

"Just get this cleaned up. I don't have time to babysit you kids. I'm going to San Francisco to wait for Norm."

What am I supposed to say? I run a whole circle of thoughts starting right here in front of Tommy Kaye's building with KILL THE JAPS painted on it, with a beat-up brother in bed next door, with a mother fresh out of her incommunicado, and now a sheriff holding back tears because she thinks her husband got killed by a Japanese attack a million miles west in some place called Pearl Harbor. And my circle ends right back here where it starts, looking up at Tommy Kaye's Look-Sea Lounge.

Alls I can mutter is "okay," but I'm so mad I don't even tell her "don't worry, Sheriff. Mr. Dutton will be fine, wait and see" or any of the other malarky people say to each other when they don't want to hear the truth.

• • •

"Come in," Mr. Kaye says from inside his apartment. Hero's on the other side of the door and licks my hand as I ease myself inside. I'm about to tell Mr. Kaye about the windows in case he hasn't heard them break, but the two bricks on his coffee table tell me he already knows. He's holding a piece of paper in one hand. I see it quiver as he gives it to me. I read aloud: "Go back to Japan, you slant-eyed traitor!"

"And, um, some jerks painted on the café walls outside. Rex is going to paint over it for you, so don't worry."

"What does it say?"

"Kill the Japs."

He just nods his head, then out of nowhere asks, "What are you now? Ten? Eleven?"

I'm not sure I'm insulted or not. "I turned twelve in August."

He nods his head again. "Just a kid. You know, you and that dog are the only two beings who have even looked at me since Sunday. My employees have quit, my deliveries have quit, my customers have canceled orders. My business associates, no one, not one soul—not even my priest has called or visited. In fact, the only phone calls I've gotten are from my bankers saying that all my assets are frozen."

"What are frozen?"

He snaps back, "Assets! Money! Cash! Don't they teach you kids anything at school?"

I don't like being yelled at because I don't know what an asset is, frozen or thawed.

"Not one person has called to see if I'm okay. No, instead I get bricks! I get death threats!" He looks at me and says, "Not even Edna Glick has come over."

"Well, she's been extra busy since you aren't open, Mr. Kaye. You know how this town drinks! And just yesterday when the McAloons started to . . ." Oh, he doesn't need to know about their sword-rattling song. "Anyway, Edna says she'll blackball anyone who says anything bad about you. She's on your side!"

He turns and glares at me. "One my side of *what?*"

"I don't know. I've never done a war. I don't know anything about assets or bricks and to tell you the truth,

I'm getting a little tired of this whole town going off the deep end about this stupid war!"

He gives a big sigh. "I'm sorry, Jewels. Look, I'm grateful for you being, well, being a friend, that's all. A twelve-year-old kid and a ten-year-old dog. My only allies." His hand goes to Hero's bony head.

I'm wondering if I should tell him about Rex and how worried I am about him. But it will only make Mr. Kaye feel bad and that's not going to help Rex feel better.

"Can you go over to the Feed and Seed? I'm worried about my bonsai. They're probably thirsty, maybe scared, maybe lonely, especially The Old Man. I moved him up there a few weeks ago."

I look around and notice his prize bonsai isn't in his usual place of honor. "What for?"

"I take him up there when he needs some warm, moist air and sometimes, well, to be with his old friends."

Yes, he's talking about midget trees.

He gives me a list with each bonsai's name. I told you how nuts-and-bolts he is about them. He tells me how to touch the soil and feel if they're thirsty. And talk to them! I must be sure to talk to them.

Then he hands me another piece of paper and says, "And here's the combination to the safe. There's a black strong box in it, and I need it. And this," he points to the combination. "Be sure to flush it down the toilet when you close the safe. Oh, and I guess I need three window panes. Those are the dimensions."

I'm actually glad I got an errand. I need to get outside where I can think and breathe.

"Jewels?"

I turn.

"You are, you know? You're my one true friend. My lifeline."

I smile and nod, but inside I wisht he hadn't said that. I don't want any of this on my shoulders. Not on top of everything else I'm lugging around on this, my fifth day of infamy.

CHAPTER 13

Mom's up and fiddling with the radio dial when I return to check on her before running my Feed and Seed errand.

"Did you kids break this thing?" she demands.

"There's a blackout."

"I know it's black out," she says. "What time is it, anyway?"

I lift the ghastly pink and green floral curtains and the black cloth behind them and when the brightness of the afternoon sun hits her, she winces and almost reels back.

"Say, what are those ugly things?" She fingers the blackout cloth.

I pick up the newspapers I was able to collect, plop them down on the table, put her reading glasses on top, and say, "Here, Mom. Read for yourself. We're at war. They make us do the blackout. No lights at night, hardly any radio during the day. Hardly anything anymore."

Mom looks pretty awful. All puffy-eyed and shaky, sitting there with horn-rimmed glasses propped on her rosy nose and a cigarette hanging off her chapped lips, eyes squinty against the rising smoke. Looking at her now, I have a hard time believing ol' Malice Alice was once a looker and, not only that, pretty smart. Mr. Kaye reminds me of that all the time. I know you can lose your looks, but your smarts? Well, if anyone can lose them, Alice Stokes can. But I always wonder where exactly smarts go when you lose them?

"Yes, I guess we *are* at war," she mumbles after glancing at the headlines and taking her glasses off. "Guess I was hopin' it was all just a big, horrible dream."

"Better put 'em back on, Mom," I say, handing her the latest stack of bills.

"What're these? Oh. *These*." She flips through the large stack.

"I stalled off Ashby's Grocery for another week. I told them you got a job on a boat." I pull that bill out and put it on the top of the stack.

She looks it over and then the butcher's bill and then the gas bill. We charge everything in town. I guess everybody does. If there was a movie called *Rob Peter to Pay Paul,* our whole town could be in it. Peter would be played by Tommy Kaye and most everyone else would play the Pauls, but we'd be the stars.

I don't like that little pout I see creeping up on Mom's face.

"Mom? You did get paid, didn't you?"

She runs her hand through her hair and mumbles, "Hope to kiss a pig, I did." She brings a weary curl in front of her eyes and adds, "If I don't get a perm soon . . . bring me my purse. Check my pants pockets, too."

Empty. Emptier. Emptiest. Purse, pockets, glove compartment. Not even loose change.

Mom gives me her "oopsy" look, which might fool men, but it doesn't fool me.

"Nothing?"

"I think I loaned some money to one of the crew and then . . . poker. Oh, hon, don't worry, Jewels! I'm back and ready to work and they'll be out fishin' again as soon as this storm blows over. Hey, why aren't you in school? I swear, Jewels, if you got suspended again for one of your pranks, I'll—"

"Mom, school's closed."

"You mean because of this war thing?"

I want to say *"Bingo!"* but know she'll hit the fan if I do. We don't need to start our own war right here at home. "There's lots to do. Like the blackout curtains and beach patrols. Committees and stuff. Men are enlisting left and right. Even Arley went to Portland to enlist."

"There, you see? There's our out right there! God may close a door but he keeps a window open! I'll take Arley's shift at the Kozy Korner and we'll be sittin' pretty in a month!"

Right, Alice, I think. God started a war just to close a door on you so you can find a stupid window and climb through. Then, as though she hears another door closing, she sits up straight and asks, "Where's Rex? I swear I'll kill him if he ran off to Portland to enlist!"

Rex? Enlist? Jeez, Mom, figure it out. But she sure doesn't need to see what condition he's in, so I say, "Mom, there's no school so he's pooped out. Let him sleep."

"Well, I'll just go in and tell him I'm home."

"He knows you're home. You checked on him last night. Remember?"

"Is he mad at me? You know, for being, well, gone? I mean, you kids are okay, gettin' so grown up and all. You know, a girl has to get out now and then and . . ." This sort of talk usually leads to The Big I'm Sorry, so I break her off.

"We're fine, Mom. We got bigger things to be mad about."

"I hate when everyone's all mad," she says. "I just do. I don't understand any of this." Her hand goes to her head and she twists some old, worn out curls around her chipped-nail-polished fingers.

"Mom, go take a nice long, hot shower, fix yourself up some, and go see Mr. Kaye. See about Arley's job. Mr. Kaye's lonely over there."

She looks at me and flashes me her worldly smile. "Honey, the richest man in town is never lonely. That's a fact."

Sometimes she makes me want to scream. I point out the newspaper editorial, grab a pencil, and make a big circle around "Never Trust A Jap." She looks at it, then back up at me, then over toward the Stay and Play where Tommy Kaye, richest man in town, lives.

It hits her and she sighs a big long, "Oooohhhh yeah."

CHAPTER 14

I'm not sure what to expect as I bike through town. Maybe Eldon's gang has left their opinions on all Mr. Kaye's businesses. Why stop at trying to kill Hero or vandalizing the Stay and Play? What if they did the same to the feed store? What about the rabbits, ducks, and chickens? What would Sea Park do without the feed store if they burned it to the ground? Everyone in town has an account there, even us, for hardware and other stuff. I bike faster. I think I smell smoke, but it's a beach town and there's almost always the smell of someone burning something.

I round the corner. The Feed and Seed is dark as death. This time last year there were strings of lights dancing over rows of Christmas trees; kids' horses were tied to the hitching posts munching oats Mr. Kaye doled out for free. I remember the crate of free Christmas puppies next to the potbellied stove. The sales counter had hot apple cider and spritz cookies for customers, paying or no, and Mr. Kaye always made his special batch of eggnog for the adults in the back room.

Now look. Nothing. The loading dock doors are pulled shut and lights are off. I ditch my bike and climb the front steps to read the note on the door: CLOSED UNTIL FURTHER NOTICE. Someone has scribbled out "Until Further Notice" and written OWNED BY A JAP! I rip the paper down and tear it up. Then I check on the poultry out back and look, there's a turkey! I'll bet it's the half-drowned one Mom got from the ship wreck. Bet Edna put it there. I give them all a pan of water and scatter some feed. They're all glad to see me.

I unlock the door and the bell over the top ding-dings a Christmasy welcome. "Probably going to be the only thing Christmasy around Sea Park," I grumble to myself. I inhale. I love the sweet smell of hay and oats and fresh cut lumber. I wisht I could live here.

I switch on the lights and head to the loft upstairs to get the glass panes. They're easy to find because everything up there's so organized. I love looking down over the feed store from here. When I was small, I used to just sit up here, my legs dangling over the edge, watching customers come and go. But not today. There's work to do. I head back downstairs.

I love Mr. Kaye's office, too. It shows a whole different side of Tommy Kaye. I mean, not the man you'd see in a tuxedo welcoming people to his fancy dances with the big bands or the man in a long white apron helping to wait tables if he was shorthanded or the man behind a bar listening to someone's tale of woe or the man at the piano playing a boogie or a waltz—and from memory, too. In this office, I see the Tommy Kaye who ordered feed and flowers and lumber and lets it all walk out the door on credit; or that man who'll give you a discount not because you are paying with cash, but because you are *paying;* I see the Tommy Kaye who let kids sit out front and give away kittens and puppies and I see the Tommy Kaye who organized our annual Fourth of July parade and fireworks show.

But my very favorite place is in the greenhouse. Mom says down south it's called a sunporch. I love the view of the ocean from here, and no matter how cold it is outside, it's always warm and there's that smell of pine and soil. The windows are a bit steamy today, so I know it's getting chilly outside. Mr. Kaye says steamy windows means there's life and breath in this room, all coming from his bonsai.

It's here I see the most interesting of all the Tommy Kayes. In this greenhouse, I see how much he loves this collection of bonsai trees. Each one has a name, an age, and a place of birth all engraved on brass plaques. Most of them come from places I've never even heard of. Mr. Kaye says each bonsai has its own life story and he knows every one of them. When I was a kid, he used to tell me some of those stories, but he was probably just making it all up. He always told me bonsai were balanced, but in a lopsided way.

I pull out the instructions Mr. Kaye gave me: "Talk kindly. No gossip or gab or gibberish. Never talk down to them—they're not children." I read on. "And tell The Old Man not to worry. All will be well."

I go over to The Old Man, Mr. Kaye's pride and joy. He's got a place of honor, sitting front row center with the younger bonsai around him like kids at his feet. This bonsai is, let's see—he's six hundred and some change years old.

"Mr. Kaye says don't worry. All will be well," I say, glad no one's around to hear me talking to a bush. The Old Man's all gnarled and sort of crippled looking. Well, who wouldn't be when you're *that* old? The pine needles are so teeny-tiny and the greens are vivid like the ocean in the summer. Even the moss shines up at me. Mr. Kaye told me that moss and The Old Man are inseparable friends and one would die without the other. That sounds over the top, but what do I know?

I finish the watering, then take some quick measurements of the windows for blackout curtains. "Hope you guys like the dark," I mutter down to them. I go back into the office.

I look at the safe combination Mr. Kaye wrote down for me. This way, stop. That way, stop. Back right, stop. Do it again. Missed it! Jeez, I can order a case of dynamite, get it delivered, light it off, and then let the dust settle in less time than it's taking me to get this dang combination to work! Okay, third try. I put my ear to the safe. Maybe I haven't been able to hear that *click*. Yep! There it is! *CLICK!* And the two large handles break loose.

The black steel doors are ice cold and I remember Mr. Kaye's remark about "frozen assets." I grip the handles and use my weight to pull back the doors. I've seen this safe open many times so I'm not disappointed that rubies and opals and pearls and coins and stocks and bonds and bundles of cash don't fall out and bury me like in the "Open Sesame" cartoons.

I look for the black strongbox and open a hatch and a little door. Well, I'm definitely going to snoop around just a little. Another door sort of peeks open. There's a ton of keys hanging on it. I can never figure out why anyone would keep a key *inside* something that's locked, but I've never had anything worth having a key to open. But Mr. Kaye sure does. Each key has a little wooden disc stating what it unlocks. I'll bet there's a hundred of them. I flip through a few and they say cabin number this or car model that, bowling alley safe, booze room, storage locker; you name it—there's a key for it.

I push the safe doors back in and man oh man, these doors are heavy! But they finally meet up. I'm halfway out of the office and then remember to flush the combination down the toilet in the office bathroom. I load the window panes and the strongbox into the wooden milk crate roped acrost the back fender of my bike and cover everything with an old scrap of tarp, then I hop on my bike and pedal off toward home.

• • •

"Thanks, kiddo," Mr. Kaye says, taking the box. "Did you check on my bonsai? How's The Old Man?"

"He asked how you were."

"What did you tell him?"

"Well, I didn't want him to worry," I say, wondering if we're joking or not. His face looks serious, so I add, "So I said you've never been better." He nods and I take it further. "I didn't think he needed to know about Pearl Harbor and all, because he's . . . you know . . . *Japanese*."

Mr. Kaye smiles at me and says, "That was very considerate of you, Jewels. Everything else okay there? Any . . . you know . . ."

"No, everything's fine. Kind of dark, kind of cold. But all the stuff is working in the greenhouse. Nice and warm in there." I don't think he needs to know about the note pinned to the door. "Made measurements for black out curtains." Then I catch a lingering whiff of what Mom calls her "signature perfume."

"Has Mom been here?"

"Yes. She told me about her latest . . ."—he pauses like adults do when they're thinking about what word to use—". . . adventure. Asked for an advance on her salary."

"Oh, she said maybe now with Arley gone, she can have his job and cook downstairs. You think—"

"Jewels," he cuts me off. "No one is going to come in for a cup of coffee, let alone a fried egg sandwich. Not for a while, anyway."

I do not want to hear anything else about this stupid war and jobs and money or no money. I'm starving and I just want out of here. I'm going home.

"Well, anyway, there's your box and window panes," I say, heading for the door.

"Maybe you or Rex can come back later and take Hero for his walk? Maybe help me with the windows?"

"Sure." And I then duck out fast.

• • •

Our cabin is chilly and silent. And there's that same whiff of signature perfume. I look around. Her purse isn't hanging on the chair and some of the bills on the table are gone. No car keys. Mr. Kaye must have given her enough "salary" to pay Paul, maybe get a perm and gas the car. She better not end up at the Inn and Out, but I'll bet she does.

So I spend the rest of the day taking care of Rex as best I can. I make ice packs and I find the leftover pain pills Mom used for her sprained ankle last year. So he sleeps most of the day and right on into the night.

Just as well Mom's out and about.

CHAPTER 15

Rex is right about one thing: I *do* care about him being called the Town Coward. It's Friday and school's back in. It's one of the worst days of my life. It's almost like I have the plague, the way kids start treating me. On our walk home, Rex tells me he's had it even worse. He's been unvoted captain of the debate team—something about his term being up with the New Year coming. But he just acts the same as always and tells me to just be cool—to act like I don't hear the jokes and pokes. Easy for him. Even with a black eye, a bandaged forehead, and a stiff walk, he makes like nothing is wrong. Well, it's not so easy for me.

It's hard to ignore words like *hero* and *coward* when the first photos of the damage in Pearl Harbor are printed acrost the front page of the newspaper—big as life. It's pretty gruesome, I'll tell you that. Huge billows of smoke rising out of a jungle of tangled ship masts, spars, and spires. Only the very tops of giant battleships can be seen rising from the waters. And the death toll's printed, too—not in dozens, not in hundreds, but over two thousand! More than two hundred of our Navy ships and aircraft are destroyed.

And along with the photos come the firsthand accounts, the names of the dead and missing, and then the blame. So now at last the whole world sees the for-real damage in Pearl Harbor. I'll never forget the look on Rex's face when he saw that first horrible photo.

But it's me who first sees the for-real damage in Sea Park as I round the corner to the Feed and Seed. It's my daily check on the bonsai and poultry. I've named the turkey Sailor, in honor of Pearl Harbor. But all the chicken, rabbits, ducks, and Sailor are gone when I arrive today. Their chicken wire cage is lying in shambles.

I go around to the front door and yep, the windows are all broken out.

My heart *tap-tap-taps* as I step into the ransacked office; it *pound-pound-pounds* as I see the open safe doors; it *thud-thud-thuds* as I look into the greenhouse. Oh no! Every bonsai is murdered! The windows are broken, the trays and bowls of bonsai are smashed, the trees are mutilated!

I ring up Sheriff Hillary. No answer, and then I remember she's in San Francisco to see if Norm survived

Pearl Harbor. Now who I am supposed to call for help? Just who's in charge?

I know! The Town Hood. Rex'll know what to do.

"It's me. I'm at the Feed and Seed. Come quick!" I say into the office phone.

Which he does.

"Oh lord, no," he whispers, looking around the room.

"Who would do this to Mr. Kaye, Rex?" I ask.

"I think the question is who *wouldn't* do this."

I look at the black safe's gaping maw. There's a red shop rag hanging out of it and it looks like a calling card. Everyone knows Eldon works at the Shell station in town. But I figure it doesn't really matter who did this. What matters is I must not have closed the safe doors all the way.

"Rex, it's all my fault! How am I going to tell Mr. Kaye? Who knows what was in that safe and those cabinets. And his bonsai!"

"Cut it out, Jewels! You had nothing to do with this! Look, I'm going to call Edna. She'll know what to do."

While he does that, I go back to the greenhouse, carefully placing the uprooted and bashed bonsai back into cracked and tipped-over pots.

"I'm sorry. I'm sorry," I whimper down to them. Now what happens to their names? Their life stories? Do they get buried?

I look around, then panic. I screech to Rex, "He's gone! He's gone!"

Rex rushes in. "Who's gone?"

"The Old Man! He's not here. Not anywhere! He's worth hundreds and hundreds of dollars. Maybe thousands. Maybe priceless!"

• • •

"Oh, no, this can't be," Edna says, finding us in the back office.

She looks at the opened safe, the riffled drawers, the tipped over file cabinets, and then the greenhouse. "Oh, no . . ." she says, taking it all in.

"This is going to kill Mr. Kaye," I say, running my coat sleeve under my running nose.

Edna puts her hand on my shoulder and says, "No, it won't. He has insurance. He'll get over this."

Then I tell her that The Old Man is missing.

"Well, *that* might kill him," she says, which puts me back into tears. "Oh, come on. I was joking, Jewels. Tommy's survived worse than this."

"Should we call the county police?" Rex asks. "State? FBI? Who do we call for something like this? I'd like to call President Roosevelt, I'll tell you that! Tell him to tell his old soldier boys to stop writing those inflammatory editorials! People are trying to get even for Pearl Harbor! Anyone can see that!"

Edna looks at Rex, who is standing under the overhead light, which makes him look more like Frankenstein's monster than my brother. "There's a lot of getting even going on around here. What's under that bandage?"

She reaches for his forehead, but he pulls back. I notice how he walks so stiffly and erect and I figure his ribs are killing him.

"Well, your mother should have taken you to the clinic," Edna continues.

"Lay off, will you, Edna?" Rex says, about as sharp as I've ever heard him talk to an adult, especially one he likes, like Edna Glick.

She looks at him, then at me. "All right, Rex. I'll lay off. Come on, kids. We have to go tell Mr. Kaye."

"I'm taking these," I say, pointing to the remains of the bonsai. "Maybe he can put them back together. They'll die here now."

We get a few boxes and place the bonsai in them, trying not to do any more damage, then carefully place them in Edna's car. She says she'll meet us back at Mr. Kaye's. Rex and me grab our bikes. I peddle as fast as I can and look back at Rex, who rides so slow it's like he's hauling a cannon. I come to Highway 101 and instead of peddling north, I want to peddle south and just disappear—find me my own incommunicado—but I don't. I wait for Rex and we ride into the Stay and Play parking lot together, parking next to Edna's car.

We each take a box with the wounded bonsai and carry them up to Mr. Kaye's apartment. Wonder what we look like—three porters carrying the worst news possible to our friend.

It's my mother who answers the door. "Well, what do we have here? Look, Tommy, it's the Three Wise Acres bringing us gifts!" she says. Per usual, my mother uses her mouth before she uses her eyes. As she looks into the first box Edna's toting, she says, "Oh, Lord."

Tommy calls from kitchen, "Don't tell me we have company . . ." His face turns to stone as he looks first at Rex, then at the bonsai.

"What happened to you, son? Put down that box and let me look at you. Alice, you didn't tell me Rex went through a meat grinder. Look at—"

"The Feed and Seed has been trashed," Rex says, breaking him off.

"It's my fault." I explain about the heavy safe doors being pulled open. "Maybe I forgot to get it closed all the way. Even the chickens, the rabbits, the turkey . . ."

"And The Old Man?" he asks, slowly sitting down.

"He wasn't there. They took him," I say.

"That explains the crank call some jerk made," my mother says, pointing to the telephone.

"What call?" Edna asks.

"A muffled voice just said, 'Leave town now and it lives,' then hung up," Mr. Kaye says. "I've been getting threats and hate calls all week. I didn't think much of that one, but I do now."

The room grew silent. Even though it's dark out and the curtains are pulled, there is still something even darker, quieter, scarier about a room that has blackout curtains hanging in it. I've never been in a funeral parlor, but I'll bet this is what it's like. Quiet as death.

"Well, you got my strong box, Jewels. At least I have that."

My mother touches Mr. Kaye's arm, looks at Edna, and asks, "What all was in that safe, Tommy? Anything from . . ." Edna gives her a sharp look and Mom closes her mouth.

They all three lock eyeballs the way adults do. "Nothing that concerns you," Mr. Kaye says. Then he turns to Edna and adds, "Or you."

Well, if it doesn't concern any of them, it sure as heck doesn't concern Rex and me. So if he isn't saying anything, I'm not either.

CHAPTER 16

I got two shopping lists—Mom's and Mr. Kaye's. Everyone shops at Ashby's. There's already talk of rationing so I figure that's why there're so many cars in the side lot. Mom's list is pretty big; we're out of just about everything, and I just hope she's paid our account down some. But since she's sporting a new perm, I got my doubts. On the other hand, no woman is more charming than Malice Alice sporting a new perm, and that charm goes a long way in the credit department. I get a dirty look from Mr. Ashby when I come in, so I'm not too hopeful.

I get two baskets anyway and go to work. Over the top of the shelves I can see that ugly peacock-blue velvet hat Mrs. Bea Johnson—Eldon's mother—always wears on her shopping day. She works at the post office and she's got the goods on half of everybody in town. She's talking to the woman who's got the other half, Mrs. Selma O'Leary. She cooks and cleans for Father Donlevy, who lives next door to his church, St. Bart's By the Sea. *The Sand Dune Telegraph*—that's what everyone calls our local gossip machine—says Selma spends too much time cleaning close to the confession room at the church and if ol' Selma's close by, you just better watch what you're confessing!

Anyway, I keep my head low and sort of lean into the shelves, keeping my mouth shut and my ears open. You can learn a lot from these two old biddies.

"I tell you, Selma, I'm scared," Mrs. Johnson says.

"Well, these are scary times, Bea. We're all scared."

"Look at the price of sugar! And only a few bags left."

"My Virgil says it's already scarce in Portland. Better stock up, Bea. At least we can still have our Christmas baking, even if we can't have our Christmas lights."

"And I hear rubber is going to be rationed soon, too," Mrs. Johnson says.

"Oh dear, I better stop at the Rexall on the way home."

They snicker again but I don't get what's so funny.

"Say, has anyone heard about Norm Dutton yet?" Mrs. Johnson asks.

"Well, his ship was in Pearl Harbor. You saw the pictures in the paper. Poor Hillary. Can you imagine? Just a sailor swabbing the deck one minute and *ka-boom!* bombed to Kingdom Come by a Jap the next."

There's a little silence and I move a cereal box to sneak a peek at them.

"And just where do you think that sneaky little Jap Tommy Kaye's been hiding?"

Then Selma O'Leary says, "You know, I have never trusted that man."

"I know! It's his *eyes,*" Mrs. Johnson says. "Between you and me, Selma, that's why my Virgil quit the Feed and Seed. He said we're not to have anything to do with him."

"And don't you wonder where he gets his money?" says a third voice. Guess half the town is over there on aisle three.

"Well, you're new here, Dottie, but that Tommy Kaye isn't exactly as pure as the driven snow."

"Driven *yellow* snow!" one of them spouts, and they all snicker.

"But all his pledges for the church and building those playgrounds," the Dottie voice says.

"*Japanese* money!" Bea says.

"I can tell you this: if it's Tommy Kaye, it's dirty money! You know it's common knowledge that him and that Stokes woman were up to no good during Prohibition."

"My Virgil said when he went to the enlistment office, the men in line we talking about locking *all* the Japs up."

"Prison?"

"Well, I guess. Either that or sending them all on a slow boat to China."

"I think China's on our side," Selma O'Leary says.

"Oh, I meant Japan," Mrs. Johnson says with a small laugh.

"Good riddance to the little traitors, I say," the third voice chimes in.

"Well, you know the governor has ordered that they're supposed to stay in their homes."

"Yes, but that's for *their* protection. What about *ours?*"

"Did you hear about the Feed and Seed? It's like a bomb went off in there. What if my Virgil had been there when that happened?" Mrs. Johnson says. I can almost see her hand going to her throat like she's saving her neck.

I want to pop over the counter and scream out that it was her own precious Eldon who tore up the building with his fellow thug, Bully, but I think better of it.

"No, I heard the government thinks some of these people *are* the enemy," Mrs. Johnson goes on. "They think some of these Japs have been *planted* here!"

"And there's that Tommy Kaye with his big fancy restaurant and all that land and forests up on Two Pine Ridge. What does he need all that land for?" Selma O'Leary says.

"Well, you *know* they've seized all their money. That should put a stop to any . . ."

Bea Johnson stalls and Selma O'Leary fills in the words, "Dirty deeds."

"And did you hear about that Stokes boy?" the third voice asks.

"Heard someone gave him what-for for defending Tommy Kaye," Selma O'Leary answers. "Serves him right."

"And what do you suppose that tramp of a mother of his is doing?"

"Well," Selma says, "it makes you think. They might *all* be in it together. Trash of a feather sticks together!"

"Wouldn't be the first time, would it, Bea?" Selma says, and I can just bet they are winking and nodding and it won't be long before this Dottie, whoever she is, will be filled in on all the details.

I can't stand it anymore and crash around the corner, upsetting a pyramid of creamed corn.

"Oh, hello, Jewels," Mrs. Johnson says to me, putting a fake smile on her face.

"For your information, it was Eldon and Bully who . . ." Then I remember that Rex made me swear to keep my trap shut about the whole incident. Anyway, she probably knows what her sweet, dearest Eldon has been up to. "Never mind! Just you be careful how you talk about my family and Mr. Kaye!"

"Don't you point your finger at me, young lady!" Mrs. Johnson says, pointing her own finger at me.

I point even closer to her nose and say, "And we're not trash!" I'm trying to find a word to call her and trying to remember that I'm supposed to be a lady-in-waiting.

She shoves her cart past me to the checkout counter. "See you at Bible study," she says to Mrs. O'Leary. I hang out at the freezer, waiting for the three women to check out and get out.

As Bea Johnson is leaving I yell, "And that's the ugliest hat in six counties!" I don't think she hears me, but I feel a little better.

I finish my own shopping and . . . well, look there. *All* the sugar is gone. Brown, powdered, and even the cubes. No molasses, no corn syrup, no nothing, and no Stokes Famous Fudge this Christmas.

I present two baskets for check out—one for Mr. Kaye and the other for us.

Mr. Ashby rings up ours first. "Six dollars and twenty-two cents."

"Um, on account, please?" Ah, it's the moment of truth that we have just about every Saturday. If you've ever had to ask for something "on account," then you know how I'm feeling right now.

"Can't let you go higher than six bucks today, Jewels. Take something out."

I look at the items and make my decision. I hand him back the two packs of cigarettes that were at the top of Mom's list. Sorry, Mom.

He gives a big sigh and pulls out our ledger card. I sign the slip and ask, "How much total now?"

"Including this, fifty-six twenty-four. Tell your mother I need to talk to her."

"Sure. Oh, this basket is for Mr. Kaye."

Mr. Ashby straightens up. "Did he send you with cash?"

"No, just this note," I say, pulling the note out of my pocket.

Mr. Ashby unfolds and reads it, sighs heavily, and proceeds to ring up the groceries. While he does, I turn the note around and read it fast. It says: "Please charge this order against what you owe me for the money you borrowed for your new freezer. T. H. K."

He makes some notes on Mr. Kaye's ledger card, then hands it to me. Written in big, red grease pen letters acrost it is: ACCOUNT CLOSED.

"No more charging?"

"We're at war," is all he says.

"You let us charge."

"We're on a person-by-person basis now."

He boxes up the groceries and carries them out to my mom's Dodge, which I've driven into town.

"Make sure you black those out, Jewels," he says, pointing to the headlights.

"I will," I say.

He looks at me and says, with sort of a smile on his face, "And you're right about that woman's hat. Ugly, ugly, ugly!"

I smile back. At least I got that one right.

"Don't forget those lights, now. There's a war on, you know."

Boy, do I know it!

CHAPTER 17

Something you need to know about me: I'm not a churchgoer.

Rex says the best way to stay even-keeled about things is not to join anything like a church or a political party or a sorority or fraternity, but since those are in colleges, I won't have to worry much about it. But Sea Park has a good assortment of churches, and they are pretty dang full on Sunday following Pearl Harbor, believe you me. Anyway, by far the top of the heap is St. Bart's By the Sea, which is on the waterfront about a block south of the Stay and Play cabins. St. Bart's has a high steeple with a bell in it. Just about every kid has snuck up there and rung it at all hours. Me, too, of course.

But Notre Dame it ain't. I know that because I saw *The Hunchback of Notre Dame* when it came to the Majestic, our anything-but-majestic theater in town. You can't compare St. Bart's dinky bell tower to the one that Quasimodo lived in with his Esmeralda screaming, "Sanctuary!" down at everyone. Talk about night and day in the Catholic Church department!

St. Bart's has twenty-five rows of pews. Most of the year, those pews aren't full, but during the summer months, the tourists cram into the joint. I always like how there are candles burning on the altar. Makes it real cozy and Christmasy all year 'round. But most of what I like about St. Bart's is Father Donlevy. He's nice to me no matter what problems my mother has gotten herself into. He isn't preachy or anything and never pushes those holy ghosts on me and says I'm welcome anytime and that I don't have to do that kneeling and water crossing if I don't want to.

There's a big basement in the church and Father Donlevy says he hopes they can make it into a kids' club or something. You know, with ping-pong and books and a radio or record player. He says he might be a Catholic priest, but he doesn't see any reason why kids can't have some fun.

A few years ago, I had this big crush on Clark Gable and started this stupid fan club with two other girls and we met down there. We could enter by a side door that Father Donlevy would keep unlocked if he knew we were having a get-together and said we could even come and go as long as we behaved ourselves, turned out the lights, and made sure the toilet wasn't running in that spooky back room when we left. It was always dark and dank down there, but we Gable Girls made it pretty nice. In our meetings, we just clipped photos from movie magazines and made our own scrapbooks. Anyway, Clark married Carol Lombard in 1939. My first heartbreak. So, to get even, I disbanded the club. No future in being a fan of a married man.

Christmas is just a few days away and I think it's going to be pretty dang cruddy for most folks this year. I keep thinking about those wool socks for some sailor named Joey at Pearl Harbor. The war is heating up and things are just awful everywhere. Anyway, I think I need some adult telling me everything's going to be okay. Alls anyone talks about is war and Japan and those Krauts, too! One minute I'm with them, and the next minute none of it makes any sense to me at all.

But just the sound of Father Donlevy's voice can make me all warm inside. He should be on the radio pitching soap or the news instead of stuck in Sea Park pitching God.

I can hear some muffled talking in the confessing room, so I wait in a pew for that to be over. The door opens and criminently! It's none other'n Bea Johnson and her ugly hat coming out. Maybe she's confessing that she's cornered the sugar market in Sea Park.

We glare at each other. "You sure you got everything off your chest?" My words are out before I can think twice.

She puffs herself up like a riled chicken and makes a step like she's going to wallop me, but she stops when we hear a door closing. Instead, she narrows her eyes, points a finger at me, says nothing, then tromps out.

I really do need to work on keeping my trap shut, especially here in church.

I open the door to the little room. "Father Donlevy? It's me, Jewels. Can I talk to you for a minute? Out here, I mean. I'm not confessing or anything."

Father Donlevy comes out the side door. "Well, hello, Jewels. Haven't seen you around in some time. What's new?"

"War, war, war! That's all anybody talks about!" I say using my best Scarlett O'Hara imitation.

He laughs and gives me back his Clark Gable, "You said it, Scaaaa-lett! Why, the confession business is standin' room only!"

"That's sort of what I wanted to talk to you about."

"Confession, Clark Gable, or war?"

"Well, war. Sort of."

"Shoot," he says. "No pun intended. Come on. Let's sit."

We take a pew. I glance around at the blackout cloth hung over the stained glass windows. Then I ask, "We're supposed to love and forgive our enemies, aren't we?"

He uncrosses his legs. I can see he's wearing blue jeans under his black priest robe. He leans forward in the pew and stares up at the wood carving of Jesus on the cross, which hangs above thc altar. "Yes, we are," he finally says. I sort of wisht he didn't have to think about it so long.

"Well, I don't think there's been too much of that going on lately, do you?"

He looks over at me. He's old, but not too old. Maybe thirty. His hair doesn't have any gray yet. He says, "War makes loving and forgiving very difficult."

"Even someone who just looks like the enemy isn't getting much loving and forgiving," I say.

"Tommy Kaye," Father Donlevy says slowly, nodding his head. "He's been on my mind a lot lately."

"People are treating him like he planned that whole attack himself."

"I know."

"So, what do you think you should do?"

"Me? There's nothing I can do." His eyes are on Jesus again.

"Don't people have to follow the voice of God?"

"In a perfect world."

"Aren't you the voice for God here?"

"Well, I'm the voice of the Pope. Only the Pope is the voice of God."

"Well, what's the Pope have to say about it?" I ask.

He leans back and touches his long, thin fingers to his forehead. Then he looks at me and says, "I don't know what any of us can do, Jewels. Mr. Kaye is . . . and others like him . . . are what they call civilian casualties."

"What's that?"

"Well, those are people who are indirect victims of war. Sort of caught in the crossfire. Like those people in

Pearl Harbor who were just in their homes or walking the dog or riding a bus and well, maybe some shrapnel or bullets hit them and they died. Not because they were the target, but because they were, well, in the way of the target."

He gets up and paces the aisle, like he's thinking of a better way to describe how Tommy has anything to do with someone walking their dog in Hawaii getting hit by a bullet. He turns and says, "Jewels, I know it's almost impossible to understand. Believe me, I'm just as confused and concerned as you are. But . . ."

I've heard it over and over and over since December 7, the date that will live in infamy. So I finish for him, "But we're at war."

"Yes, we are."

There's a church silence that is somehow more silent than regular silence. Then Father Donlevy asks, "How's Rex?"

"Fine." I hate to lie while sitting in a church and face to face with the man in charge, but Rex and me have a pact.

"I hear he took it pretty bad."

Cripes! I think. Looking down at my fists, I say, "He took it. He just . . . took it." I feel Father Donlevy's eyes on me.

"I was welter weight boxing champ at Gonzaga. I'd be happy to give him a few pointers."

I think about that, then say, "I thought churches were for peace, not for fighting."

"We are. But we also have to defend ourselves, if it comes to that." He doesn't sound too convinced, though.

"Guess you're in that crossfire, too," I say.

"Maybe we all are. But tell Rex if he needs . . . you know . . ." I look at him and see both his hands are fists now, too.

"Rex doesn't want what he needs. He needs what he wants," I say. Mom's been saying that for years.

"And what's that?"

I get up to leave and look back at him. "Don't you know?"

"No."

"You should." I point to the cross. "Peace."

He starts to walk with me toward the door. "Peace comes at a price, Jewels."

"Well, Rex paid it, all right," I say, feeling a hurt someplace deep inside me. I'd come in here to feel better and now I'm feeling like someone just kicked *me* in the gut.

"Look, Jewels, any time you want to come and, you know, chew the fat . . . just say the word. I'll be here for you. I promise."

CHAPTER 18

Just when I think it can't get any worse than a Christmas without sugar or lights or peace and good will on Earth, it does. Mayor George Schmidtke has come to collect all the cameras and radios owned by Tommy Kaye. Happy New Year! It's another order from the government. Seems orders are coming every day and from every direction—getting us on the coast all geared up for war, right here on our very beach.

So, Mom and me have to go through all forty cabins at the Stay and Play and collect all the shiny new Bakelite radios Mr. Kaye just bought the year before. Well, there's no way I'm going through any war without *my* radio, so I hide it in my closet, even though I think it's legally ours since Mr. Kaye gave it to us for Christmas last year—our last real Christmas.

Mom, me, and Rex have to haul down Mr. Kaye's big, expensive mahogany radio, the one with a record player in it. Mayor Schmidtke's waiting with his Best Meats delivery van to haul it to wherever they're taking all Mr. Kaye's things.

Next come the cameras. Mr. Kaye sort of laughs as he comes out of his bedroom with three cameras around his neck and two in his hands. "Here. This should make Schmidtke's quota. These are all Japanese. Love 'em or hate 'em, those Japanese make one heck of a camera."

I nod my head, feeling horrible that I got to help take away anything of his and hand them over to that Schmidtke. Alls I say is, "I'm sorry. Maybe I can talk Schmidtke into letting you keep one of these."

"Don't bother, Jewels," he says.

• • •

"Well, I feel just horrible about zis. It's all for our country's security. Orders are orders," Mayor Schmidtke says as I hand over the cameras. He says he's sorry, but he's looking through one camera's view finder and I figure it's being confiscated, all right—right into his delivery van's glove compartment.

"Hate orders," Rex says.

Mayor Schmidtke sighs and says, "Yes, Stokes, we know all about your political opinions! And zeir outcome." He grins as he points to the yellowish leftovers of Rex's black eye.

"Don't you point your fat finger at my son!" Mom says. *Good for you, Mom! Let him have it!*

There's glaring between them.

"Where's the list for all zis stuff? I have to sign for it," Mayor Schmidtke asks, closing the van doors.

Mom hands him the list we've made of the stuff surrendered and the value.

"What's going to happen to all that?" Rex asks, pointing to the van.

"Going to be safely stored in a warehouse up at Camp Clatsop, compliments of our national guard."

"But we advertise that all these cabins have radios in them. It's not fair to take them," Rex says. "What does having a radio have to do with being Japanese?"

"We don't question orders, son. And orders say 'property of Japanese' and zose radios are property of Japanese," Mayor Schmidtke says. "And let me give you Stokes a bit of friendly advice," he adds, through his diver's side window. "Giving aid and comfort to the enemy is treason." He drives off without even so much as a "happy new year" or a "danker shame" or whatever they say in German.

Rex, me, and Mom stand here watching him drive off. Finally Mom says, "That man makes my blood boil! He's pretty darn German braggin' about his Schmidtke's Hand-stuffed Sausages, but not so much cartin' off Tommy's belongings!"

Rex says, "Yeah, and did you notice how he's smoothed out that German accent of his? Used to be you couldn't understand half of what that fat, old Kraut said. You gotta love what a war does to one's social standing."

I don't know what tangent he's about to go on, but I will say this: I've never liked the butcher/mayor even before Pearl Harbor. Even when he's wearing his mayor suit, he still smells like blood and meat, and I don't think he ever cleans under his fingernails.

When we get home I look up the dictionary definition of *treason*. Now *my* blood is boiling. If anyone is betraying anyone, it's Sea Park betraying the best man in town. I grumble to Rex and he tells me to get lost. He's working on an editorial for the school newspaper. Alls he lets me see is the title: INJUSTICE IN THE NAME OF WAR.

• • •

It's late Sunday afternoon, February 1, 1942. Things have been pretty quiet until the newest editions of the papers get to town, then everyone starts talking about the war all over again. I'm reading an old *Silverscreen* movie magazine Mom swiped from the beauty parlor and Mom's painting her toenails. Who knows where Rex is.

There's a knock on the door. Mom and me look at each other. We don't get company very often, especially in winter, especially on Sundays, and most especially now that Rex's editorial is printed and gets picked up by the *Sand Dune Telegraph*. We're what Rex calls *personas non gratises*.

Carefully, Mom opens the blackout cloth acrost the door, keeping the chain in place so the door opens just a peep. "Who's there?"

The answer comes in the form of a card being offered by a long, big hand, white shirt cuffs, gold cufflinks, and dark suit sleeve. Mom takes the card, reads it.

"Mom, who is it?"

Mom turns around and mouths the letters "F-B-I" to me. I take the card and read SPECIAL AGENT IN CHARGE, HERMAN BOOTHBY, PORTLAND, OREGON.

"Uh, this really isn't a good time," she calls through the door opening.

A man's deep voice says, "This'll only take a minute."

"Um, I'm really not presentable right now." She has cotton stuffed between her toes, her old chenille robe is ajar, and her hair is in curlers.

"Please, Mrs. Stokes."

"Uh, well, can you, uh, well, uh, just wait there then, will you?"

The hand disappears as Mom closes the door. She leans against it and looks at me. "Where's Rex when we need him?" she says. She scrambles to her bedroom and I follow her.

"What do we do? What does he want?"

"I have no idea! Get me my black pumps!" She rushes about pulling her curlers out and popping the cotton wads from her toes as she pulls on her red, white, and blue dress, reserved for Edna's float in the annual Fourth of July parade.

Mom says in an urgent whisper and motions to "Quick! Hide the radio!"

I snatch it up and toss it into the refrigerator, then close the door.

Mom gives her lips a fast smack of lipstick, crunches the waves of her still-wet hair, cinches her belt, and opens the door.

"Come in," she says. "Be careful. The blackout rules, you know." She opens the blackout cloth just a bit for him to slip through. He is so tall he has to duck to get under it.

"My," Mom says, "you're a tall one."

I mean it—this Agent Boothby fills our tiny room. And man is he strange looking! His face is long and square—no, that would make it a rectangle. A horse's face! That's what he has—a horse's face!

"So, if you don't mind, Mrs. Stokes, I'd like to ask you a few questions about your . . ." he pauses.

"About my what?" she asks, fingering the dime store paste pearls she's tossed on.

"About your employer," he says.

"My employer?" she answers, exhaling.

"Isao Kiramoto."

Mom's face goes blank. Then she waves her hand in the air and says, "Oh, well, y'all have the wrong person, then. I never heard of that personage. My employer is Tommy Kaye." Out comes the Southern accent.

"May I sit down?" he says. He indicates one of our rickety chairs and Mom suggests the sofa instead. Agent

Boothby adds, his face all serious, "You see, Mrs. Stokes, according to our records, they are one and the same person."

Most of what I know about the FBI is J. Edgar Hoover going after the likes of Baby Face Nelson, Al Capone, John Dillinger, and some of those other gangsters back east, not any of us here in Sea Park. Got to admit, I'm scared. Wisht Rex would come home.

"Shouldn't I have a lawyer here or something?" my mother asks. "I mean, isn't that how these things work?"

"What things?" he asks and smiles at her.

"Well, you know, y'all askin' questions and writin' down my answers. I mean, I might say something that might, what's that word you G-men use, in . . . in . . . incinerate?"

I look at her. Did she really say *incinerate?* Then, she fumbles with, "No, *insinuate*." She chuckles. "I can never get those two words straight."

"I think you mean incriminate," he says. I watch him watch her.

"Oh, yes, incriminate! How silly of me. Thank you."

Look at her—smiling, gushing! Cripes, is she *flirting?* If she keeps going like this, she's going to incinerate us into deep water. I glance at the clock and wisht to heck Rex would get his butt home. Forget a lawyer—if anyone knows anything about any legal FBI business, it's Rex. His bed is held up with stacks of textbooks some law student renter left instead of paying his summer bill. I think Rex has read every one of them.

"Now, if you don't mind, please tell me a little more about this Tommy Kaye," the FBI agent says, licking the tip of his pencil and aiming it toward his notepad.

"Well, I've known him for, let's see . . ." A freshly painted bright red fingernail goes to her powdered cheek as Mom figures out the years. While she's figuring that out, I'm figuring out how we can get this giant FBI man out of here.

Incinerate? Yes, I got an idea! I go to the stove, grab the coffee pot, and mess around with the gas and a match.

"Owww!" I holler. I turn to my mother and whine, "Mom! I burnt my finger!" I seize a finger and squeeze it, turning it as red as Mom's fingernails. "Owwwww!"

"Oh!" Mom says, popping up. Then, to Agent Boothby she says, "Will y'all excuse me just a minute? We got us a little emergency." He makes a half-attempt to rise as we leave the room.

Once in the bathroom, I close the door. She grabs my finger, looks at it, then down at me. "We got to get him out of here!" I whisper up to her.

"Shhh!" she says, turning on the hot and cold water taps.

"I had to do something, Mom. What's he want to know about Mr. Kaye for?"

"I don't know." She pulls open the medicine cabinet and gets the gauze out. "Here, make a bandage."

"What should we do?"

She starts fixing her hair and looking close at her lipstick.

"Mom, you think this is the time to primp?"

"Jewels, honey, there's a time to play it dumb and a time to play it smart. If you ever learn anything from your ol' mom, it's that. Now, I don't know how the FBI got involved, but he's here now. So you just let me do the talkin'. Now wrap that finger." Then, she calls out, "Only be a minute, Agent. . . " She looks at me.

"Boothby," I whisper.

"Boothby!" she sings out.

We come out of the bathroom. I hold my bandaged finger to my chest and she says, "I'm sorry, Mr. Agent Boothby. I guess our little emergency isn't so little after all."

"Anything I can do? I've taken several Red Cross classes," he says, rising.

"No, no," Mom says, handing me my coat. "Can't mess around with burns. We're goin' over to the clinic. Come on, Jewels. Momma's going to get y'all fixed up." I should have known Mom can really come through when the scene calls for a little drama.

"Well, here, let me drive you there."

"No, thanks. I have a car. I'm sorry to cut this interview so short. But y'all'll understand." She hands him his hat and grabs her coat from the nail in the wall.

"Yes, but I have—"

"Jewels, keep that hand high so it doesn't throb so much," she says.

"But, I was going to ask you. . ." he begins. He might be FBI and all, but I don't think he's had much practice dealing with women of a Southern nature.

“My child is in pain!” she snaps.

“I was going to ask if there’s someplace in town to get a bite to eat,” he says, buttoning his overcoat.

Mom’s face goes blank like that’s the last thing she’s expecting him to ask her.

“Oh, yes. Uh, try the Crab ’n Cakes, just south of town. But hurry. They close at six on Sundays.”

I have my coat on and before I can say “ouch” again, she scoots him out the door. “I’ll be in touch,” he says while Mom holds the blackout cloth aside for him.

“Yes, fine. Y’all’ll excuse us now, won’t you?”

We wait about three minutes, then Mom says, “Well, come on.”

“But he’s gone.”

“And he’s probably outside waitin’ to see if we leave for the clinic.” And sure enough, there he is, still loading himself into his car.

“Good Lord, I suppose he’s goin’ to follow us,” Mom says, getting the engine to turn over. We back out, and the FBI agent backs out. We head north on Pacific, but the FBI agent heads south toward Highway 101.

“Sorry, Mom, this mess is my fault. I thought we could get rid of him if—”

“Never mind. He’s out of sight,” she says, looking in the mirror. She pulls over and we just sit there for a few minutes, relieved and wondering what the heck is going on. “What kind of a war is this? Lyin’, runnin’ from the FBI, and for what?”

I wisht I knew. "Hey, where we going?"

"Edna's."

I should have figured Alice needs a drink. "If you think I'm sitting here in this car while you go in and have yourself a few belts, you are so wrong, Mom!"

"I'm not having a few belts, Jewels. Haven't you noticed I've been sober for a few weeks now?"

I think back. Hmmm, come to think of it . . . "Well, then why—?"

"To warn Edna the FBI is snoopin' around and to . . ." Her voice trails off and we pull over again. "No, we're not."

There, in the parking lot, we see Agent Boothby unfold himself out of his small car and head into the Inn and Out.

So now we're heading south, winding through the back roads toward home.

CHAPTER 19

"I don't get any of this," I say, unwinding the finger bandage and letting it fly out the window. "Let's go find Rex and see what—"

"I'll tell you exactly what this is all about," she says, wiping the fogged-up window with her coat sleeve. "That FBI man must think Tommy Kaye is a spy for Japan or something."

"Is he?" I asked. "I mean, he isn't. Is he?"

"If he's a spy, I'm Mata Hari."

"Who's that?"

"Never mind. I can't see anything with that stupid slit of light and that useless defroster!" she grumbles, peering over the steering wheel. We turn right onto Occidental Street, and Mom pulls over. She turns off the headlight and we can see the full moon coming up behind the clouds, reflecting light off the ocean straight ahead of us. It's sort of pretty and serene.

"Seems sort of stupid not having any lights when that moon's so bright. How you going to black out a moon?" I ask. "Why do we have to have everything so black anyway?"

"I think it's because we're . . ." she says, sort of low, like maybe we're surrounded by the enemy. I look at her. "Targets."

I look back over toward the ocean.

"They say they're out there," she whispers.

"Who? The Japanese?"

"Yes. They say maybe Germans, too. Who knows?"

"Who's 'they'?" I ask.

"'They' always means anyone airin' their opinion, Jewels. You'd be amazed what 'they' say on our party line." She looks back over the ocean. "*They* say they're out there. Somewhere."

"You mean, if our lights were on right now, some Japanese gunner would see us and bomb us to Kingdom Come?" I ask.

Mom turns and looks at me. "I guess," she says. She runs her hand over her face, purses her lips, and sighs heavy like she does when she's thinking things over.

"Do *you* think they're out there and will come ashore and invade us?" I ask.

"I don't know."

Just then, the car chugs, rattles, and conks out. We look at each other, exhale as if to say "not again," open our doors, and get out.

My mother puts her arm around me and says, "Jewels, honey, we're goin' to be fine. Everything will be just fine." And we walk arm in arm along the shoreline, two perfect targets for the Krauts or the Japanese or the FBI or the McAloon Twins Beach Patrol or anyone, but it's sort of nice. Most arm-in-arming Mom and me ever do is ol' Jewels helping ol' Malice Alice home after a long boozy night at Edna's Inn and Out. But not tonight.

We stop in front of the Look-Sea Lounge and glance up. It's pitch dark now but was once so bright and gay and full of life. Sometimes I used to sneak over and hide in the dunes when there were big things going on. Holiday dances, special events, parties, and such. Dancing people and music would spill out onto the patio and the spotlights from the roof would light up the whole beach. Hard to believe all that fun and life once came out of this big, dark building.

"Sort of sad, huh, Mom? Seeing this place so dark and dead."

"It's not dead. Maybe just snoozin'," she says.

I can smell cigarette smoke and there, sitting on one of his teak deck chairs on the patio, is Tommy Kaye, bundled in a blanket and smoking. Hero comes to meet me as we walk up.

"You're not supposed to be out here," Mom says.

"Neither are you," Mr. Kaye says back. He kicks out a chair to invite her to sit.

"Nice evening, for February," Mom says, sitting and taking in a long breath. "Maybe a Chinook comin'."

There's one of those silences that all kids come to understand. You know, where adults want to talk or something but they won't if you are standing right there. So either they're going to say something like "don't you have some homework to do?" or "be a good kid and make us a drink" or maybe even the old standard "put an egg in your shoe and beat it!"

"Mom, I got . . . I *have* some homework to do. What do I do if that FBI man comes ba—"

Mom shoots me a look but Mr. Kaye picks right up on it. "FBI?"

"Oh, you know those hotshot G-men, always snoopin' around. Askin' questions about you. So, maybe we best go inside," she says.

"Why? You think I should just hide from the FBI? You think I have *something* to hide?" I pick up the anger in his voice, and you don't hear that too often from Mr. Kaye.

"No, I meant, maybe . . . Come on, Tommy. Don't get mad."

"Well, I *am*! I am sitting on *my* deck chair, on *my* patio, on *my* property. I have nothing to hide! Why the heck should *I* go inside?"

"Well, because I'm gettin' cold. And you could probably use a drink," Mom says as she ticks her head up toward his apartment.

CHAPTER 20

"Shut up! I can't hear!" Rex barks at me, holding a glass of milk in one hand, half a sandwich in the other, and peering through the swinging kitchen doors into the Look-Sea Lounge. We're here doing homework and laying low from the FBI man while Edna, Mom, and Mr. Kaye sit talking.

"What're they saying?"

He shushes me again, then says, "Edna was grilled by the FBI man. Wanted to know if Mr. Kaye has any family."

"Well, he doesn't," I say. "And his parents are dead."

Rex stops chewing, looks down at me, and asks, "How do you know?"

"He told me. Guess what else he told me?"

"Shhh! Things are heating up in there."

We open the doors and sneak into the big, darkened room.

"This is the FBI!" Edna shouts. "God knows what information they have—on all of us!"

"*All* of us?" Mom snaps. "What are you hiding? Two clams over the limit? As I recall, you got off scot-free!"

"Well, I'm pretty sure you don't want any government man snooping around your past," Edna snaps back.

Rex and I look at each other.

"Ladies, please," Mr. Kaye says. "Are you forgetting our pledge? It was right there behind that very bar when we all put our hands on the Bible and swore we'd never talk about it again!"

Mom and Edna are nose to nose, but settle back into their seats. Edna and Mom are what Mr. Kaye calls the "best of enemies." They both love and hate each other so much, you'd think they were sisters.

Mr. Kaye says, "Now, Edna, what else did this agent ask?"

"He wanted to know how much money you have, but I said, '*You're* the FBI. *You* tell *me!*'"

"What else?" Mr. Kaye asks.

"He asked about family and if you travel and well, it was the third degree. I tell you, it was the third degree."

Mr. Kaye runs his hand through his hair and turns to Mom. "And did you get the third degree, too?"

"No, we got rid of him. But he wants to come back tomorrow!"

Edna gets up, saying, "I need another drink."

Rex and me quickly slip back into the kitchen. We sit at the table and he mutters, "Crud. It's going from bad to worse."

"Because of the FBI man?"

"No, Jewels, because the toilet in cabin twelve doesn't flush. Of course! They don't send the FBI unless it's something big. I wonder who Mr. Kaye's lawyer is."

"Ed Simcoe, who else?" I say. There's only one lawyer in Sea Park and everyone uses him. Town joke is he spends most of his time in court suing himself. Then I remember. "But it doesn't matter. Becky Simcoe said her dad already went to Portland to enlist."

"Pretty soon it'll be just us kids left in Sea Park," he says. "Guess we have that to look forward to, since all the adults are acting like children."

Then I ask what I got to ask, have been wanting to ask but have just been too scared to: "Do you ever think, well, wonder . . . what if Mr. Kaye really is . . ." I stumble until Rex stops me.

He throws his pencil acrost the room and shouts, "Stop it, Jewels! Just stop thinking that!" That starts him coughing a little and he grabs his side.

"Rex, you better do something about those ribs."

"I read they take a long time to heal. Maybe months," he says, polishing off a glass of milk. "It's just hard to breathe being all bound up like this. A sneeze would kill me." Then he looks at me and says, "Anyway, you just stop thinking like the rest of the town about Tommy Kaye!"

"What'd you think's going to happen to him?" I indicate the Stay and Play around us. "I mean, if there's no customers, won't he go broke?"

"Yes, I guess so. Unless that strongbox from the safe is filled with thousand-dollar bills."

I shrug my shoulders. I'm thinking about the family photo of Mr. Kaye and his parents. "Everyone wants to know where he got all his money."

"Maybe he inherited it," Rex said.

I get up and put the milk away. "Maybe. His dad was a military man. Do they make much money?"

"The Japanese military?" Rex asks.

So I tell him about Mr. Kaye's folks—a white father and a Japanese mother.

"Huh. He doesn't look biracial," Rex says. He catches my face and says, "Half and half."

"He's not half and half. He's adopted."

Just then the doors swing open and the three adults stand there like they've been the ones eavesdropping on us.

"Aren't you kids supposed to be doin' homework?" Mom says, pointing to our notebooks and textbooks still stacked on the table.

"What about the FBI man?" I ask. "What if he comes asking questions again?"

"I will deal with him," Mr. Kaye says. "If he asks you anything, just say to ask me. Tell him I'm always here like a good little Jap, obeying Governor Sprague's orders."

"Come on, kids," Mom says. "Let's go home. It's a school night."

Mom and Mr. Kaye hug each other goodbye, which sort of alarms me because folks in Sea Park aren't big on hugging, and when it happens, it's usually at funerals.

We walk home and Rex goes to his room to do homework, and I go to my room to read, and Mom finishes painting her toenails.

• • •

Sometime in the middle of the night, Rex pulls me awake. "Jewels!" he whispers. "Wake up!" He jerks me upright.

"Knock it off, creep!"

"Shhh." He sits on my bed and tugs on my overhead light.

I squint and look at him. "You sick?"

"No. Tell me again about Mr. Kaye being adopted."

"What time is it? Can't this wait?" I lay back down but he pulls me up again.

"Wake up, Jewels. This is important."

"He told me he was adopted when his folks were stationed in Japan. So what?"

"Uh oh."

"What?"

"We were learning about it in Modern Problems. If he was born in Japan, that means he's Issei."

"What say?"

"Issei. Look, when it comes to the Japanese in this country, there are Issei and Nisei. Nisei are Japanese *Americans*. You know, *born* here, but of Japanese parents. Issei are people who were born in Japan but *live* in America."

My head is spinning, but it usually does so when Rex is figuring things out. "But what do they call the ones who were adopted by an American major and a Japanese woman?" I ask, yawning.

"I don't know."

"It's stupid. If you live here you should be an American and that's that. Enough of that Issei stuff," I say through a yawn.

"Nothing's that simple. One thing I *do* know: there's going to be a big push to send the Issei back to Japan."

"Why?"

"Because they think their loyalties are to their fatherland."

"I thought the fatherland is that Nazi Germany thing," I say.

"Fatherland is the place of one's birth, Jewels."

"I guess that's why the FBI man said his real name is Iso? Moto? I can't remember those weird names. Anyway, he called Mr. Kaye a Japanese name."

"Because he was born in Japan and that's his Japanese name," Rex says, nodding his head like he does when he's thinking deep.

"Well, he's here now and he's not a Jap. He's Tommy Kaye and our neighbor and boss and plus the man who paid for your broken leg operation five years ago when you were dumb enough to play Tarzan trying to impress that stupid summer girl. Ambulance ride all the way to Portland? Or did you forget?"

His hand goes to his knee where he still has two long scars. "No, I didn't forget."

He stands up and pulls the light switch off.

"Rex?"

"What?"

"Do you think they'll send him back to Japan?"

"Well, the FBI being here isn't a good sign. Lots of people want to send them all back. Think they're all traitors, just because their eyes slant." He sort of chuckles and adds, "Lord knows, folks in town wouldn't mind if Mr. Kaye just vanished."

"Why? Everyone used to like him."

"Sure, they did. When it comes to credit and borrowing. You know, like in the game of Monopoly? Tommy Kaye owns Boardwalk and Park Place but everyone who owes him money gets a big fat get-out-of-jail-free card."

"I hate Monopoly," I grumble, lying back down. "I always lose."

Alone in the dark, I just want to fall back asleep, forget everything I don't understand. But alls I can think about is that fat little Monopoly man with the spats and the mustache, holding the "go directly to jail. Do not collect two-hundred dollars" card. So I try to remember that name the FBI man told us—something Moto, which makes me think about Quasimodo and *The Hunchback of Notre Dame*. Then that makes me remember that Maureen O'Hara was only eighteen when she made that movie. I use my fingers to count the years. Six. In six years, I'll be eighteen and man, I'm going to need every one of those years to fill into something like Maureen O'Hara! So, that does the trick. Thinking about how much work that's going to take makes me really . . . really . . . tired. . . .

CHAPTER 21

The FBI hasn't come calling again, but according to the *Sand Dune Telegraph*, he stayed two nights at Babs Bishop's Boarding House—"A View From Every Room." Bet after those two days, he knows more about everyone in town than Father Donlevy, Selma O'Leary, and Bea Johnson put together. Then, just that like, he's gone. Wisht it could be a case of out of sight, out of mind, but you just can't get a man like a FBI special agent out of your mind.

• • •

My bike tire is, per usual, flat, and I got to walk to school today. It's Friday, but I can take just about anything on a

Friday. Rex says he'll walk with me. Now, you don't see brothers doing that very often. I don't know if he's scared that more FBI will come around or that the new club of rah-rah-rah do-gooders might bother me. The club calls themselves the SPORTS, which stands for the Sea Park Outdoor Reconnaissance Team, formed by none other than Eldon Johnson, Bully Hallstrom, and five or six of their toadies. I don't exactly know what reconnaissance means, so I ask Rex on our walk.

"Well, reconnaissance is sort of like spying, like scouting out a situation and reporting back," Rex says.

"Who they reporting back to?"

We stop. "I don't know," Rex says, sort of out of breath. "That's a good question. The principal is letting them meet at school, so maybe that's who they report to. But it's nothing short of vigilantism, if you ask me."

"Come on, Rex. Quit already with those big words. It really cheeses me when you talk above my head. I'm not your debate teacher or . . ."

"It's taking the law into your own hands. Like martial law or militia or . . ." I cross my eyes—my standard "huh?" look. "Okay, it's like exactly what's happening to Mr. Kaye. Someone's been vandalizing his property and no one's doing anything about it. It's like the whole town is the law and no one is doing anything to protect the common good."

"But Sheriff Hillary is gone. There isn't any law in town."

"Go to the head of the class!" he says. "So everyone thinks a self-appointed gang like the SPORTS is okay. And it's not. So Mayor Schmidtke steps in and gives those thugs a uniform. They're just old jackets and caps from the Sea Park band, but that's not the point. Giving them a place to meet and a uniform sanctions them." My eyes go crost again. "It gives them permission. And just kids with wooden rifles is one thing, but I read that guerrilla groups with adults and real guns are forming everywhere," he goes on.

"Go-rilla?"

"Yeah, like a bunch of armed monkeys," Rex laughs. "I tell you, Jewels, we are one step away from martial law."

"Oh," I say, noticing I don't have to walk so fast to keep up with him like I used to.

"So, you don't have anything to do with the SPORTS, got that, Jewels?"

"Any of them? What if—"

"Don't even give them the time of day." He stops and looks at me. I see how his looks are changing. He looks like—I don't know—more like a man, not a boy anymore. It's like that shellacking he took sort of made his looks different. Harder, maybe.

"Anyway," he says, "you see those jerks in those uniforms coming, you just turn around and go the other way. Uniforms should really be outlawed."

"Well, I'll bet a uniform helps knowing a Kraut from a Yank," I say.

He smiles at me and nods. "That's pretty darn smart, Shorty." I like it when he has some pride in his eyes when he looks at me.

"Mom says there's a time to play it smart and a time to play it dumb."

"Well, she'd know," he says, heading off toward the senior high wing of our school.

I notice that he's walking like he's older'n The Old Man.

• • •

So here I am, sitting in first period, my thoughts about as far away from the history of the Oregon Territory as, well, Tokyo. I let my mind search for something funny after worrying all through homeroom about Rex. So I think about Eldon's SPORTS and how funny they looked marching into school today in those cornball, circusy band uniforms. Then I think about Rex's idea of uniform-outlawing. What if some fairy sprinkled magic dust over a German battlefield and wammie!—all the soldiers are bare-butt naked! Naked armies hit me as pretty funny and I got to scrunch my lips to keep from laughing.

I look out the window toward the beach and my eyes land on the church steeple anchoring down St. Bart's By the Sea. Then it hits me! It's genius! I swear, it's genius! I spurt out loud, "Quasimodo!"

The whole class laughs and Miss Thackery says, "Jewels, do you have something to share?"

"Uh, no. Well, yes, I mean, I need to use the girls' room."

Kids always think that's funny like they don't know about the call of nature. Miss Thackery hands me a hall pass and I go straight to my locker, collect my coat, and dash out of the school, heading back home. My brain is overheating; I'm planning things so fast. And I got the whole weekend to put my plan into action.

I'm not going to tell anyone—not even Rex. Nope, this is going to be just me and, well, of course Tommy Kaye will have to be told. Eventually.

• • •

"The Gable Girls?" Father Donlevy says after I ask for the key to the church basement. "I thought you were done with Clark Gable."

"Oh, no, I was thinking of another club, you know, something to maybe support the war?"

"Like the SCOUTS?" he asks. I can tell by the look on his face that he isn't big on them, either.

"No, not like them. They say we're going to have to ration and stuff and maybe, well, who knows what? I thought a group of us girls could just have a club and meet and sort of, you know, do stuff."

"Stuff? That covers a lot of territory."

I haven't put a lot of brainwork into this part of my plan. Father Donlevy is usually so easygoing and never asks many questions. "Um, maybe we could roll bandages and I don't know—whatever people do in a war. You know, war work."

"Sure, why not? Girls need clubs. I'll get you the key and tell Mrs. O'Leary it's okay for you girls to be coming and going. Just remember to keep things quiet. Turn out the lights when you leave and make sure that toilet isn't running."

"Thanks!"

"And remember, Jewels, if you girls make any money on whatever 'stuff' you get going . . ." and he points to the polished brass donation plates stacked on a side table. "Always nice to remember the Founder of our feast."

"Oh, I'll remember him, all right," I say. I know he means God. But he doesn't know I mean Tommy Kaye, who sure as heck founds lots of folks' feasts and payrolls that end up in those very same collection plates.

I start with Cabin 39, the one farthest away from ours. I use the cleaning cart and just make like I'm tidying up inside. But what I'm really doing is pilfering a little of this, a little of that, from each one. And no, I am not stealing. I'm on the ol' Robbing Peter To Pay Paul program. Perfectly legal.

Then I box the things up and use the hand cart to haul them down to the church basement. Things are going pretty smoothly. Everyone's too busy with their own war work to bother with me.

Until now. I'm hauling down a box into the church basement and stop dead in my tracks when I see her shadow.

"Whatcha doin' down there?" a voice calls down, pointing to the two boxes of this and that in the hand cart at the top of the steps.

It's Little Janie Johnson, working on a sucker, glaring down the stairwell at me.

• • •

Egad, why does it have to be her? Daughter of Bea Johnson, town gossip and all-around know-it-all. Janie's about eight and has buck teeth, big thick glasses, frizzy hair, and a dim future. The other strike against her is she's Eldon Johnson's little sister and she's learning the art of bullying from the expert. Anyway, she's a spoilt-rotten brat, and I stop cold when I see her.

"Buzz off, termite," I say.

"I don't hafta! You moving in down there?"

"No, I'm making a clubhouse, not that it's any of your beeswax," I say, coming upstairs and grabbing another box.

A lock of her hair blows onto her sucker and she unsticks it with dainty fingers, then asks, "What kind of club you making?"

"A big girls' club. Don't you come down here, Janie! It's dangerous!"

She backs up a step and calls down, "Can I join?"

"No!"

"Aw, I never get to join any club. Eldon won't even let me be a SPORT."

"You don't want to be a stupid SPORT," I say.

"You don't know what I want," she says. "What's your club do, anyway?"

I think of something I know she won't like. "A book club."

"I like books."

"Books on politics."

The sucker goes back in her mouth and it bobs as she talks, "What're politics?"

"You know, government and news and, well, I said you wouldn't be interested."

Janie's sucker smacks as it comes out of her mouth. "I know some news."

I put the box back into the cart and look down at her. "Do you? What's that?"

"We got us a live turkey. Eldon found it, and Momma's gonna feed him and get him all fat for Easter. Then we're gonna eat him. I kinda wish he found a pig 'cause I like ham and not so much turkey." The cherry sucker makes her lips gooey and red.

"That's nice," I say. Well, at least Sailor the Turkey made it through Christmas with his drumsticks intact.

"I got some other news."

I put the box down. "I'll bite. Shoot."

"There's gonna be a *big* explosion."

"A what?" I ask, now giving her a little more interest. "What kind of explosion?"

"Can I join your club?"

"Who said anything about an explosion?"

She shrugs her shoulders.

"Janie, explosions are serious. If you know there's going to be an explosion, you better tell."

"I might. Can I join?"

"Ah, get lost, Janie. I'm too busy for games."

But I stop again when she says, "Uh huh. I heard Eldon and Bully talking. Eldon said when word of this gets out, it'll blow this town sky high."

"Word of what, Janie?"

Her expression changes. “I don’t know. I didn’t hear that part, but can I join anyway? It’s not news now but it’s gonna be news. That should count.”

I bend down toward Janie’s face and say, sweet as her sucker, “Okay, tell you what, Janie. You can be our *secret* member.”

“Okay! What’s that?”

“Your job is to just do what you do best. Hang around and listen. When you hear of something, you come tell me. Especially what those stupid boy SPORTS are up to, okay?”

“Okay!” she says, her face now glowing. “And we’ll tell those FBI men to leave us alone. One is big and ugly and the other smells like cigars.”

“The FBI came to see you?”

“Sure. My daddy called them long distance all the way to Portland, and Momma was yelling about the money and Daddy said he was reversing the charges and told her to clam up. Is that news, too?”

“That depends,” I say, trying to act like I don’t much care. Janie Johnson can be tricky, even if she is only eight. “What were they talking about?”

Janie’s eyeing a framed photograph of the race horse, Man O’War, fresh off the bathroom wall of Cabin 13. “Gee, he’s pretty,” she says.

“Janie, what news did you hear from the FBI man?”

“I like horses.”

I hand the picture to her. “Here, take it. Now what did he say?”

"Um, I don't know. Eldon has these keys."

"Keys to what?"

"I dunno."

"Give me the picture back."

"No. Wait! I remember! Something about a bulldozer."

"Huh? What's a bulldozer have to do with blowing this town sky high?"

"I dunno. Maybe they meant blow the warehouse up."

"Warehouse?"

"The warehouse they said the bulldozer is in."

I think fast—then I remember the keys in the big safe. But a bulldozer? What the heck does that have to with anything?

"They have some big maps, too," Janie pipes up.

I hand her back the picture. "Maps of what?"

"I dunno. They called it a bonker."

I roll that word over in my mind. "Bonker? You mean bunco?"

She shrugs her shoulders. "Can I join your stupid club or not?"

"Okay, raise your right hand," I say. "No, your other right hand." It goes up, sucker skyward. "Repeat after me."

"After me."

"Not yet. Wait till I finish. I, Janie Johnson, being of sound mind . . ." She repeats seriously.

"Do hereby swear to be a member of the secret, sacred society . . ."—I stop, not only to let her catch up, but to figure out our club name—". . . of the Sea Park See Girls."

"When do we meet?" she asks, sucker now back inside her mouth.

"That's secret," I say. "When you have some news, you find me. Got it?"

"Got it. Shake!"

I know how sticky that grimy little hand is, but to seal the deal, I shake.

I go back to my "war" work, thinking about the bonker. Janie must have meant bunco. That's what the FBI is on to. That's it. Mr. Kaye must be in some sort of bunco racket trouble. And I'm not even sure what a bunco is!

Which makes my mission all the more important.

CHAPTER 22

I continue to raid stuff from the cabins and think hard about my next step. Can I pull this off all by myself? We've learned plenty in the last few weeks about the Allies and Axis. The good guys are the Allies. That would be us—the United States, Canada, England, and I think France; and the bad guys would be Germany, Italy, and Japan. They're the Axis. An ally is good; an axis is bad. When I think about it, we have our own little Allies and Axis tug-of-war right here in Sea Park. Most of the town is the Axis and just a handful of us are the Allies. And Tommy Kaye is the line in the sand we're all tugging of war over.

• • •

Saturday night. Usually Mom's busy getting ready for a night out, which is occupying a barstool at Edna's. Only, it's weird, but I've noticed Mom hasn't been doing much of that lately. But tonight I really need her to get out of the house if my mission is going to work.

"Thought you'd be all gussied up by now, Mom," I say, peeking in at her. She's filing a fingernail at her dressing table but is still in her robe. She's gotten some work on the docks cleaning fish and Mr. Kaye's been paying us for keeping things locked and clean and dark at the Stay and Play. So, it's not as though we're broke.

"Oh, thought I'd just stay in tonight. Play a little gin rummy with Tommy."

"Not going to Edna's? I heard the Oly Olsen Trio's coming down from Astoria to play. You usually like to sing with them, don't you?"

"Oh, these foggy old pipes can barely blow out smoke let alone a decent tune anymore," she says, sort of wistful-like.

I do *not* want her playing any gin rummy with Mr. Kaye tonight.

"So, what are you doin' tonight, Jewels?"

"Maybe call a meeting of the See Girls," I say.

"You and your little clubs. Whatever happened to the Gable Girls?"

"Disbanded. The rat got married."

She turns on her vanity stool and looks at me, frowns, and says, sort of sadly, "Oh, did you hear? Carole Lombard died in a plane crash yesterday."

"Huh?"

"Yep, she was goin' someplace for a War Bond rally or, I don't know, something to do with this disgustin' war! How do you like that? One minute on top of the world, big famous actress married to Clark Gable, and the next, planted into the side of a mountain because you're raisin' money for the war. You know, Jewels honey, this is one crazy world."

"Which is why I think you owe it to yourself to go down to Edna's and have yourself a high ol' time."

That brings her eyes to me in the mirror's reflection. "You think? I have been a bump on a log lately, haven't I? Can you see any roots?" She pulls back her hair and inspects the grow-out from last month's henna rinse job.

"You look fine, Mom. Go on. I've been adding money to the toffee tin. Take some and go have yourself a good time."

"What's Rex up to tonight?" she asks, checking out more roots using the two mirror system.

"He's probably off fixing something for Mr. Kaye."

"Is it just me or does it seem like that boy doesn't . . . I mean . . . ever since Pearl Harbor. Well, he used to be so social. Always had a date or that debate team of his."

I'm not going to say anything if Rex hasn't. "Everyone's changed since Pearl Harbor."

"Ain't that the truth. He just seems, well, I guess mothers and their sons just grow apart sooner or later."

"Mom, there's lots of work to be done when there's a war going on."

She looks right at me. "Promise you and me won't ever grow apart. You know what they say: a son is a son till he takes a wife, but a daughter's a daughter for the rest of your life."

That's too far in the future for me to think about. I'm just thinking about tonight. "Okay, I promise," I say. "Look, get dressed, and I'll get the toffee tin."

She comes out a few minutes later, perfumed, lipsticked, and looking not half bad.

She turns around. "Are my seams straight?"

"Give me a pen so I can connect all those dots," I say. Mom's stockings have polka dots of nail polish here and there where she's tried to stop them from running. Silk stockings were expensive before the war and now impossible to get.

"Fine thing when a war gets in the way of a woman looking her best," she says, reading my mind. Or maybe I was reading hers. Uh oh. Put that on my "worry about later" list.

"Well, how do I look?" She pulls out her ratty, secondhand fox stole from the closet, swirls it around her neck, and clips the fox's mouth to its tail. I don't care how much money I may have someday, I will *never* wear a dead fox biting its own tail around *my* neck.

"You look good, Mom," I say, just as I've said nearly every Saturday night for the last how-many years. "Come on. I'll drop you off."

"It's a good thing Sheriff Hillary is out of town or I wouldn't be lettin' you drive at night," Mom says. Then comes the sheepish grin. "If things get roarin', I'll stay in Edna's back room so's you won't have to come get me. And there's that stupid curfew to worry about. But I'm goin' to try to be good, Jewels. I really am."

She hands me the car keys and we leave.

Jewels's Mission, Part One:

Rex out of the way. Check.

Mom out of the way. Check.

Now, for Jewels's Mission, Part Two:

Kidnap—I mean dognap—Hero the bloodhound.

CHAPTER 23

Have you ever thought you had the best dang plan in the world and then it all goes ka-blooey when someone sticks his big, giant nose in it? Well, the big, giant nose is on the face of that big, giant FBI man, Herman Boothby! I find him sitting at the same table that just a few nights earlier my mom, Mr. Kaye, and Edna Glick had been sitting at in the Look-Sea Lounge. The same lamp light makes the white tablecloth glow. And there, sitting acrost from him is none other than Tommy Kaye. They're having a drink together! How do you like that? Ka-blooey with a capital K and extra blooies!

"Oh, excuse me," I say. "Didn't know you got—you *have*—company."

"Oh, he's not company so much as he's a customer. And who am I to turn away a customer?" Mr. Kaye says, smiling. "A *paying* customer."

"RubyPearlOpal Stokes, I believe," Mr. Boothby says as I stand here probably looking as bright as all three Stooges put together. If Mr. Kaye had been sipping a martini with Adolph Hitler, I could not be more shocked. Okay, close your mouth, Jewels. Think fast!

"Uh, time for Hero's walk."

"Like Emperor Hiro, huh?" Agent Boothby says. "Cute. Very cute."

"Not very. It's h-E-r-o. As in laying down your life to save another. You FBI men do it all the time," Mr. Kaye says.

I take Hero into the kitchen, but that's as far as I go. Something serious is going on. I peek back through the swinging door. Now they're standing, facing each other. Agent Boothby towers over Mr. Kaye. The talk is loud and echoey in the big empty room. I see hands gesture toward the ocean.

Then Agent Boothby slaps some papers on the table and puts on his hat and coat. "And don't say you haven't been given a choice."

"You call this a choice?"

"Consider yourself lucky, Mr. Kiramoto."

"My name is Kaye!" he hollers. "Thomas Hardin Kaye!"

Agent Boothby points to the papers. "Not in the eyes of the government. Born in Japan, family in Japan, investments in Japan. We have records of every money transfer to Nagasaki. Sir, I don't make up these rules. I only enforce them. But as of Sunday, December seventh at oh-seven hundred forty-eight hours Hawaiian Time, you and your race became enemies of the United States of America. And that's on looks alone and not counting all our evidence against you from our files. So, you can either pack your bags for Japan or pack your toothbrush for Leavenworth."

Leavenworth? That's a big lock-up somewhere. What the ka-blooey is happening?

"Ever hear of a lawyer? A hearing? A trial? I can explain everything you think you have on me."

"And you'll be given all those opportunities in Portland," he says. "Maybe you can clear these things up. Frankly, your past history with us won't exactly help your case."

"That file was closed years ago!"

Agent Boothby has his hat now and he says, "I'm sorry, sir. You must know there's no place to hide. Not now. You have to understand, this is war. So, I can either slap some cuffs on you now and anchor you somewhere, or I can post a man outside your apartment door."

"I'll . . . I'll have to make some arrangements," Mr. Kaye says, gesturing at the Stay and Play around him. "I can't just leave. I have obligations."

Agent Boothby walks toward the side door, turns, and says. "You have until nine in the morning. I'll send my man up." He dons his hat. "Like I said, I don't make up the rules." And he leaves through the blackout cloth and into the night.

Mr. Kaye turns and just stares into the empty room. He picks up the papers on the table, scrunches them, and tosses them toward the side door. He screams something, but don't ask me what. It's in another language—probably Japanese.

He goes to every lamp in the room, every light switch, and flips them on, each one with a swear word and a kick and toss of something. Then he goes to the huge blackout curtains and yanks them aside.

"Here I am!" he screams. "The enemy! Come get me!" He waves his hands like a mad man. "Here I am!"

I've never seen Mr. Kaye this upset. I'm sort of scared that the McAloons or maybe even Boothby or his partner might shoot him from the beach below. I slowly walk into the bright room and he glowers at me while trying to catch his breath. His eyes are on fire.

"I swear by God they aren't taking me anywhere! This is my home! They'll have to blast me out of here!"

"I got—I mean I *have*—a better idea," I say. "Hurry! I'll show you."

"Show me what? Jewels, this has nothing to do with you."

I look up at him. "Yes, it does."

His face softens back into his calm, kind one. "No it really doesn't."

"But I have a surprise for you. You can't go anywhere before you see it. I've been working hard all week and if that man is going to take you away and . . . I mean, will you ever come back?" I can't keep the crack out of my voice.

"Oh, Jewels," he says, pulling me into his arms and holding me. "Please. Don't cry."

He sways me a little like I've seen him do with my mom, as if he's hearing music no one else can hear. I step out of his arms and look up at him. "Come on. Come with me. It'll only take a minute. Quick, before that FBI man returns."

CHAPTER 24

We go through the kitchen and back hall, down the stairs and to the darkened café. Just as we slowly open the door, I stick my head out and get the scent of cigar smoke. I plaster myself against the door.

"Shhh," I say, putting my finger to my lips.

"Jewels, if I didn't know better, I'd say you and I are making a run for it," Mr. Kaye says.

"No, we're not," I say. It's not a lie. We are not running. Creeping is more like it.

We ease out the door. I peep around the corner and there acrost the parking lot is the cigar-smoking FBI man, leaning against a car.

Mr. Kaye stops on the pathway as a gust of wind reaches us. He stops, takes some deep breaths. "Oh, I love salt air," he whispers.

"Come on, Mr. Kaye. Just over here," I say, leading him toward the church basement door.

"Jewels, where are you taking me?" he says, feeling his way along the dark pathway into the basement door. "What the . . ."

I unlock the door, slide aside the blackout cloth, and turn on the light. We stand on the landing and look down into St. Bart's basement. Alls I say is, "Sanctuary."

I close the door behind us. I've done a pretty darn good job of creating a homey atmosphere, if I do say so myself. Chairs, rug, lamps, books, and even a homemade painting of the Last Supper someone left in Cabin 9.

Mr. Kaye turns to me and says, "Excuse me?"

"You know, sanctuary."

"What do you mean by sanctuary?"

"*The Hunchback of Notre Dame,*" I say, a little miffed he doesn't see the genius of my plan. "This is the Catholic church. You're a Catholic. No one can get you here. Not those sword-rattlers, President Roosevelt, the FBI men, or anyone. You'll be safe here. Come on, let me show you." I pull him down the steps and into the main room. "Here's your library, your den, your kitchen, and your bathroom is behind the curtain over there. Make sure the toilet doesn't run. Father Donlevy's a stickler about that."

Mr. Kaye looks like he's just seen a ghost. "You mean to tell me Father Donlevy agreed to this?"

"Well, not exactly. I mean, he said I could use this as a meeting place, you know, for my new club. We're doing war work. He's all for us doing war work." I pause and look down at the holey Oriental rug at our feet. I add, "He just doesn't know that you're my war work. Anyway, he's a priest. He has to agree to sanctuary."

Mr. Kaye folds himself into the overstuffed chair from Cabin 19 and puts his face into his hands and sort of quivers. Is he crying?

"Mr. Kaye? Are you . . . ? Mr. Kaye?"

His head comes up. "I . . . I don't know whether to laugh, cry, or spit nails. To strangle you or to hug you, Jewels." His face is red like he's been laughing and crying at the same time. He looks around the room. "This is probably the stupidest, kindest, worst-thought-out, most loving thing anyone has ever done for me."

"You think it's stupid?" Yeah, there's hurt in my voice. I might not be a genius like Rex, but I'm not stupid, and I've worked and planned and planned and worked!

"No, no, no, Jewels. Not stupid. I take that back. Look, sweetheart, there's no such thing as sanctuary anymore."

My head pops up. "Huh?"

"The church outlawed it centuries ago."

"No sanctuary?"

"Only in fiction, Jewels. I'm sorry."

What is he saying? "Um, well, okay, so what? No one needs to know you're here. Even Father Donlevy. He thinks it's just us girls down here with our club. So you can just stay here and no one will know. And everyone says this war won't go on long and—"

"Oh really? Have you seen how the Japanese have squashed our entire Pacific fleet? It's going to take years just to rebuild, let alone defeat anyone."

"I heard what that Boothby said. They can send you back to Japan. He said Leavenworth or Japan. I heard it! They're taking you away!"

He looks up at me, his worn smile gone. "Yes, they are."

"Because you're Issie or something," I say. "Rex told me. He knows all about this stuff. You're Issie because you were born in Japan."

His eyes search my face. "Issei. Yes, I was born there. But, Jewels, you're just a kid. This isn't your problem."

"You can't let them send you back."

"Well, it's either that or prison. So I can either get shot here as a Japanese spy or lose my head in Japan as an American spy. If I'm lucky, they'll give me my own sword to fall on," he says. "I'm pretty much dead either way."

"Don't say that!" I holler in my loudest whisper.

"No, I was speaking metaphorically."

"I don't know what that is! Alls I know is they are going to take you far away!"

"I'll find a way out of this problem," he whispers, but there is not one ounce of courage in his voice.

"I already *have* found a way out of this problem," I say, indicating the basement around us. "Sanctuary."

He sort of sniffs a laugh, looking around. "I don't suppose you have anything to drink down here."

At least I did that right. I open the moldy curtains I hung along a wall, and there's the liquor cabinet—well, it's just a cupboard with dry rot that fell out of Cabin 30. I open the doors and show him all the booze I've been swiping from the Look-Sea Lounge. "And I'll go get the rest, if you want."

He pours himself a stiff one and sips it. "Looks like you've thought of everything."

"Well, not the FBI part," I say, my voice a bit low.

"So, who all knows about this sanctuary?"

"No one, I promise! I did this all by myself, Mr. Kaye."

"Now, if your mother came up with this harebrained idea, I would understand. But you, Jewels? Whatever made you think this could work?"

My face goes blank. I guess I'm hurt, and okay, maybe a bit peeved. I fold my arms. "Well, what was *your* plan? It's not like you can just fade into the crowd. I mean, no offense, but you look pretty dang Japanese."

We glare at one another. Then, slowly, out comes his strange smile. "I never thought it would come to them sending me back on a technicality. Just because my parents never legally adopted me, just because I was born in Nagasaki, just because . . . oh, Boothby's got me and he's got me good!"

"No, he doesn't. St. Bart's has you. I don't think the FBI has jury . . . juru . . . what is it?"

"Jurisdiction?"

"Yeah, that over the Pope. Do they? Well, Father Donlevy speaks for St. Bart's and St. Bart's speaks for the Pope and the Pope speaks for God."

He looks at me and says, "Jewels, sweet child. I can't just stay here. Sooner or later, they'll find me. And don't you see? Running away only implicates me further."

"But you're *not* running away. You're staying right here in Sea Park where you can oversee your businesses and you can wait out the war with all the comforts of home. Out of sight and out of mind. You know, like my mother when she's incommunicado."

"They've already frozen my accounts. I can't even write a check for a can of dog food! They'll confiscate everything I own." He refills his glass. "If they haven't already."

"What was in that strongbox you asked me to bring you?" I'm feeling the ratty old Oriental rug being pulled out from under me.

"The usual legal stuff that proves who I was, but not who I am. Some keys, some cash, a few memories. I should have married your mother two years ago when she asked me," he adds. His head comes up to meet mine and he says, "Oh, I'm sorry, Jewels. That was a cruel thing to say."

"Rex and me have known all about you and Mom for years. I don't know why adults think they can hide something like that. Anyway, why should you have married her? What difference would that make?"

"Well, as my heir she'd inherit everything I've worked so hard for all these years."

"Doesn't there have to be a corpse before there can be an heir?"

"I'm dead six ways to Sunday and I'm about to lose everything! Sure! Give it all away!" he hollers, kicking the couch.

Down goes another shot and it's doing something to him. Something I've never seen before.

"They're taking me away tomorrow. Jewels, Jewels, Jewels. This is war. We are at war with Japan. *I* am at war with *me!*" He thunks his chest. "I was born in Japan. I am not an American citizen. And that's not the least of it."

Uh oh. When my mother says that after downing a couple shots of booze, yelling and kicking a couch, you know to brace yourself. He says, "They have all the records of my money wires to Japan."

I'm seeing a long telephone wire all the way to Japan with dollar bills attached like undies on a clothesline. Funny, the things you see when you don't want to see the truth.

"There is no way anyone is going to believe that money was going to my sister in Nagasaki. She runs an orphanage there. The same one my parents plucked me out of and the same one they left her in. No, that's going to be seen as funneling."

"What's funneling?"

"To J. Edgar Hoover and to Sheriff Hillary Dutton and to everyone in between, Jewels, any money sent to Japan is giving aid and comfort to the enemy."

Treason. "Well, then I guess I'm as guilty as you are," I say. I indicate the basement around us. "Guess I'm giving aid and comfort to the enemy, too." I point to the whiskey bottle and add, "Maybe a little more comfort than aid right now."

He truly smiles at me, then—his warm, wonderful smile that always makes me feel like everything's going to be okay. "You're a good kid, you know that?"

He wobbles to the bar and polishes off another shot. I wonder how much booze this war is going to take to get him through it.

There's a creak up on the landing and we both look toward the door. It slowly creeps open. I didn't latch it tight! This might be the shortest sanctuary in history!

Mr. Kaye steps in front of me like there's danger coming.

Then, shyly, in pokes Hero's long snout. He looks around on the landing, looking like Goofy with one long ear turned back on itself. He sees Mr. Kaye and bounds down the steps. I rush up and latch the door then come back downstairs.

Mr. Kaye slumps into the couch and Hero climbs up next to him, plunking his great big head onto his master's lap. Mr. Kaye lays his head back and closes his eyes. "Well, Hero," he whispers. "Here's another fine mess we've gotten ourselves into." Then to me, he adds, sounding pretty old, pretty tired, "Does this establishment have a wake-up service? Tell the front desk I have a very important appointment at nine in the morning."

"Sure," I say, knowing I won't wake him or hand him over for anything in the world.

I give him the ratty, crocheted comforter from Cabin 3. He tucks himself into it and falls fast asleep. I pat my leg and Hero follows me upstairs. I can tell he'd rather stay down there with Mr. Kaye but when this dog starts his howling, it can be heard all the way to Tok-e-yo. I turn off the light, careful to replace the blackout curtains acrost the door and padlock it behind me.

I check around each corner now before I walk around it. I'm almost home free when someone says, "Jewels?"

I know that deep, dark voice but I keep walking, pretending I don't hear him.

My arm gets pulled and I turn and look up into Boothby's huge face, which is scary now in the dark shadows. "Are you all right?" he asks. "It's late to be out. And it's past curfew."

I'm thinking fast and scramble for my excuse. "Um, I'm scared," I say. I lift Hero's leash and add, "I went to take Hero back and Mr. Kaye said—"

"You talked to him? When we went back up there, he wasn't in his apartment or anywhere we looked. Now, you tell me, Jewels. This is about our nation's security. I know he's a friend of yours, but if you know something, you best tell."

"He, um, said he was, well, he was mad. And he said he was just . . . um . . . leaving town. Had enough. And he said he's done with everything and he was mad as a hornet and he was getting out while the getting out was good." Do not ask me where this is coming from!

"Did he say where he was going?"

Oh, someone just hand me a shovel to dig myself deeper. "Well, no. Well, maybe. Let me think. Oh yeah, he said someplace where he could breathe." My eyes land on the old rusty, bent DRINK CANADA DRY sign outside the café. "Canada. He said he's going to Canada."

Agent Boothby looks around the parking lot. There's only one car parked there—the Stay and Play car. "And did he say how he was going to get there?"

"No. He just grabbed a big suitcase, put on his hat, and told me sigh-o-nar-a. Locked up and left. Just like that."

I am glad it's dark out because my face is stinging hot and I know my lying face is pure red right now.

"I see," he says, like adults say when they probably don't believe you but don't want to call you a dang liar until they know for sure you're a dang liar. "Well, that certainly adds more to the case," he says, jotting down some notes on a pad. He smiles and actually tips his hat to me and says thanks and goodbye.

"Oh, and Jewels?"

Uh oh. I turn.

"Don't forget the curfew."

Well, I don't like adding more to the case, but if him and his cigar-smoking partner will just leave town then pretty soon everyone will think Mr. Kaye *is* gone and forgotten. Incommunicado.

I go home and feed Hero. Now I can add lying to the FBI to my record. How old do you have to be for the firing squad? What's the weather like in Leavenworth? Where the heck *is* Leavenworth? I can't believe what I've done.

Four times I get up to go unlock the church basement. Who do I think I am? It's stupid. How come plans that seem so clever in the daylight are just plain harebrained in the dark of night?

CHAPTER 25

"Hey, Shorty," Rex says, pulling on the light. "Where's Mom?"

I'm all foggy. I love those few brief seconds when you wake and you can't remember the trouble you've gotten yourself into. "Huh?"

"She's not in her room. She go incommunicado again?"

"Uh, no. She said she was going to Edna's and then spend the night if it got too late."

"Well, it's too late."

"Where've you been?"

"Feed and Seed. Studying. It's quiet there once I got it all cleaned up and the windows blacked out."

"Only *you* would study on a Saturday night."

"Got to ace my finals. If I do well on those, I can get out of this crappy town. Get anywhere but here."

I sit up and look at him straight on, not sure if my ears are buzzing or if there's a bit of wheeze in his voice. "What's out there besides 'anywhere but here'?"

"A life. College, maybe."

He's the only boy in town thinking college right now—this February after infamy. Most're thinking about war and signing on the dotted line to go kill some enemies.

"College costs money," I say. "You stand just as much a chance of going as traveling to the moon."

"Mr. Kaye says if I can get a scholarship somewhere, he'd front the rest of the bill."

Mr. Kaye. Zonked out in the basement of the church one block south of us. Agent Boothby trying to pick up his fake trail to Canada. Now it all comes back to me. And you know what? It's another good reason why maybe my plan *has* to work. No Mr. Kaye, no college for Rex.

"Rex, I think there's something I should tell you."

My voice is quavering and he takes notice. "What?"

So I spill my guts, starting with the words and papers being tossed between Agent Boothby and Mr. Kaye, passing through Leavenworth then on over to Japan, and ending in the basement of St. Bart's and my harebrained idea of sanctuary.

"Jewels! There's no sanctuary anymore! If there was, every church in the world would be filled with thieves and murderers!"

"Well, I didn't know that when I put him there!" I snap. "But I'll be blasted if I'm going to stand by and watch that

FBI man haul him off to prison! Or worse! They shoot spies, you know!"

I think for the first time ever, Rex is speechless. He looks at Hero snoozing on the floor, then back at me. Then he screeches out, "Are you out of your mind? You can't . . . he can't . . . Jewels! You can't do this!"

"Well, I did! And as far as the FBI is concerned, Mr. Kaye has run off to Canada, so they don't even have to bother looking here anymore."

"What's that about Canada?"

So I tell him that part of the story.

Rex sputters in and out of a cough, "Jewels, you have no idea what you've done. Leaving his apartment, leaving Sea Park, leaving Oregon is one thing. Leaving the country is another. And Canada! That's where draft dodgers and conscientious objectors go!"

"But he *hasn't* gone to Canada. He's gone to church!" I say, pointing toward St. Bart's. How come no one but me is getting this? "He's only a block away. Safe and sound."

Rex is pacing my room. Finally, he stops and, face contorted, asks, "And Mr. Kaye actually agreed to this lunatic idea of yours?"

"Well, after a few drinks I think it was looking pretty darn smart to him, all things considered."

"He's in hiding and we're accomplices! They could arrest us all, Jewels! " He turns and points at me. "What am I saying? *You're* an accomplice! I'm not going to jail for something my idiot sister did! No sir! I—"

"Well, at least I did *something!* What did *you* do? You curl up in a ball and let Eldon and Bully beat the crap out of you! I'd rather be an idiot than a coward!"

Now we're both standing face to face. I give him a hard shove. He seizes his side and yells as he doubles over. I couldn't have hit him that hard. He turns and grabs me by my pajamas shirt and pulls me toward him. He makes a fist and puts it close to my face. For a second, I think he's actually going to hit me.

We glare at each other. I pull myself out of his grip and yank aside the curtain-door to my room—my suggestion for him to leave. Which he does. I hear what he calls me as he passes.

I hate everything and everyone in my life right now!

CHAPTER 26

An hour later, I'm in Rex's room. I pull on the light and say, "I take it all back."

He doesn't move but says, "Me too."

"Here. I made cocoa."

He sits up with a groan and holds his side.

I hand him his mug and say, "Don't you see? I had to think of something. Everyone's saying he's the enemy. And you know he's not."

"I know. But being the enemy isn't half as bad as being a Benedict Arnold."

"Who?"

"You know, a turncoat? A traitor? Cripes, even Benedict Arnold hightailed it to Canada!"

"Look, I don't know anything about any Benedict Arnold. Alls I know is Mr. Kaye's probably the best friend any of us ever had. Me, you, that dog, and even Malice Alice. What's going to happen to us if the FBI takes him away?"

Rex looks down at his steaming mug. I've always known him and me are as different as Mutt and Jeff. Him and me nearly fist-fighting an hour earlier is about as close as we've ever been to seeing eye-to-eye. I never have a clue what runs through that mind of his. He's smart and logical, and I'm nothing like that. He thinks ahead of himself and even behind himself—sort of like when he's in the middle of a problem he turns a whole circle around and looks at it from every angle. I just go from here to there, no stopping in between.

"Think I should put him back?" I ask.

That makes Rex chuckle a little. "What? Like a toy on a shelf?"

"You know what I mean."

Then, the oddest thing happens. Rex says, "Are you sure only you and me know about this?"

"Well, Hero, but he ain't talking."

"You, me, and Mr. Kaye. Right, Jewels? You didn't tell Edna or Mom? Father Donlevy?"

"Crost my heart and hope to die," I say, making an X over my heart.

"None of your little Gable Girlfriends know?"

"I said 'hope to die!'"

"Well, maybe we can pull this off for a few days. Until we know the FBI has left for good. Maybe I can find some lawyer for him or something."

"Maybe by then we'll have won the war and things will be like they were before," I say.

"Do you ever pick up a newspaper? This war is going to go on for years."

"Oh," I say. "Guess that's a long time to live in a basement."

"It's never going to work long term," he mutters, shaking his head.

"Do you really think we could get into trouble for doing this? Go to jail even?"

He sighs and sort of smiles. "Yeah, the Benedict Arnold Lockup for Juvenile Traitors."

"'Cause you're eighteen in September and if we could get into trouble—real trouble—then I'm quitting. Boys your age can go to real jail, Rex. I'm a girl. They won't do much to me."

"Don't sell yourself short. Ever hear of the Girls' Betterment Reformatory in Eugene?"

"You're just trying to scare me."

"Sometimes you need scaring, Jewels."

"Well, at least if you're in jail, you can't get your head blown off in the war."

His eyes blaze at me. "It's just like you to think like that! Jeez, Jewels. I'm not going to jail, and I'm not going to get my head blown off! Unless it's by one of those

McAloonatics on their broken-down beach patrol horses or those SPORTS with their pop guns!"

"Okay, okay. So, what do we do?"

"All we can do is wait until tomorrow morning and see what Mr. Kaye wants. It's his life so it's his decision. Kill the light. I'm tired."

"What about Mom?"

He sighs heavy. "We'll just tell her Mr. Kaye left. The less she knows, the better."

He's asleep by the time I close his door.

CHAPTER 27

"What's that fleabag mutt doin' here?" Mom asks the minute she walks into the front door. Odd, she doesn't look hung over and it's only eight-thirty in the morning. Maybe she really has been "bein' good."

"Hi, Mom! You're up bright and early," I say.

Rex starts to say something, but sort of chokes, then starts coughing.

"Rex, you okay, darlin'?" Mom asks, stepping toward him.

I'm *this* close to telling her that no, Rex is *not* okay! But Rex just points to Hero and says, "I'm allergic, that's all." His glare at me is a hint of our pledge to tell her only so much.

"Then what's that fleabag mutt doin' here?" Mom says.

"Well, Mom," I begin. Hero's snoring and draped acrost our saggy half couch. "He's sort of . . . sort of . . ."

"Mom, sit down. We need to tell you something about Mr. Kaye."

Her face is stony as she sits. "What's wrong? Has something happened?"

I let Rex do the talking. The FBI, the threats, the choices, the future, and finally, his flight.

She looks at me and Rex, sitting now acrost the table. "What do you mean, Tommy left? Left for where?"

"Canada," I say, edging a cup of coffee closer to her. The lie is getting a bit easier each time I say it, or maybe it's just easier because this is Mom. "Yep, last night. He just shows up with a suitcase and hands me the leash and says goodbye, he's off to Canada."

"Canada? What's in Canada?"

"I don't think he was going *to* something so much as he was going *away* from something," Rex says, adding some milk to his coffee.

"For how long is he gone to Canada?"

"For the duration," Rex replies.

"Duration? Duration of what?"

"You *do* know there's a war going on, don't you?" Rex says, smiling, but with some snap to his voice—something he's doing a lot of lately.

"Of course, I do! And I'll thank you to keep that tone out of your voice, son." Mom's face scrunches up as she rolls the tip of her cigarette in the ashtray, a clear sign she's thinking.

"Wait a minute," she says. "His car's in the parkin' lot. How'd he get to Canada? Walk?"

"Um, guess someone gave him a ride. Maybe he flew?" I say.

Mom turns to me and asks, her voice odd, her eyes watching me carefully. "Flew? How? Sprouted wings?"

"Or more likely he chartered a boat," Rex says.

"Oh, this whole thing's a big mix-up. He wouldn't just leave. Not say goodbye or anything. Especially to . . ." her eyes catch first mine, then Rex's, and finally rest on Hero. ". . . to me."

She puts her coffee cup down, gets up, and looks out our cabin window. But she isn't looking at any view. She has her hand over her eyes. Uh oh, I think. I sure didn't see this coming. She's going to cry.

"I can't believe he would just up and desert us," she says.

Rex and I look at each other. I don't think he's seen this coming, either. "Well, if it'll make you feel any better," I say, trying to sound a bit brighter, "it was just a *small* suitcase."

"But he can't just leave. What about these cabins? The Look-Sea? What about everything?" When she turns to look at me, I can see her eyes are filled with tears.

"Oh, he said you're supposed to run things for him," I blurt out. Okay, that's also a lie. Rex shoots me a look like I'm crazy.

"Me? Run the whole shebang? Me? Ha. Tommy never let me even so much as flip a pancake without him lording over me."

"Well, he said you know how it all works. Said Rex could work the Feed and Seed after school, and you should see if Corliss can come back to the Kozy Korner to wait tables and help with the reservations. And I already know how to take care of the cabins and all. And Hero won't be any trouble. I promise."

Just then, as though to prove his worth, Hero lifts his head, perks his ears, and grumbles a *grumpf!* He looks toward the door. Then, there's a knock. Mom looks out and quickly leans against the door.

"It's that FBI man! What do I tell him?"

"What's he doing here? I told him Mr. Kaye left last night. What's he want?" I say, glancing at Rex.

Mom adjusts her dress. She opens the door and Agent Boothby takes up the whole jamb.

"Why, hello, Officer Booth," Mom says, very sweet and very Southern.

"I'm an agent, not an officer," he says, taking off his hat. "And it's Boothby. May I come in?"

She lets him pass. Hero just thunks his tail and goes back to sleep.

"My, you're up and at 'em early. Good to know Uncle Sam's got a handle on everything," Mom says.

"Well, I'm just on my way out of town. I was hoping Mr. Kiramoto—well, Mr. Kaye I guess you know him as—I was hoping he'd change his mind and come with us back to the Portland office. But apparently he's made other arrangements."

"Oh really?" Mom asks.

"Yes, seems he's fled to Canada," he continues. "Isn't that what you said, Jewels?"

I raise my face, and I'm praying it's not red. "Maybe he's fled to family." That's the best I can do. He must know I'm lying.

"I can tell you, I'm just as shocked and surprised by all this as you are," Mom says.

"Well, I'm neither shocked nor surprised, Mrs. Stokes," Agent Boothby says casually while jotting down some notes. "I don't get paid to have an opinion." He looks up and smiles at her.

"Then what *do* you get paid for?" Rex asks.

"To trust my feelings—my gut."

"And what is your gut telling you?" Mom asks.

"That a man you care very much for just hurt all of you." He gives each of us a kind smile. "Now, I see Mr. Kaye's car is still there," Agent Boothby goes on. "Any explanation?"

"No gas?" Mom suggests, with a feminine shrug of her shoulders. I remember what she'd told me about there being a time to play it dumb and a time to play it smart. Wisht I knew which one she's playing now.

"Perhaps he had operatives," Rex says.

We all looked at him. "Operatives?" Agent Boothby asks.

"Well, isn't that how spies work?" Rex says.

"Rex!" Mom says. "Do you have the gall to suggest that our Tommy Kaye is—"

"No, *he* is," I say, pointing to Agent Boothby.

Mom says, “Now you listen to me, all y’all! Tommy Kaye may be many things, but he is not a spy, and he certainly doesn’t have operatives!”

Agent Boothby looks at her and says, “I admire your loyalty, Mrs. Stokes. I just hope it isn’t misplaced.”

Mom tightens her dress with a tug on the belt, showing her hourglass figure. “If you’ll excuse us, we have Kaye Enterprises to run.”

“Oh, I’m afraid we’re going to have to close down Kaye Enterprises.”

“What on Earth for?” she asks.

“They’re owned by, well, an enemy of the state at best—a spy for the Empire of Japan at worst.”

She sits. “I see.”

Rex is ready to say something, but Mom shoots him a shut-up glance. “Agent Boothby, this whole town is dependent on Mr. Kaye’s establishments. I’m sure your intentions are not to close down all of Sea Park. Over just one . . . Japanese whatever-he-turns-out-to-be.”

“Well, no, of course not, but—”

“With all the importance on the home front, I’m sure throwin’ people out of work is not what this war is all about. In fact, it seems to me if there is *anything* good about a war, it’s jobs. Now y’all don’t want anyone to go hungry on account of your silly red tape.”

“Mrs. Stokes, this is war. If we err, it’s going to be on the side of caution. Times like this, there is a good reason to have that red tape.”

"But it's not fair!" I say, getting my two cents in.

"No, Jewels," Rex says. "He's right. Rules are rules, especially in war."

"Well, we wouldn't want the FBI to err on *anyone's* side, would we?" Mom says.

"Well," Agent Boothby says, fiddling with the rim of his hat, "needless to say, if you hear anything from Mr. Kaye, anything at all, it will be your obligation, your patriotic duty, to let me know. My card."

"Yes, I have one just like it on the table," Mom snaps.

"Look, I don't want to be hard-nosed about this. I'll take my time about filing my report. Maybe you can keep the restaurant and the feed store open. For now, at least. But from what I've seen, you might have a hard time getting people to stop throwing rocks and start throwing money at them. Well, we'll be in touch." He puts on his hat, shakes Rex's hand, gives Hero an ear-scrunch, tips his hat to Mom and me, and leaves.

Mom closes the door and falls into the nearest chair. "Well, I'm glad that's over. G-men are the most annoyin' people! Rules and red tape. Obviously, he's never lived in a small town."

"He's right," I say. "What does it matter anyway? It's like everything of Mr. Kaye's is poison or something."

"Well, not so fast," Mom says, looking like some wheels are turning inside that hennaed head of hers. "Now I'm mad as hornets that Tommy left, sneakin' off in the night like he did. But once word gets out he's not around, you wait and see. We'll get customers back again."

"But he said *for now*. What about for later?"

Mom just swishes her hand and says, "Oh pish posh. He's got bigger fish to fry than to worry about a two bit, one horse town like Sea Park. If you think justice grinds slow, you should see how slow government grinds."

That makes Rex laugh, and he starts coughing again. "Good for you, Mom," he spits out.

"Jewels, take that dog out of here," Mom says. "Rex is allergic."

Mom sips her coffee and says with a thoughtful expression, "Tommy wants to leave us high an' dry. Fine! Him turntailin' might be just the shot in the arm Sea Park's been needin' since Pearl Harbor."

She gets up and heads toward her room. "I'm takin' me a nice long nap. Now, when I wake up, please tell me this has all been just one big nightmare, and oh yes, if that Tommy Kaye ever does show up, well, he'll sure as snakes wish the FBI *had* taken him!"

Once we're alone in the room, I whisper, "Well, so far so good, huh, Rex?"

He shoots me a dirty look. "Yeah, for everyone *but* Tommy Kaye."

From Mom's room we hear her crying.

"And maybe Mom," I say.

CHAPTER 28

I rustle up some breakfast and a pot of coffee for Mr. Kaye. We hide everything in an old wooden toolbox with a latch cover, just in case someone sees us on our way to St. Bart's. It's too heavy for Rex so I carry it, and Rex acts as lookout with Hero leading the way. Church is still going on strong.

"Think he's still in there?" Rex asks.

"He couldn't get out if he wanted to," I say, showing him the key to the padlock on a string around my neck.

"Isn't there a way to get into the basement from inside the church?"

"Nope."

"Doesn't Father Donlevy have a key?"

"Nope. It's the lock from Cabin 16." The lock slips open and I carefully push the door against the blackout curtain. We step onto the landing. Everything is dark below.

"Mr. Kaye? It's me. I brought you some breakfast and here's Rex to—"

I switch on the light and see Mr. Kaye on the makeshift bed I'd made with two chairs and a sofa. He turns toward us and puts his hand over his eyes.

"What?"

"Breakfast," I say, pulling out a plate of bacon and eggs. "Get it while it's hot."

He scrunches his eyes and slowly blinks them open. He looks at me, then at Rex, then at the room around him. "Where am I?"

"Incommunicado," I answer, pouring him some coffee. He sits up and takes the cup.

"What's that awful noise?" he asks, looking toward the rafters.

"Organ music," I say.

Mr. Kaye glances up to the rafters and then says, "Lord, it's true. I'm in the basement of a church. I was hoping I'd dreamt it." He runs his hand over his face. Then he springs up and says, "What time is it? The FBI! I was . . ." Then his eyes narrow like he's trying to remember something important.

"You said the only way you'd go with them was for them to blast you out," I say, reminding him of last night.

He turns, mouth open, staring at me. "Yes, but, that was just an expression. No, I have to go with them, to face it all." His eyes go to Rex. "And you, Rex? You're in on this . . . this madness?"

"Well, they can't take you if they can't find you," Rex says. "There's a certain amount of logic to that. I don't see how this is going to work past a few days. Jewels, we better tell him everything."

"Well, I was scared and sort of cornered and, well, it was that FBI man," I say, my voice a bit shaky. "I mean, I didn't think saying you'd gone to Canada was such a big deal. I just had to think of someplace far away for you to go. You know, sort of throw them off your trail, and there was that Canada Dry sign and—"

"Hold it right there. Where am I?"

"In the church basement, but everyone thinks you're in Canada," I say, sort of low.

"I see. Canada." He seems to be adding it all up. "That would make me a traitor." He sighs and adds, "But, Boothby and most of the country think I'm one of those already."

"There you go," I say. "And some even think you're a spy, so—"

"Mr. Kaye," Rex says, breaking me off. "It doesn't matter much how you got here. But what does matter is what to do with you."

"Firing squad at dawn?" he says, lifting the cover off the plate of breakfast.

"Look, we know you're not a spy or a traitor or anything they say you are," Rex says. "But there's something else. Here, I brought over the paper."

Rex points to something on the first page. Mr. Kaye scans it, takes off his reading glasses, and places a hand on Hero's head. "I know where this is going," he says, more to Hero than to us. "It happened to the Germans living in England during the Great War."

"This relocation thing?" Rex asks.

"They gathered them up, Bavarian accents and all, and sent them away—to the Isle of Man. I always thought that had a touch of irony in it, the Isle of Man."

"What was that?" I ask, somehow knowing I'm not going to like the answer.

"Prison," Mr. Kaye says. "Well, they didn't call them prisons. So they called them internment camps, relocation centers, concentration camps, detainee's camps. Sort of like our own Indian reservations here," he says. "Put everyone together in the same place where you can keep an eye on them. Just in *case* . . ."

"I never heard anything about that and we just finished a whole unit on the Great War," Rex says.

Mr. Kaye tosses the newspaper on the floor and says, "And your grandkids will probably never know about what's happening now, either." He taps his foot on the editorial. "You know, maybe I *should* go to Canada. Just disappear."

"Do you know anyone in Canada? For real, do you think we could get you there?" I ask.

"Don't know a soul. No wait, my bookie finally moved to Vancouver."

"Least here you got us," I say.

"Does your mother, I mean, does she know about any of this?" He indicates the basement around us.

"No, she thinks you're in Canada," Rex says.

Mr. Kaye nods, still looking down at the newspaper. "So, everyone thinks I've just run away. Nothing says 'guilty' like hightailing it," he says, then looks up at me. "Was she mad? Hurt? Did she say anything?"

Rex and I look at each other. I don't know what to say. What can possibly make this any better, for any of us?

"I think she was both," I say. "Then she went back to bed."

"That's my Alice," he says, standing up and helping himself to another cup of coffee. "Well, then. I guess it's just you kids, that old dog, and me."

• • •

I leave the basement first, look around, then Rex follows with the empty box and Hero. We lock the basement door behind us and dash into the pathway that leads to the Stay and Play cabins. Rex and me go to Cabin 7 where we clean up the dishes and sit down to make our schedule and plan.

Criminently! Everything's happening so fast now, the right hand needs to know what the left hand is doing, as they say. We have to figure out how to get food down to Mr. Kaye without making anyone suspicious as well as help Mom to get Kaye Enterprises up and running.

By noon, Rex is looking pale and tired and says he's heading home to rest before attacking his stack of homework.

"You, too, Jewels. Mom sees our grades take a nose dive, she'll get suspicious."

CHAPTER 29

I told you about our *Sand Dune Telegraph*—fastest way to spread news in a town like Sea Park. Well, it's only Wednesday, and guess what? The Kozy Korner Kafe is open for business. I'll bet word of Mr. Kaye's hightailing it was on everybody's lips by Sunday night.

Mom had me make up a big sign, UNDER NEW MANAGEMENT, and taa daa! Folks are back just like usual. Even Corliss Ainsley, lisp and all, has come back to work the counter while Mom cooks. Rex and me are liking it because it keeps Mom on the straight and narrow and we get hot food to bring back home, making it easy as pie to sneak down to Mr. Kaye.

Finally, Sea Park is throwing money, not bricks. Ever hear of a sea change? That's where something big—like a sea—changes all of a sudden. I'm watching Sea Park have its second sea change. The biggest sea change for everyone was Pearl Harbor.

I help at the café after school and Rex opens the Feed and Seed for a few hours after school and you know, things are working out pretty dang well, considering how lousy the war is going everywhere else in the world.

You know how big I am on that whole out of sight and out of mind program? You would be amazed how easy it is to fall for it. Yesterday, I forgot to take Mr. Kaye the latest papers and one of those things to make soda for his whiskey and, well, did I hear about it.

To make up for it, I told him I'd bring him a wine with today's blue plate special, Spaghetti à la Alice. When I come into the café, I hear the wonderful sound of money. The ding of the bell over the door, the ding of the cash register, and ping of the order counter bell and Mom calling out, "Order up!"

Corliss whisks the plates away and says, "Hurry up that spaghetti. Frank and Leo are whining already."

"Tell those old coots to keep their shirts on!" Mom hollers back. She sees me and says, "Just in time, Jewels! Check those noodles, will ya? And get started on them dishes."

"Hi, Edna!" folks call out as she enters. When you run a roadhouse in a town like Sea Park, you know just about everyone. She comes around and stands in the kitchen door jamb.

"Well, well, well," she says to Mom, who looks pretty rattled in Arlie's big cooking apron, cigarette dangling off her lip, and with her hair all scrunched into a hairnet. "Look who's got herself a cooking job."

"Look who's got herself a whole café," Mom says, sounding a bit proud of herself. "Besides, someone had to do something. No use letting this whole place just rot and fall into the ocean," she says, picking a cigarette ash out of the spaghetti sauce.

"So, it's true? Tommy ran off to Canada?" My ears prick up, but I keep my hands in the dishwater and make like I don't hear. Edna dips a wooden spoon into the sauce Mom's stirring, tastes it, and proceeds to add some salt.

Mom snatches away the shaker and says, "Guess so. He sure isn't anywhere around here. He even gave that fleabag dog to Jewels."

"You know Tommy as well as I do, Alice. He's no coward and he'd never . . ."

The doorbell dings. We all look over the counter to see who's entered.

"Uh oh," we all mumble at the same time. Corliss Ainsley doesn't realize she's just given her sweet, bucktoothed smile and a menu to Special Agent in Charge Herman Boothby.

Corliss comes into the kitchen and Mom whispers, "What'd he want?"

"Who?"

"That big stranger," Edna says.

"A cup of coffee. Why? Who he?" Corliss asks.

"The FBI," we reply together.

Corliss puts her hand to her top blouse button like something's showing. But it looks like she's the *only* person in the café who doesn't know who Boothby is. No sooner does the agent sit down then there's five people around him, the McAloon twins included. Father Donlevy always tells me when two or more gather with God in mind, that's a congregation. He should also have told me when two or more are gathered with war in mind, that's a battle—even in a tiny little café in a Podunk town like Sea Park, Oregon.

I go to the front counter, pulling away from my mother's grasp. If I keep my head low and pretend to wipe the counters maybe folks won't even notice me noticing them.

"I'll tell you why he's gone!" someone says. Mr. Boothby looks up with interest and gets his notepad at the ready. The coffee cup gets pointed east to the hills that Mr. Kaye owns. "See them hills? Well, you can't see it now, but you can when the fog lifts. He built this big tower-like thing and calls it a forest lookout, but you get one fine view of the whole coastline up there."

"Ah, that's nothing," Leo McAloon says. "Me 'n' Frank've lived here since before God, and Tommy Kaye just showed up here one day and buys up everything. Me 'n' Frank always did wonder why a Jap would want to do that. Well, it's as clear as the nose on my face, now."

Frank adds, "Invasion, of course! He was sent here by ol' Hiro Hito to get everything ready for them Japs to just pull up to the beach and have us all on a plate!"

Leo says, "Tell him about the light."

"What light?" Frank asks. His twin points toward the ceiling. "Oh, *that* light. It's a dang search light up there on the roof. Helped him wire it myself."

"Tell him what he said," Leo prompts.

I am filling a salt shaker as I look carefully over the counter. "He says to me he wants a search light so bright that folks can see Sea Park all the way from . . ." and then both twins say, "Toe-Ke-Yo!"

Frank continues, "Yep, them's was his very own same words. My mother's nightcap it's to bring in tourists. It's to bring in Japs!"

Mr. Boothby asks for their names and how to get in touch with them. Now everyone else in here wants to get in on the act. They all spout their own stories and suspicions and names and numbers.

"Step aside, boys," Mayor Schmidtke finally says. The crowd splits for him. He offers his hand to Agent Boothby and introduces himself. "George Schmidtke, Mayor of Sea Park and purveyor of Schmidtke's Fine Meats," he says. "I'm the 'govern-meat' here in town. Zat's our little joke, isn't it, boys? Zat's Schmidtke, with a d and t and k-e."

I grab a tub and start busing the table next to the crowd surrounding Agent Boothby.

"Now, it occurred to me the other night, zinking zis whole mess over," the mayor goes on, like it's an election year. "I seem to recall him talking with some men last summer. Right here in zis very café. Zat booth right over zere, in fact. Now, zees were strangers. Vell, as you can see," he glances at the business card, "Agent Boothby, when a stranger comes to town in a suit and tie, he—" he snorts a little laugh, "—well, he gets noticed."

Agent Boothby looks at the mayor and asks, "Do I detect a bit of a German accent?"

You can hear a bead of sweat drop. All eyes go to the mayor. "Austrian," he says. "But you have a good ear, Agent Boothby."

Liar, I think. Everyone knows he's more German than polkas and sauerkraut.

"Anyway," Mayor Schmidtke goes on, "I heard the vord *bunkers* several times in zat conversation."

It was like the whole room takes a deep breath when they hear that word.

But where have *I* heard that word? Oh, Little Janie Johnson said "bonkers." It must have been "bunkers." I know what a bunker is. We kids used to make them all the time playing war in the sand dunes.

"Bunkers?" Agent Boothby asks. "You're sure?" He writes something down.

"Well, get this," Sadie Moran butts in. "Once I came to collect for the monthly paper delivery and he pulls out this wad of bills like some bootlegger and flips through it for a few measly Washingtons. Gives me a sawbuck tip! Now, I don't care how good business is in this town, nobody goes around with that kind of cold hard cash in their pockets!" Then, she asks the crowd, "Now exactly where does he get money like that?"

"Did any bills have pictures of that Jap king on them?" someone asks, nudging the man next to him and laughing. "Say, how many of them yens to a Yankee dollar these days?"

Folks laugh and I got an odd feeling in my stomach. Like I'm going to be sick.

"Well," Agent Boothby says, putting away his notepad and rising. Still others in the room are all talking to him and it looks to me like he wants out of there as much as I do. He says, "I think I have all I need for now."

"Vell, zese are frightening times in zeh world today," the not-German-but-Austrian mayor says. "Ve all need to be vigilant and cautious."

"Well, I don't think you have much to worry about anymore. Mr. Kaye reportedly went to Canada. So it's no longer my case. I'm handing this off to Interpol. I'll be in touch if need be." He finishes his coffee, gets up, and tosses some of his cards down on the table. Everyone grabs for one.

"Me 'n' Frank are doing our parts. We're already signing men up for the beach patrol. Got the SPORTS signed up. They're just boys, but it'll prepare them for what's to come."

"And what's to come?" Mr. Boothby asks, smiling cordially.

"Zeh vest coast invasion, of course," Schmidtke says. "Isn't that vhat zis is all about?" He points to the notepad in Mr. Boothby's coat pocket.

Boothby smiles as he puts on his hat and repeats that he'll be in touch if need be.

Then, he leans acrost the lunch counter toward the kitchen and says, "Mrs. Stokes, I know you'll be sure to let me know if you hear from Mr. Kaye."

He leaves the café and a chilly breeze seeps in. And with that, my stomach scrunches even more. I hate this! I hate it because I'm thinking about bunkers and lookout towers and search lights and wads of money all the time. And I'm thinking about us Stokes. Do they hang or shoot aiders, abettors, accomplices, operatives, or even friends?

CHAPTER 30

It's been two weeks since Agent Boothby left town, and now things are finally smooth sailing. Mom's agreed not to open the Look-Sea Lounge in exchange for the breakfast and lunch trade, while Edna takes the dinner and the booze trade. We Stokes are pretty dang busy, believe you me.

We've moved into Mr. Kaye's apartment above the café, and it sure was nice having heat at the push of a button instead of the kick of an oil heater; a porcelain bathtub instead of a rusty metal shower; and no groaning refrigerator waking you up at all hours. If Mom gets curious about Mr. Kaye's personal belongings slowly disappearing, she doesn't mention it.

Even Mr. Kaye is doing—well, I won't say fine, but he's doing okay. Rex and me keep to our schedule. I check on him in the mornings before school and Rex checks on him around dinner time. He uses the hot plate for coffee or he can open a can of soup if he wants. We are just as careful carrying out garbage as we are carrying in food and supplies.

I sneak Mr. Kaye out late at night for fresh air, and if the coast is clear, we let him shower and clean up in one of the empty cabins. I make the big sacrifice and loan him my radio so he can catch up on the war news and hear the latest tunes. I make sure he gets the newspapers and magazines folks leave lying around the café.

But it's getting a little tiresome for all three of us. Make that four. Hero is pretty darned confused just who his loyalties belong to now.

Sheriff Hillary Dutton is back in town. Word is there isn't enough of her husband's body left to have a casket funeral so they're going to hold a big memorial for him at St. Bart's. It's like there's a big blackout curtain over the whole town of Sea Park. He's our first war dead.

Mr. Kaye asked me to smuggle over his black suit for the event. And so him and me and Rex set up three chairs in the basement and we're sitting, listening as the service is held upstairs. The music that drifts down is pretty moving. Mr. Kaye, on account of him being Catholic, gives himself a sip of wine and a cracker and he does some up and down kneeling and praying.

Rex looks at Mr. Kaye. "That organ isn't playing 'Ten Cents a Dance,' is it?"

Mr. Kaye nods, dashing away a tear with his hankie. "That was Norm and Hillary's song," he says. "I've played it for them on their anniversary for years."

So, now we have our first war dead memorialized and put away and we have our sheriff back.

• • •

One of the Town Hood's jobs is to keep the bulletin board tidy in City Hall, just outside the police office doors. With Sheriff Hillary being gone so long and then having to mourn and bury her Norman, the stack of flyers she hands Rex and me is pretty big. So, we're busy pulling notices, pinning things like wanted posters and other legal mumbo jumbo to the board one afternoon.

"Sure hope we don't find one with Mr. Kaye's face and 'wanted dead or alive' on it," I mumble. But Rex isn't listening. He's reading a flier.

"Lord almighty. Look! They're doing it! Just like Mr. Kaye said! This is going to kill him."

I read over his shoulder. At the top in big letters it reads;

EXECUTIVE ORDER NUMBER 9066.
INSTRUCTIONS TO ALL PERSONS OF JAPANESE ANCESTRY

"Is that what I think it is?" I ask.

"The order to lock away all Japanese people living on the coast," Rex says, wadding up the flier and throwing it into the hallway. But just doing that makes him wince and grab his side.

Sheriff Hillary has come out of her office. She looks at us, the paper at the tip of her Wellington boot, then back at us. She picks it up, un-wads it, and reads.

She nods her head and there's that downturn of her lips that some people think is a sad smile but I know is anger. She looks at us and says, "Too bad our little resident Jap traitor has vamoosed! I could kill him with my bare hands!"

Alls I can see is Mr. Kaye being right under *everyone's* noses during the memorial service for *her* husband and him doing the communion and crying over "Ten Cents a Dance." Nothing makes any sense. Rex and me play dumb and keep working, but Sheriff Hillary keeps talking. "Word is he was going to clear a runway so Jap planes can land. Why else would he have those coastal maps and that bulldozer? Now I ask you, what does he need a bulldozer for?"

"Logging," Rex says flatly. "He owns all those tracts of timber on Willits Mountain."

"Bingo! He was going to log the inroads to the landing strip," she says. "Now, the sooner you Stokes stop defending Tommy Kaye and begin to see the light about this whole war, the better off we'll all be!"

Rex and me look at each other. "There's so many rumors out there about everything and you know they aren't true!" I yell.

"Watch it, missy!" the sheriff warns.

Well, I won't watch it, and I hate it when someone calls me missy. "One idiot even said Mr. Kaye was in some Japanese gang," I go on.

"Jewels," Rex warns.

"Go ahead and tell her what some dingaling said about that gang thing," I go on.

"Yazuka—the Japanese Mafia."

"I know what it means," Sheriff Hillary snaps. She points her cigarette at us and adds, "And don't think I'm not doing my share of detective work on all this. Like where he got all his money during the Depression when none of us had a pot to pee in! Man, you think you know someone and then, all this! Right under our noses! Now hurry up with those fliers. And this is going up!" She tacks up the 9066 flier. "Folks need to know how our government is protecting us!"

She hands the box of tacks back to Rex and says, "I have to lock up and go on patrol." We watch her retreat into her office.

I look at Rex and say, "What Mr. Kaye told me is true."

"What's that?"

"War changes everything and everyone."

"Well, it's not going to change me," Rex says, tossing old fliers into the garbage. "I'm going to study, graduate, and then *I'm* going to hightail it out of town and pray I don't get drafted."

We walk outside and the chilly February air hits us. Rex starts coughing again.

"Don't worry. That cough'll get you Four F or worse, if they got it." He spits into the road. "So when you going to do something about that cough?" I ask.

He points toward City Hall. "Allergies. That place hasn't been cleaned since the last war."

"Bull. I know you're still strapping your ribs."

"No, I'm not."

"Prove it," I say, reaching for his shirt.

"Get lost." He grabs his bike from the rack and takes off toward home.

Well, I don't need to see his ribs. I've caught him wrapping that bandage and belt around his chest twice in the last couple of weeks. And his coughing at night almost brings down the apartment's walls. Mom's been giving him cough syrup and he slugs it down. But it's not allergies, and it's not a cold, and it's getting worse, and just about anything starts it off. I think he's starting to lose weight, too. Every time I warn Rex I'm telling someone about his broken ribs, he tells me he's on the mend. We'll see.

I untie Hero from the bike rack and look up at City Hall and, just as Sheriff Hillary is locking up, I run back to the steps.

"Now what?"

"I left something."

"Well, hurry up!" she growls.

I run to the bulletin board and rip down the flier, pocket it, and run back out. I bike over toward the church,

Hero lumbering by my side, wondering if we should even tell Mr. Kaye about that executive order 9066 thing.

Hero stops. I stop. Hero bays. I hush him.

Then, from the shadows, Father Donlevy appears, standing on the walk in front of the church.

"Oh, you scared me," I say, relieved it isn't the McAloons or the SPORTS or the FBI or Sheriff Hillary on patrol or—okay, I admit it—or even the Japs invading the coast.

"Hello, Jewels. I wonder . . . could you come with me?" he says. "Maybe answer some questions?"

CHAPTER 31

"You can bring your friend with you," he says, pointing to Hero. We walk inside and through the alcove of the church. It's cold and quiet and sort of spooky. Lots of candles flicker on the altar. Probably all for Norm Dutton. I follow Father Donlevy's swishing black robes and squishy shoes into the church office. This room is small and musty smelling and cluttered with books. He tells me to sit, which I do. The lamp on his desk must be only a 20-watter because it doesn't give much light. You better dang well believe my heart is thunking.

"Jewels," he begins, "I've noticed something very odd since you and your See Girls took over the basement."

"Really? What's that?"

"This," he says, handing me a piece of paper. North Coast Public Utilities. I look at it, then back at Father Donlevy. "The meter reader wondered if there was a problem, so he comes around every week to take a reading. Just what sort of war work are you girls doing down there? Riveting battleships?"

I'm speechless. This is what Mr. Kaye would call a technicality. Like him never being officially adopted. A mess-up in the paperwork at the head office. Red tape stuck smack dab acrost a dang light bill.

"Jewels?"

"Um, we're, um . . ."

"And there's something else," he goes on. He points to my side where Hero sits, panting, watching something that probably isn't there on the carpet between his paws.

"Hero?"

"Yes, Hero. I know dogs bay at the moon, but this is the first one I've seen who bays at a basement doorknob. And the other morning, I get the most delightful aroma of bacon. You girls curing hams down there?"

"Um. Well, we were having a breakfast meeting," I say. This is not going well.

He gets up. "I think you better just show me," he says, untangling a key chain from a bunch of those Catholic bead necklaces that they use to pray with when they've goofed up like I'd be doing right now if I was a Catholic and might anyway if it can get out of this one. "And another thing. When I went to check, this key . . ."

"I know. Doesn't work." I hold up the key and string around my neck.

He gives me a stern look and puts his hand out for my key.

On our way out of the church and around the side to the basement entrance, my mind is going like sixty. We have a code for an emergency like this and I'm praying Mr. Kaye remembers it.

When we get to the basement door, I knock three times and call out, "Ollie Ollie Unguentine!" I turn to Father Donlevy and say, "That's our password to be let in. Don't tell anyone."

"But the door is locked from the *outside*, Jewels," he says, unlocking the padlock. He opens the door and gestures me inside first.

I look down and see Mr. Kaye's digs, neat and orderly just like he always keeps it, but he's nowhere to be seen. We go downstairs.

"Say, this is quite a layout," Father Donlevy says. "You girls did a great job."

"Yeah, but you're right. We shouldn't leave all these lights on. We'll kick in some money for the bills."

"Yes, all the comforts of home." He turns to me and adds with a big smile, "If one of you runs away from home, we'll know where to find you."

He looks at the hot plate, the boxes and cans of food, the few dishes washed out and draining next to the dish pan. "Keeping tidy. That's good." From there, he looks at the stacks of newspapers. "Keeping informed. That's good." Then he stands in front of the four bonsai plants and the string of bare light bulbs over them for warmth and light. Father Donlevy turns and looks at me.

Cripes, done in by a stupid midget tree, I think.

"You know, these little guys have always fascinated me."

Next comes the liquor cabinet. He opens the door, examines a few bottles like he's shopping at the liquor store, nods his head, and turns back to me with folded arms.

Then, Mr. Kaye emerges from the darkness, holding an electric coffee pot.

"It's not what you think!" I holler, standing between them.

"It isn't?" Father Donlevy says.

"It's sanctuary," I say.

"That's what I thought," Father Donlevy says.

We hear Hero wail from outside the door. "Jewels," Father Donlevy says, "you better let that dog in before the whole town comes looking down here."

I scramble up the steps, let the dog in, and scramble back down.

Mr. Kaye says, "I was just about to make some coffee. Perhaps something a little stronger is in order?"

"I see you stock my favorite scotch," Father Donlevy says.

I didn't know priests drank. The two men raise their glasses. Then, to me, Father Donlevy says, "Sanctuary, huh?"

"Uh huh."

He looks at Mr. Kaye, who smiles and says, "Sort of an interesting slant, isn't it? At first it was harebrained, then it was, well, convenient. If anything, it's allowed me time to think."

Father Donlevy seems to be letting it all sink in. He looks at me and says, "Jewels, this is very, very . . ." He's searching for words. "Very . . ."

"Serious," Mr. Kaye says.

"Yes, but, Tommy, you are . . ." He's looking at Mr. Kaye almost like he's never seen him before. "I mean, you're wanted or . . . what exactly are you?"

"Well, I'm a member of your flock," Mr. Kaye says. "What I'm *not* is a spy or a Japanese operative. But I'm also *not* an American citizen, but only because my parents never legally adopted me. So now I'm a fugitive from my own government, hiding in a dank, dark, moldy basement, dependent on this girl, that dog, and her brother for everything."

"And there's something else you need to know," I say, pulling out the Executive 9066 flier. I hand it to Mr. Kaye and feel like I'm handing him Execution Order 9066.

I'm waiting for him to go ka-blooey over it, but he just hands it to Father Donlevy. "For our own safety, I'm sure."

Then it hits me and I say to Father Donlevy, "So, what's the difference if he's locked up with the government or if he's locked up here?"

"I know it all sounds that simple, Jewels, but this *is* different. This could mean big, big trouble for all of us. I mean, there is no sanctuary, and Mr. Kaye is . . ."

"You don't have to mince words with me, Father. I'm the enemy. In the eyes of the State Department, I am the enemy." He taps his chest with each word.

"I can't—the church can't—harbor the . . ."

"Enemy!" Mr. Kaye shouts. "Just say it!"

Father Donlevy looks down at his hands and he whispers, "Enemy."

"He's not the enemy!" I say. "And you know it. You can't turn your back on him."

"Jewels, what a small-town priest in a rundown parish thinks has nothing to do with any of this. I have no say. I have no power. No one in the church will back me on this." He looks at Mr. Kaye and adds, "It's not like you just stole a loaf of bread and need food and shelter for the night."

"No, it's not," Mr. Kaye says.

Then another angle hits me like a ton of bricks. "Well, Father, aren't church confessions supposed to be secret? I mean, what if Mr. Kaye were upstairs in that confession room and confesses he's hiding in your basement? Wouldn't you have to keep it just between you, him, and God?"

"Jewels, this is different," Father Donlevy says. "This basement isn't a confessional. This is—"

"A church," I say, pointing upstairs. "Isn't it just a technicality where you learn about folks' sins? Like maybe on death beds and firing squad walls and such?"

Mr. Kaye sort of smiles and looks at the priest. "I think this is one of those 'out of the mouths of babes' moments. I believe she has a point there."

Father Donlevy sighs heavy and says, "Jewels, I think the dog needs a walk."

I leash him and go up the steps. When I look back down, I see Father Donlevy, back turned on Mr. Kaye. He's looking down, hands clasped. Mr. Kaye kneels.

I close the door and wait outside.

A few minutes later, Father Donlevy comes out. The dark afternoon makes his face look almost bluish and pale, like he's been put through a wringer.

"Sometimes, I wish to heaven I'd stayed in medical school," he says, handing me back the key to the basement and brushing past me.

I guess that brings us Allies up to a total of four—five counting Hero the bloodhound.

CHAPTER 32

We don't hear much about all the Japanese–American folks being rounded up and sent off to the relocation centers, which is what they call them. There are some Japanese families down in Depoe Bay we know about and a lot more in islands in the Columbia River where they farm and fish and such. Portland has lots of them, too, and we see a few photos in the papers of them lined up with luggage. No one smiles like they usually do when they get their pictures taken for the newspaper, though, and I wonder who's going to take care of their farms, their boats, their pets, their businesses while they're being relocated. April 7 is the deadline for them to report and that date is coming up fast.

As for Kaye Enterprises, well, I got to admit that ol' Malice Alice is stepping up to the plate pretty good with all of it. Not that tourists are breaking down our doors. Everyone's still scared we're going to be invaded. There've been sightings of Japanese submarines right off the coast, and now there's talk of big blimps coming to Tillamook where they can float above the coast and look for the enemy. Not sure what the men onboard will do if they find them. Seems to me a blimp isn't much of a match against a ship's cannon or a dive bomber airplane and it sure can't turntail too fast. I know, because I've seen newsreels of blimps and they move slower'n glaciers.

Most towns have raised up an official Home Guard and so the coast is pretty busy with horse and German Shepherd patrols. Some folks have taken to the hills to look for enemy planes from lookout posts. They have some outfit who does shooting practice at targets they set to float on the ocean. Latest rumor is some joker sunk a whale. Mistaking a whale for a submarine is one thing. Mistaking Mr. Kaye for the invading enemy is another, and as all this practicing for war heats up, I got to pledge to be more careful taking him out at night. Too many trigger-happy fingers around Sea Park nowadays.

Just like Mrs. Johnson and Mrs. O'Leary said those months ago in the grocery store, we're rationing things like sugar, meat, butter, rubber, and gasoline—another reason why we aren't getting any tourists as spring comes to Sea Park. You might have the gas to travel, but you might not have the tires or vice versa. There's ration books on all that and even shoes, which makes me mad because I never did get those Oxfords for Christmas.

Our Austrian-not-German mayor appointed a few folks to be air wardens and they'll take turns walking around town, wearing tin hats and whistles around their necks, and toting buckets of sand. At first, I thought they were supposed to throw the sand into the face of the enemy, but Rex informs me it's to put out any fires from bombings. Yes, they are *that* worried the war is coming to us right here in sleepy ol' Sea Park. The mayor has appointed himself Chief Evacuator, which I think means he gets to be first in line to evacuate town if we're invaded.

Us kids are asked to collect scrap metal and grease and newspapers, so everyone has something to do here on what they're calling the war home front. I've got enough to do with my own war home front. In fact, I'm getting pretty worn out. And so is Rex. I don't know how much longer we can go on like this. And Mr. Kaye, he's starting to look pretty ghostly and pale and I think he's losing weight. The whole sanctuary plan is wearing us all down.

Mr. Kaye even says maybe life would be better in one of those relocation camps down south where the weather is nice and warm and where he could maybe get up a bridge game or ride a bike or help sew uniforms or roll bandages. "I sure would like to feel the sun on my face," he says. He sort of smiles upward and closes his eyes, like he's remembering sunlight and warmth and salt air.

"Where's that Leavenworth lock up?"

"Kansas," he says.

"Lots of sun there," I say.

And he just turns, fixes himself a drink, and says, "Never mind. I'm just getting so bored, so itchy, living like this."

"You like to read," I say, pointing to the stacks of books I've been bringing over.

"Wish the library wasn't closed," he says.

"Maybe Rex can get some from school or something."

"High school textbooks?" I can tell by his face that's not so exciting.

"Mom's cleaned out all your closets. Those books were all I could find," I say, wondering if it's going to be a sore point.

"She's up there and I'm down here. Of all the times I've asked her to move in with me . . ." he says, shaking his head. Then his eyes catch mine. The point is sore all right. He adds, "After we'd be married, of course."

I'm not sure what to say. It kind of makes me mad, though. The Town Hood, Town Clown, and Town Bimbo've been poor and struggling and getting laughed at and all and maybe Mom just marrying Mr. Kaye could have changed that. Might have gotten ourselves a little respect. Then again, maybe we'd all be getting our pictures taken boarding a train to some relocation place in the middle of nowhere or have visiting relative rights at Leavenworth. Or steaming our way to Japan. Or being shot as traitors. I don't like this train of thought.

"But it's strange. She always said marrying me would be the easy way out," he says, looking into his glass of whiskey.

Strange, he says? I'll say strange! "Are you kidding? Mom's always taking the low road out and back in again. Last time toting a turkey!" I say. The embarrassment of her last stunt still stings. "She says you can't fight city hall so you just may as well float on the tides. Like flotsam and jetsam."

He smiles at me and says, "Well, for every low tide, there's a high tide." I just want out of this basement. "Okay, no more philosophy. Say, I know where to look for books. I have some crates in storage."

"But I thought they, you know, the FBI, already cleared out your warehouse."

"I don't think they know about this place. It's up on the landing strip in Warrenton, off Beach Berry Road."

He gets a key out of his strongbox along with a five spot. "I have a hangar up there. I've owned it for years. Actually, your mother owns it. I needed a tax dodge. It's all legal."

"*My* mother owns an airplane hangar?"

He smiles and says, "In name only. Bet she forgot about it years ago. The hangar is where I keep, well, things that mean a lot to me. Like books."

"Like things you don't want the FBI to get?" It's out of my mouth before I can think better of it. Okay, I admit it, when he said "landing strip" alls I could see were enemy planes landing on it. And now what's this about a tax dodge and my own mother owning something she forgot all about?

"Yes, things I don't want anyone to get. *My* things," he says.

"And why do you need to dodge taxes?"

Now he's looking at me sort of narrow-eyed. "If I didn't know you any better, I'd say *you're* beginning to doubt me."

"Well, it's just . . ."

"Look, I'm just as American as everyone else and want to pay the least amount of taxes for the most amount of government. It's something my accountant cooked up." He hands me the key. "You know where it is?"

"Sure. Kids party up there all the time."

His eyebrows spring up. "Really? And how would you know?"

"I get around," I say, sounding just like my mother.

"This key unlocks Hanger 4. It's the big one with three sections. I stored crates of books way in back of the second section. Better take a flashlight. I haven't paid the light bill since, well, December. Oh, and here's a five for gas and get Rex an ice cream. He could use some fattening up."

• • •

"Come on, Rex, we're on a mission."

"I'm getting tired of your missions. First your mission to paint those ugly lions' eyeballs, then your mission to save Tommy Kaye from the world."

"Get your nose out of those books," I say, before he can turn this into a lecture about growing up. "It's Saturday.

Come on. Mr. Kaye gave us money for gas and there's still some coupons in Mom's book."

"Nah. You go. I'm in the middle of something."

"Homework on a Saturday afternoon?" I say. "Heck, Rex, you could fail every class from here to Doomsday and still graduate at the top of your class. Come on. Mr. Kaye gave me extra money for ice cream."

"No, I don't feel like it."

"But if Sheriff Hillary catches me driving again she'll throw me in the girls' clink. And crates of books are heavy and . . ." I don't play the scaredy little sister act too often. But it always works when I do.

He slams his book shut and tosses his pencil down. "All right. Just up there and back. No ice cream. No nothing."

• • •

"I didn't even know there were any airplanes around here," I say, looking down at the hangar key. "You hardly ever see or hear them anymore."

"Don't worry. Now you'll see plenty of planes. Are you forgetting the Japanese are going to invade us?" he says, giving me a shove.

"Yeah! Tommy Kaye Invasion Air Force!" I joke back, returning his shove.

He yells, folds into the door, and almost drives us off the road. He pulls the car back straight and stops.

"When you going to see a doctor?"

"Doctors cost money."

"So do funerals."

"Shut up."

"I mean it! We got money. Mr. Kaye still has cash."

Rex's gotten his breath back and keeps his eyes on the road ahead. He just nods and says, "Okay. I'll talk to the nurse at school. She comes in on Tuesdays from Tillamook."

"Okay."

"Look, Jewels," he begins in a voice I don't hear too often from him, "it's just that I've been working so hard on these college entrance tests. If they want to operate or whatever on me, well, it's going to mess everything up." He looks at me and adds, "I have to think of a way to get out of this lousy town."

I hate it when he says things like that, and my nose is going all prickly like I got to sneeze. I don't want him to see my eyes well up, so I look out the window and just mutter, "Fine. You just go ahead and get out of this lousy town. But what about the Feed and Seed? What about me and Mom?"

"Come on, Jewels. Before long, you'll be doing all you can to get out of Sea Park, too. Wouldn't hurt you to start thinking about what you want to be. College and life and all that."

"Mom says the best way to take life is one day at a time," I said. "Just float along."

"I think you misheard her. She says the best way to take life is one *drink* at a time."

"Hey, she's been pretty good lately, don't you think?"

"Jewels, Mom is a lush, and you and I both know it. Face it."

You know, I've heard plenty of people call our mother lots of things over the years. But hearing it from my own brother, well it hurts. We've pulled up to the landing strip and he stops the car and looks over at me. "Jewels, Mom's mom. I don't know what makes her that way. I just know that if I stay in Sea Park, I'm going to end up the same. And you will, too. I don't care how I get out. I'm just getting out by fall."

"You going to enlist?" I ask, joking, because I know all about him being against the war.

But when he says "maybe," I look him right straight on, surprise and worry on my face. "No, don't," I whisper to him. "Don't go to war."

"Hey. We have plenty of time to worry about that. Come on. Let's get those books and get out of here. I'm feeling like a chocolate cone after all."

CHAPTER 33

"Jeez, they've really let this place go," Rex says, pointing to the runway, which is pretty much just sand-covered tarmac and weeds growing up between the cracks in the old pavement. Mounds of blackberry bushes have taken over just about everything on the hillside, including some old shacks.

The big hangar is made out of that wavy kind of metal with rust bleeding along every seam. "Wow. I hope little Janie Johnson doesn't see this place. She says she's going to win the Lions scrap drive, and it would be just like her to sneak up here and take this place apart piece by piece," I say.

A misty rain begins to fall and Rex zips his jacket up, saying, "Come on. Let's just get this done and get out."

The lock on the door doesn't work until we jiggle the key back and forth. "No one's been here for a while," Rex says.

We enter and we're struck smack dab with the smell of mold and mildew and maybe even something dead. "See if the lights even work."

I hand him the flashlight from my coat pocket. "They don't."

There're rows of windows way up high, so once our eyes adjust, we can see enough not to crash into anything.

"He said the crates are stacked in the back of that middle section," I said, pointing with my flashlight.

The three hangar sections are separated with high chain link fencing and gates. The first hangar has pieces of old cars and boxes and a lot of old tools stacked all around and inside them. Chains, ropes, and crab pots hang from the high rafters and with the shadows and smells, well, I'm just as glad I talked Rex into coming.

"Does all this stuff belong to Mr. Kaye?" he asks.

"I guess." I duck through some cobwebs and follow Rex through the second door. This one is heavy metal and it takes both of us to push it aside.

"All right, let's start digging our way to the back," Rex says, setting the flashlight on a ledge to light the way. But I grab it and continue through the third door, which is wood and easy to creak aside. "Jewels, leave that alone!"

Unlike the other two sections, this one is cleaner and clear of stuff. Except this one has a big huge something under a tarp held down on four corners with ropes and stakes. It's big as a whale.

"What do you suppose that is?" I get on my hands and knees and peer up under the tarp like a kid sneaking into a circus tent. I come back out. "It's an airplane."

"Gee, and here in an airplane hangar, no less. Who'da thunk?" Rex says. "Come on, Jewels. Can we just . . . leave that alone!"

I unhook one of the ropes from the stake and lift back the tarp. "I've never seen an airplane up close. Relax, let's just look. You used to be nutty about airplanes, remember?"

"That was before I saw what they did to Pearl Harbor," he mutters.

We flip back the tarp so we can see half the airplane. It has a big propeller on each wing. "There. See? It's an airplane. Twin Beech. Mint condition. Satisfied? Come on!" Rex says. "I'm hungry."

I use the foot step and the handle to pull myself up. I peer into the cockpit. "Hey, this is cool! I'm going inside." I pull open the door and climb into what looks like maybe a cargo area because there aren't any seats like you see on airplanes in the movies. I use the flashlight to zero in on the cockpit.

Rex pokes his head inside. "You shouldn't be in there. Come on out!"

Heck with that, I think. This is my first and maybe last chance to be in a cockpit. I sit down in one of the seats and make like a pilot, playing with handles and pedals. "Get me! The Amazing Interplanetary Adventures of Jewels Gordon!" I call back to Rex and show him my big goofy grin.

"Get out of there!"

"What, you afraid I'm going to start this thing and fly off?"

"Come on!"

"Hey, you said you wanted to get out of town! Come on! I'll fly you!"

"You're going to break something!"

Rex climbs inside and sits down in the other cockpit seat, and I love seeing the little-boy grin on his face as he looks at the dials and controls.

"Wouldn't you love to be able to fly?" I say, pumping the paddles on the floor. "I sure would!" I look over at him. He's holding an old photo. "What's that?"

"I'm not sure. It was tucked into this panel here," he says. "Shine the light on it."

"And you think *I'm* a snoop. Hey, doesn't that look like Mr. Kaye?" I point to the man standing in the shade of the wings.

Rex takes a closer look. "Hmm. Maybe. Hard to tell for sure."

"My eyes are better. Let me see," I say, snatching the photo. "Look at that old-timey airplane."

"It's called a biplane. Bi, as in two wings."

"I know that."

He snaps his fingers to get the photo back and he looks closer at it. "I think that's a Curtiss JN-4. They called them Jennys. Surplus from the Great War."

"Everyone keeps talking about the Great War. What was so great about it?"

"I don't know. Maybe inventions like this biplane made it great," he says, tucking the photo back into the side pocket he'd found it in. "Come on. Let's get those books."

I start to get up and Rex pulls me by the arm. "Now, don't you go asking Mr. Kaye about this."

"Why not?"

"Look, he's kept this plane up here hidden away for a reason."

"What?"

"I don't know the reason! But it's none of our business, and besides, it only shows that you've been where you aren't supposed to be, doing what you aren't supposed to be doing."

He climbs out of the cockpit and while his back is turned, I take the old photo and tuck it into my shirt. I climb out of the plane and we put the tarp back just like we found it.

From there, we find and load four wooden crates of books. The only thing that has me worried is the writing on the sides of the crates is in those funny Japanese characters. We crack open one crate and sure enough, it's filled with books. Japanese books. I pull a heavy one out. I point to what I think is the title of the book and mutter, "I sure hope this doesn't say *How To Invade Oregon In Five Easy Steps*."

Rex takes the book and looks at me. I wonder if he's thinking what I've been trying not to be thinking about all day now. He gets this odd smile on his face looking at the front of the book. "Huh," he says. "More likely *A Farewell To Arms* or *The Sun Also Rises*." He shows me a signature. "Hemingway."

I hate to admit it, but I'm still trying to put two and two together and coming up with five. The bulldozer, the bunkers, the landing strip, this airplane. And now these crates of books in Japanese, one of them signed by Ernest Hemingway who even I know of.

Who the heck really is our Tommy Kaye?

CHAPTER 34

"Oh great," Rex growls, spotting Eldon and Bully as we come out of Salty's Sweets. They're leaning against our car, probably waiting for us. The back door next to the curb is ajar. This isn't good.

They must have given up on the old band uniforms, because now they're just wearing navy blue shirts, red belts, and tan pants. They got themselves badges for their yellow bandanas that read SPORTS. They make me sick.

"What'd you think those jerks want?" I mumble through my Neapolitan cone.

"You kiddies enjoying your widdle tweats?" Eldon says, coming toward us on the sidewalk. "You're out of uniform, Ethel."

"I told you, I'm not interested in joining your little vigilante group," Rex says, looking over their heads to the gray of the ocean.

"Just you and that little cripple Dickie Knowlton are the only two jellyfish who haven't taken the oath," Bully says. "And since Dickie's planted in a wheelchair, well, he gets a pass. But you? What's your excuse?"

"Buzz off, jerk," Rex says.

"Oh yeah?" Eldon says, smacking Rex's hand, knocking the scoop of chocolate right off the cone. "Oops," he says. "Now don't cry, Rexy. Mommy'll buy you a new ice kweeem cone!"

Both the jerks laugh. And I'm standing here, frozen to the ground, thinking *oh no, not again!* In a way, I want Rex to fly into a rage. In a way, I want to be as big as Agent Boothby and take them apart myself. In a way, I want to just evaporate into the atmosphere and come back down as rain somewhere a million miles from Sea Park.

Rex just looks at his empty cone, then back at me. "Here, hold this."

"Ree-xxxx," I whisper, now holding a cone in each hand.

And then Rex hauls off and belts Eldon so hard in the cheek that he reels back against our car, slamming the door shut. I hear a snap and I sure hope it's Eldon's face bone and not Rex's hand. Rex picks up the ball of ice cream as Bully jerks him around and *smash!* The ice cream goes right into Bully's face! He falls over backward under Rex's shove.

Well, as much as I love ice cream, I take my scoop of Neapolitan and smash it into Eldon's face while he's down, stunned and red and hurting, and now there's two surprised SPORTS sporting ice cream beards on the ground!

Rex says, "Come on, Jewels. Get in the car. You drive."

We climb in and pull away. I look at them in the rearview mirror. "I can't believe you clobbered Eldon!"

"I can't believe you sacrificed your ice cream," he says.

"For real, Rex. You clobbered him!" I repeat, prouder than ever.

"I lost control. I just saw red," he says. "Enough is enough."

His tone makes me glance at him. He's not looking he-mannish or cocky or full of himself. He's leaning into the door and looking outside the window.

"Hey, he needed hitting, Rex! And the ice cream to the face was the cherry on top!" I say, grinning ear to ear. "Wait till that gets around town!"

But Rex isn't sharing my excitement. He's holding his side again. "What's wrong?"

"I don't know. Something let go when Eldon grabbed me. Must have pulled a muscle." He reads my face and says, "I told you. The nurse comes on Tuesday." I glare at him and he adds, "I promise! Keep your stupid eyes on the road before you get us both killed."

I give him a glance and he says after twisting around in his seat, "There. Better all ready. Besides. It was worth it." There's his small grin.

"Well, I hope you broke Eldon's face when you hit him," I say, pulling into our parking lot. "And I hope you gave him a good ugly scar! I hope every time I see that jerk . . ."

"Look, Eldon's already enlisted," Rex says, cutting me off. "He reports the day after we graduate. Along with the other eleven boys old enough including that Neanderthal Leroy Parker who can barely sign his name on the dotted line. So you won't have to look at Eldon's ugly face for a long, long time. If ever again."

Rex gets out of the car, slams the door, and walks away. I take off after him and catch him heading toward our old cabins. "Wait up! What's with you?" He keeps going like he hasn't heard me. I pull him around. "We don't live here anymore, remember?"

He opens the door to his old cabin and hollers, "Look, I helped you get those books! I got you your ice cream cone and I clobbered Eldon Johnson! What else do you want from me?" Then he slams the door in my face.

What the heck just happened? Fine. I'll leave him alone. Anyway, I got to smuggle those books down to Mr. Kaye before the Ladies of St. Bart's start arriving for their Saturday Supper Social. Still, I can't get it out of my mind. How strange things have become. How this war's making all of us, now even Rex, into people we aren't, and I hate it.

Everything, everyone is changing. Even me.

CHAPTER 35

The rain's really coming down now and I hotfoot from Father Donlevy's toward home, but stop short when I see Sheriff Hillary's squad car in the Stay and Play parking lot.

I peek into the café and see the sheriff sitting in a booth with Mom acrost from her. I catch Mom's eyes and she glares at me. She gets up, refills Sheriff Hillary's coffee cup, and over her head she mouths the words, "Go away." I know to turntail.

I hide in the covered stairwell that leads up to the Look-Sea Lounge. When I finally peek around and see the sheriff's squad car leave, I slip back into the café.

Mom's cleaning the booth. She tosses down the rag—*whap!*—when she sees me. "Sit down," she orders. I do, noticing the booth seat is still warm from Sheriff Hillary.

Mom looks down at me with her arms folded over her greasy apron. "I need to ask you some questions."

"Mom, don't be mad. Rex just had enough and hauled off and let that Eldon Johnson have it smack in the kisser!"

"What are *you* talkin' about?"

"Ah, what are you talking about?"

"You mean to tell me our Rex *hit* Eldon Johnson?"

"A . . . well . . ." I can hem and haw alls I want, but Mom sees right through it.

"He was in a fight? Has the whole world gone mad?"

"Well, actually, yes, it has," I say. "Well, you know, Mom, he's Town Hood. He has to take matters into his own hands once and a while."

"Town Hood is supposed to keep the peace, not—" She stops short and shakes her head. "I'll deal with him later. What I want to know is what you kids were doin' with my car this afternoon."

"Uh, ice cream cone. We went to Salty's Sweets. We heard what with sugar rationing and cream being scarce and all that ice cream won't be coming in much longer and—"

"You drive a car two blocks for ice cream?"

"My bike tire is flat," I say, which is not a lie because it's always flat.

"Well, do you know what Sheriff Hillary just told me?"

"No."

"She said Eldon Johnson said the back seat of *my* car was loaded with crates. And what were in the crates?"

“Uh, books. Text books,” I manage.

The bell on the door dings, and I think I’m home free. But it’s only Rex. “Hold it right there,” Mom says.

Rex stops in his tracks. She holds her hand up to silence me, then asks, “Rex, what was in the back seat of my car today?”

“Crates,” he replies sort of slow and looking at me.

“And what was in those crates?”

“Scrap metal. For the Lions’ drive.” Dang, why didn’t I think of that?

She looks back at me. “Rex, sit down.”

He scoots in the booth next to me.

“Now, accordin’ to your sister, those crates were filled with books.”

“Sure,” Rex says, easy as pie. “And some newspapers. For the scrap drive.”

I just nod and add, “Yeah. Books and newspapers and scrap. Think there’s some old pots you can give us?” I ask, pointing to the kitchen ceiling where the utensils hang.

She says, “Accordin’ to Sheriff Hillary, the crates were filled with books. *Japanese books*,” she goes on. Looks like we’re still on the firing squad wall.

Rex and me know better than to look at each other, sitting side by side in the booth. One look can tell all.

She plops a book down on the table, “Now, just where the heck did you kids get boxes of Japanese books?”

“Uh, at the Feed and Seed,” I say. “They were in this closet in back and—”

"Jewels, give it up," Rex interrupts. "Just tell her. Sooner or later . . ."

"Sooner or later *what?*" Mom asks.

"Rex! No! Don't!"

"Tell her," Rex says, staring at me. "Just get it over with!"

"Well, somebody better tell me something and *now!*" Mom hollers.

"We were getting books for Tommy Kaye," Rex replies, so casual it's like we do that every Saturday. "The books were stored in this old airplane hangar."

"*Your* airplane hangar," I add.

"What the devil are you talkin' about?" she says, her eyes narrowing and her voice lowering.

"Mr. Kaye said it was *your* airplane hangar. A tax dodge," I say.

Then I spill out the whole story. I start with *The Hunchback of Notre Dame* and end with four crates of Japanese books and one signature from Ernest Hemingway smuggled down to Mr. Kaye just a half hour ago. I'm trying to keep my voice calm but just looking over at Rex makes me want to cry on account of he's the one who's done the big suffering.

Her face goes the blankest I have ever seen it go as she slowly drops into the booth seat acrost from us. Guess my own face would go like that, too, if I'd just learned my two kids were breaking only-J.-Edgar-Hoover-knows how many laws and right under the whole town's noses—her's, Sheriff Hillary's, God's, and everyone's.

I can usually figure Mom out just by her expressions. I know she's tired, I know she's confused, and I know she's mad. But she gets up from the booth, goes behind the lunch counter, and I think she's probably reaching for a drink, but instead pulls out her cigarettes, lights one, and sits on a stool while she smokes and looks like she's thinking all this over. The silence is killing us, but Rex and me have no idea what to do. Every time we look like we're going to say something, she raises her hand to silence us.

At the end of the cigarette, she finally says, "I'll be upstairs, soaking in a hot tub. You kids lock up. There's leftovers in the fridge. Some scraps for that dog of yours."

"Mom, are you mad?" Rex asks.

"At you two nitwits? No. At Tommy Kaye? Oh, yes!"

"Why?" I ask.

"I can't believe he put you, me, all of this, at risk with this *insanity!*" she says.

"Well, it was *my* idea, Mom. Not Mr. Kaye's," I fess up.

"And what if that Agent Boothby comes back snoopin' around?" she asks. She runs her hand though her hair. That's never a good sign.

"Why would he?" I ask. "I mean, as far as the world knows, Mr. Kaye has vamoosed to Canada."

"Jewels, you can't keep a man hidden for the whole war," Mom says, clipping her words. "What I can't believe is how *you* went along with this"—she's looking for the right word—"*balloonitic* idea, Rex."

Losing her Southern accent is not a good sign, either.

"Would you quit giving everyone else credit for *my* balloonitic idea?" I shout.

I don't mean it to be funny, but first Rex cracks up, then Mom, then finally me. Yeah, that was a pretty balloonitic thing to say. I admit it.

"What about Sheriff Hillary?" Rex asks. "What are we going to tell her about the books?" We all look at each other.

Mom goes to the window and looks outside. The sky is starting to turn pink. Then, she turns to us and asks, "How long have you pulled this off?"

"Since January. You know, since he *left* for Canada," I say.

"Hmmm." Her pointing finger taps to her lips, a sure sign she's thinking.

"Mom," Rex says. "Sheriff Hillary? Those books?"

"Well, I'll just tell her what you told me. I almost bought it. You found some of Mr. Kaye's books at the Feed and Seed and were going to donate them to the paper drive. Certainly won't be the first lie I've ever told that woman." She starts toward the back stairs. "Anyway, Sheriff Hillary is the least of our problems."

"So, you're not going to tell?" I ask.

She turns. I can't tell, but is that hurt in her face? "Do you really think I'd rat on my own children?" She looks at us and adds, "Besides, how would I run Kaye Enterprises with you two in the reform school?" She gives us a very weary smile and starts down the hallway.

"Mom, what are you going to do?" I call out.

"I told you, take a hot bath," she says, taking off her greasy apron. "Then, I'm going to fix myself up, pull myself together, straighten my seams, fix a pitcher of martinis, and go down into your 'sanctuary' and see how in heaven's name I am going to get us out of this mess."

She closes the hall door behind her.

I get up, turn, and look at Rex, who's fiddling with the little peg board kid's game on the table. "Why did you tell her all that?"

"Jewels, get off it. How much longer did you think we could keep this up?"

"But . . ."

"And something else! Can't you see? Mom and Mr. Kaye—how they've changed? Both of them."

"It's war! Of course, they've changed!"

"No, you dimwit! Can't you see? I thought girls were supposed to just feel these things! Mom and Mr. Kaye. It's like they *need* each other!"

I run my own hand through my hair. No, I do not see that at all. "I don't know about you, but I feel like my whole brain is coming apart."

"Good. Maybe that will be an improvement!" Rex starts to storm out, then turns. "I'm sorry. Look, there're only two choices. Either Mr. Kaye comes out and surrenders, or we keep doing what we've been doing and just hope to high heaven that no one else finds out."

"Yeah, but the finger gets pointed at *us* if he surrenders."

"I know it!" Rex yelps. "I warned you from the beginning. They aren't going to think of us as just a couple of goofy kids who didn't know any better. This isn't as though we're just hiding that old bloodhound from the dog catcher!"

"Yeah, and thanks to *you*, Boy Genius, now Mom's involved! What if she gets drunk and spills the beans to, oh gee, I don't know, *everyone*!"

"I don't think you're giving Mom enough credit. She . . ."

"And what if those McAloons find out?" I holler, then mimic a McAloon and add, "Say, Frank, looky here. I just killed me my first Jap!"

At that, Rex turns on me and points his finger. "Go ahead! Make a joke out of it like you always do! But I'm telling you this, I am not going to jail for harboring the enemy! If I have to go to Canada myself, I will."

"Well, I don't want to go to jail, either," I say, tears springing to my eyes. "Or you or Mom or Mr. Kaye or Father Donlevy."

"Stop blubbering. I'm going back to my cabin. Let me know when Mom's 'seams are straight.' We'll all go down to talk with Mr. Kaye. And Father Donlevy better be there, too."

• • •

Most interesting to me is the look on Mr. Kaye's face when Mom descends those steps ahead of us into the basement.

She stops suddenly. It's like he can sense her or maybe smell her or knows the sound of her heels. His head comes up, they lock eyes, and for the first time ever, I think I know, I mean really understand, what Rex was talking about. They're in love with each other.

Mom walks down the steps, all fixed up in her Saturday best, then sashays over to Mr. Kaye and slaps him a good one acrost the chops. His hand goes to his face. Then, she turns to Father Donlevy who takes a step back like maybe he's going to be hit next. She says, "Forgive me, Father, for displayin' violence in the house of God."

He give her an air-cross and mutters, "You're forgiven."

"What'd you do that for?" Mr. Kaye asks, rubbing his cheek.

"For making' me think you were nothin' but a two-bit coward! How can you put my children at risk by goin' along with this . . . fiasco?"

"I don't know, Alice. It sort of just happened," he says.

"You look horrible," she says, handing him the pitcher of martinis she's made.

"So would you if you'd been living in a cave for . . ." he walks to the wall calendar from the Feed and Seed and looks at the days Xed out, "for fifty-seven days. Although I can't really call them days because I haven't seen the sun for fifty-seven of them! At least Dracula gets to fly around at night."

"I think this is a case of 'you've dug your own grave, now lie in it'!" she says.

"But he didn't dig it," I say. "I did. This was all *my* idea."

"Everyone, please," Father Donlevy says. "It hardly matters how he got here. The question is how to get him out without ruining us all."

"Out to what?" I holler. "To jail? Back to Japan? How come he can't just stay here until . . . ?"

Their expressions pretty much answer my own question. "Until what, Jewels?" Mr. Kaye says. "Until peace is declared?"

"Well, should we get Agent Boothby down here and tell him everything? He seems like a square shooter. In fact, maybe he can do something to help. Like call the adoption people or the citizens' office or Eleanor Roose—" I stop talking. It's pretty useless, me talking like I can actually get anyone out of this grave I've dug. "Oh, never mind!" I bolt up the steps and Rex follows me.

So, the adults stay underground. I suppose they're sipping martinis and thinking what to do next. Rex and me go back to the Kozy Korner.

"You happy? They're all down there now and we're up here. How about I just lock them *all* in for the duration of the war?" I dangle the key around my neck. "Serve 'em all right."

"Well, Jewels, you can't blame them for—"

"I know! It's all *my* fault. So shoot me!"

Rex makes a pistol with his hand, aims at me and says, "Pop!"

"Do you ever just wisht you've never been born?" I ask, plopping down into a chair.

"At least once a week," Rex says, sitting down. "And it's wish*ed* not wisht."

I feel something scrunch in my pants pocket and pull out the old photo from the airplane.

"Jewels! You were supposed to put that back!" Rex says, taking the photo from me. "You little thief."

"So shoot me twice," I say, grabbing at it.

"Why'd you take that?"

"I wasn't done looking at it. I want to see what that writing is on the bottom."

I hop up and grab a pair of Mom's reading glasses next to the cash register and use them to look at the photo. Some of the ink is chipped off but I can make out "'Bar . . . storming . . . ross Was . . . gton, nineteen twenty-something.' Bar storming?"

"Barnstorming. Sort of a circus-type show, only with airplanes. You know, back in the olden days. Women walked on wings and pilots pretended to have dog fights. Like the airplane fights in the Great War."

"Tommy Kaye did that?" I ask. I take a closer look at the man in the photo. "Yeah, that's him all right. Look how young he looks."

"You should show that to Mom. She'll probably get a kick out of it."

"Rex. There is another person sitting in the back cockpit, waving." I hand him the glasses and the photograph. "I swear, it's . . . Mom."

CHAPTER 36

"Look, for once, let's just play this smart," Rex says. "Don't show this photo to anyone. So just put this someplace and forget it." Rex is using his I'm-older-and-smarter-voice, so I agree.

Now that we've moved into the apartment, Mom hardly ever goes to our old cabins. I'm thinking I'll hide the photograph there and maybe after this war is over, we can all play one big game of Twenty Questions.

Mom keeps this old wood footlocker under her bed. She says it's her hope chest, which is something ladies keep for when they're hoping they'll get married. You're supposed to put junk in it you'll need when you get married like tablecloths, candlesticks, nighties, and a divorce lawyer's phone number. She says I'll want a hope chest someday but I'm still hoping just for a chest. She tells me to wait. Chests come all in good time.

I sort of miss the talks we used to have like that—fun and sister-like. Even when she was the good-time girl, ol' Malice Alice, she was kinda fun. It's like this war has even changed her. Anyway, I slip the old crusty photograph through the slit between the lid and the rest of the box and shove it back under her bed. Rex is right. It's none of my business.

• • •

So, what do the big, smart adults come up with as a plan for Mr. Kaye? Absolutely nothing. We are keeping things what Rex calls *status quo*. No one has a solution. Kaye Enterprises is hanging on by an eyelash, but it is hanging on. Mom and Mr. Kaye keep company and Father Donlevy keeps quiet. But at least Rex and me are getting help now. But, I'm worrying that it'll be five of us now, six counting Hero, lined up against that firing squad wall if we get caught.

• • •

The deadline for all Japanese Americans to report for relocation in Portland was April 7, which has come and gone, and which means there aren't any Japanese people left anywhere on the whole west coast. This also means that Mr. Kaye would stick out like a sore Japanese thumb if found. He jokes that he's going to get a switch of long black hair, braid it, glue it to his head, get some black pajamas, leave sanctuary, and pass himself off as a Chinaman.

All of us are changing in some way or another, though. Or at least that's what it seems like to me. My grades have gone from Cs to Ds, and Rex had become more of a hermit, always studying and filling out college tests and stuff like that. Sometimes I think he's older'n Mr. Kaye. He prefers his old, cold, and moldy cabin to our warm, spacious apartment. And yes, he did see that visiting school nurse who told him broken ribs just take time to heal and wasn't he lucky that scar on his forehead healed so good and next time lead with your right.

Mom is now a sober chain smoker, Mr. Kaye is about as pale as sand and drinks more than he ever did before, and Father Donlevy has developed this annoying facial tick. I think Hero is the only accessory to our crime who is his same old self, as long as I don't forget to feed him.

I tell you, some days I wisht that Agent Boothby *would* drift back into town and do some real detective work. I would just let Hero's nose point the way to the church basement. No one could arrest a dog! But I guess the FBI and police are too busy finding and locking up other people with the *Japanese stain*, as some editorial writer calls them.

Not only that, we were getting our butts kicked in the Pacific War until finally, a few days ago, we learned that some flying ace named Doolittle led a bombing raid on

Japan. Man, we sure needed to hear that and so did the Japs, according to the news reports. It was sort of a big, patriotic "take that!" I guess the enemy didn't think we could hit 'em where they live and fly away to tell about it, which the Doolittle raiders did. Anyway, lots of folks are celebrating. Mr. Kaye just wanted to know what towns had been hit and he looked pretty relieved Nagasaki wasn't one of them. After all, that's where his sister keeps her orphanage.

This war is forcing me to think about a lot of things I don't want to think about. I keep thinking about poor ex-sheriff Norm Dutton, just a sailor on deck one minute then *whammo!*, smithereens the next. Some Japanese pilot wins, Norm Dutton loses. Then a pilot named Doolittle wins, some Japanese welder in a shipyard loses, and some Nagasaki orphans win, so how do I keep score? It all seems so, well, flip-of-a-coinish. Heads, you live. Tails, you die.

Of all of us, Rex is the one I worry about the most. He keeps typing and mailing off his essays and applications. But it's like he's just going through the motions. We barely have money for gas, even if we do have the ration coupons, let alone college—scholarship or no. It's like he's lost his spark. There was always something so hopeful looking about Rex. Talking about how he'll go here and do this and study that. His graduation is coming up and instead of doing all the fun senior things, he just backs away. No parties, no sneaks, no nothing. He won't turn eighteen until September, but I know he's worried about where that number leaves him in terms of the war.

And I'm worried about it, too.

That's not alls I'm worried about. See, I got a big report due so I better start worrying about my grades. Mrs. Simmons keeps harping that beginning in eighth grade, grades all start going on a transcript, whatever that is. She says we need transcripts to get into college, but alls I can think is let's just worry about getting us out of this war before we worry about getting us into college. College is a hundred years and a million dollars away, but this report is still due in a week.

Our library finally reopened, getting ready for summer tourists. It isn't too big, but it's loaded with Oregon history books and since my report is on the Whitman massacre, I know I can find what I need there. Little Janie Johnson's wagon, loaded with enough scrap to build a battleship, is parked in front as I enter the library.

I see the topknot of her little knitted cap bobbing up and down the short stacks in the kids' section. "Well, Janie. Looking for a book on shipbuilding?" I ask her.

She gives me her screwy look and says, very importantly, "No. I'm looking for a book on trees for Mother's Day."

"Janie, these are library books. You can't give them as Mother's Day presents," I say.

"Well, I don't have any money so I'm going to get a book and draw my mom pictures and rules on care and stuff."

"Oh, well, that's nice. What kind of trees?"

"This itsy bitsy tree that Eldon's going to give her for Mother's Day," she says.

I stop cold. I knew it! Of course Eldon took The Old Man, along with Sailor the Turkey and lord knows what else from the Feed and Seed. But I play it cool. "I think it's called a bonsai. Say, that's good news for the See Girls. Tell me more, and I'll put it in our newsletter."

"How come I never get to see your newsletter?" she asks, her eyes narrowing.

"You know, because it's secret. Our whole club is secret."

She screws up her mouth while thinking that one over.

"Come on, tell me about your tree and maybe I can help you find a book."

"Well, it's about yay-by-yay big," she says, holding her hands a few feet apart. "And all prickly if you touch it. It's kind of ugly, but anyway, Eldon's been hiding it in our shed so's he can give it to Momma. And on account of he's going to report to war in a few weeks, he says I need to help take care of it. He calls it a prisoner of war, but I don't know why. Eldon's stupid sometimes. How can a tree be a prisoner of anything?"

Yeah, good question, Janie, I'm thinking. *Good question.*

CHAPTER 37

"Come on, Rex, we got to do this. We need an adventure, and besides, it's getting back at the Johnsons. Who doesn't want to do that? And if anyone's going to eat that poor turkey, it's going to be us!"

"Stealing a bonsai and a turkey in the pouring rain is an adventure?" he says, leaning back in his chair. "Sounds like another one of your balloonitic missions." He whirls his pencil in the air.

"It's not just *a* bonsai; it's The Old Man! You know how important he is to Mr. Kaye! Come with me. This'll be fun. We need fun!" I say.

"I think you can handle swiping a plant from a garden shed all on your own, but that turkey might keep you hopping. Just don't get caught. I'm still Town Hood for two more weeks, you know."

So, I scope it out and give it a good think. I can either skip school and do it in broad daylight, or do it at night under the cloak of darkness. Each has its own special risk and danger. During the day, Mrs. Johnson keeps her tattle-tailed little pug dog in the fenced backyard while she's at work at the post office. But in our blackout hours, it's really dark at night and a flashlight will stick out like a light house beacon. Then I might have the civil patrol, McAloons, SCOUTS, and the entire Japanese navy taking pot shots at me.

So I choose dusk. I got it all planned out. In fact, I'm already planning the reunion between Mr. Kaye and The Old Man.

But it isn't as though I can take The Old Man and the turkey and hide them under my jacket like I was shoplifting a Baby Ruth or a hamster. That bonsai is pretty dang big and probably heavy, too. The old Dodge has been running on gas fumes for at least a week, so my getaway car is out.

But we do have nine handcarts propped up against Cabin 40 so I pick the best one. I've got on my slicker with the hood and my rubber boots—the kind that everyone in town wears—in case I leave footprints at the scene of the crime. I put two wooden crates in the handcart and head out. To be on the safe side, I use the Janie Johnson routine and put a few pots in the crates. I'm just another kid out looking to win the scrap drive now.

Mrs. Johnson has already pulled closed her blackout curtains. That's a good sign. Now, about that little rat dog. I make a few short whistle-toots to see if it's close by. Nothing. I look up and down the street. No one's there.

Now, this is the Oregon coast and every gate has rusty hinges, I don't care what it's made of or how old it is or how well you oil it. So I pull at the gate slowly. Cripes, the Johnson gate just falls off and over and clanks onto the grass! I freeze and listen. Slowly, I step over it and continue along the side of the house and into the backyard. The shed's toward the back and I make my way through the huge collection of scrap Janie has stacked along the walkway. I pick my way carefully because one catch of my boot and I'm going to make a huge clatter if I fall.

There's a chicken wire pen next to the shed and I figure by the faint garbles that's where Sailor the Turkey of War is kept. Here's a hint: turkeys do *not* like flashlights flashed in their faces. I turn off the light fast. The scared bird hovers in a dark corner but I scoot him out and he makes his escape, gobbling off toward the sunset.

Gates rust and shed doors swell. It's an Oregon law. So I know to give the door a bit of a shove, but it opens so fast I almost fall inside. I give the shed a once over, trying to keep the flashlight low. I spy tools, cans, boxes, sacks, and a pitiful looking poinsettia leftover from Christmas. I move toward the back, thinking Eldon would probably keep The Old Man hidden until Mother's Day. There's another smaller room with a sign over the doorframe. I remember this place! Eldon's old clubhouse. No Gurlz Aloud.

I push aside some crates and sure enough, there's The Old Man sitting on a shelf under a high window. At least he's been getting some daylight, but he looks pretty sad.

"Don't be afraid," I whisper. "I'm breaking you out."

Yep, The Old Man is heavy, especially as I carefully pull him off the shelf. How could I live with myself if I end up being the one to kill him? I pocket my flashlight and get as good a grip on him as I can. It's going to be a shaky trek back to the sidewalk in the dark, walking around all that scrap.

I'm pretty strong for my size and I'm through the backyard and halfway down the side of the house in no time. I see some light quickly flash toward the back of the house and I think that's a screen door slamming. Dang! To be safe, I duck into the hedge and hold still. You know how you hold your breath so you can hear better? Alls I hear is the sound of the rain. I count to thirty, then finally continue to the sidewalk, hugging The Old Man like he's Clark Gable.

It's nearly dark now and I got to get home and fast. Pretty soon the Air Warden will make his first rounds, and I feel like I'm smack dab in the middle of No Man's Land, toting a prisoner of war no less.

I get The Old Man into the crate and plan on taking the side streets home. I look south toward Highway 101 and think I see some shadows moving. Then I hear something.

Barking. I turn toward the direction of the sound. Finally, sound and sight work together and I see them. It's Hero chasing the turkey pell mell and Mr. Kaye on the other end of the leash running pell meller!

Hero passes me, then catches my scent and whips around. He's just about to galumph into my arms when I pick up another noise. A higher, faster noise. Hero spins around again as the Johnson's little pug tears into him. Poor Hero stops and howls as the little dog nips his legs. I don't think dogs know their own sizes. Sure can't tell by the yelping and baying who's murdering who. Hero's all tangled in his leash and I think he's getting the worst of it.

Mr. Kaye hollers and pulls. I try to grab at the fast little dog who turns her nips on me.

There's such a ruckus, I figure all of Sea Park is going to be on us, but look there, it's none other than little Janie Johnson, screaming, "Teko Teko Teko!" She swoops in and grabs her dog. And now Hero is running off toward home. So much for loyalty.

That leaves Janie Johnson looking straight up into the face of Mr. Kaye. Her eyes triple in size, her mouth drops open. She takes that kind of deep breath that comes just before a huge holler. Then three slow steps backward.

She turns, hugging her dog for dear life, and bellows out her warning to the town, the state, the world! "Japs! Japs! Japs!"

How do you like that? All my hard work. Undone by a scaredy-cat bloodhound, an escaping turkey, an eight-year-old big mouth, and a pug with guts enough for all of us.

We watch helplessly as Janie disappears, screaming, into the dusk. A miniature Paul Revere.

Alls I can say is, "I'll bet that little brat's gonna tell."

• • •

"Mr. Kaye! Run! Please! Back to the church!"

But he just looks at me and says, "No."

"I mean it! Janie will tell everyone! How did you even get out?"

"I broke out. Took the door off the hinges. I've done it a dozen times." He turns his head to the sky and lets the rain pelt down on his face. "I miss the rain."

"Mr. Kaye, come on," I say, pulling him by the sleeve.

He shakes my hand off his arm and says, "I'm tired of this, Jewels. I'm just tired. I can't breathe in that tomb. I need sun and rain on my face. I need life around me! I need to go bowling! I need to play eighteen holes! I need to dig clams! I need—"

"Can we talk about this later?" I'm seeing all my work about to go down the sewer because Mr. Kaye needs gutter balls and clam bakes!

He takes off his cap and runs his hand through his hair. "How I've missed the rain." He starts to sway like he's hearing some far off tom-tom rhythm.

He's going batty, nutty, balloonitic, shellshocked, stir crazy! "Mr. Kaye," I plead, "look what I got you." I pull the tarp off the box and show him The Old Man. "I got him back for you. I got back The Old Man. Come on, you don't want him to see you dancing in the rain like a lunatic, do you?"

Mr. Kaye stops twirling. "The Old Man?"

"Quick. Help me push this cart back home. I don't think he likes the rain, do you?" Okay, if I got to get the help of a six-hundred-year-old tree to get Mr. Kaye back into hiding, then I'll do it. I don't care how crazy it is. I'm not the one dancing in the rain when Janie Johnson is probably spilling her guts to her mother and Eldon and everyone else.

"The Old Man?" he asks again, looking down at the bonsai. Then he snaps back to real life and adds, "No! No rain! Cover him back up!"

We each take hold of the cart and push it back lickety split to St. Bart's without tipping it over.

"You go down," I say. "I'll go get Rex to help us with The Old Man. Then we have to figure out how we're going to get ourselves out of this one."

"Keep him out of the rain," Mr. Kaye says.

I look back toward town and I bet you anything every phone behind every blackout curtain in every house is ringing with the news. I suppose there's always the chance Janie's reputation as a miniature con artist might mean no one will believe her.

"Oh please *please* let her mother call her a liar!" I chant as I come around the corner to Rex's cabin.

"Whose mother?" Rex asks, scaring the bejesus out of me.

I give him a rundown of the last half hour.

"Well, you've really done it this time," he says.

"It was only Janie Johnson. Who believes her?" I say. "Come on. I need your help with The Old Man."

He follows me to the church basement door where I've parked the bonsai out of the rain. "I can carry it if you'll get the door," I say.

"No, I'll help." We one-two-three hoist it.

"Just kick the door open! Hurry! I'm losing my grip!"

Crash!

"Rex!" I holler.

It isn't a really bad fall. Not like you see in the movies when the guy goes tumbling down twenty steps. Rex has caught himself on his second roll! But The Old Man doesn't catch himself and has fallen, splattering his six-hundred-and-some-change years on the cement floor.

But that isn't who Mr. Kaye or me go to. It's Rex. He's holding onto his side and is gasping for breath, groaning in pain.

"Can you get up, son?" Mr. Kaye asks.

"I . . . don't . . ."

We support him on each side and slowly get him downstairs and to the couch. "My chest . . . it's . . . I can't catch air. It . . . hurts." He takes some breaths and his face is all white. He swallows and some color comes back. "I thought this was over."

"What was over?" Mr. Kaye asks, looking at me.

Rex coughs and it's like he's snapped in half with pain.

"He got into a fight way back just after Pearl Harbor. He was hurting a long time. But ribs take a long time to heal, don't they? He was getting better, I thought."

Mr. Kaye has his fingers on Rex's wrist pulse and says, "Get your mother and Father Donlevy. Now!"

I run upstairs and outside, first to the church office and then to the café.

"It's Rex," I scream out. "He's hurt. Bad!"

• • •

"What's the closest thing to a doctor we have left in this town?" Mom says, kneeling down next to Rex.

"Me," Father Donlevy says, helping me remove Rex's jacket and shirt. "Easy, son."

"You?" Mom asks.

"Two years of med school and five years missionary work in Alaska," he says. "Rex, tell me when I've hurt you." He gently begins to feel down Rex's ribs.

"You've hurt me!" Rex hollers.

I step back and feel tears sting my eyes.

"It hurts to breathe, doesn't it?" Father Donlevy asks. "Right here?"

"Yes," Rex whispers, his arm over his eyes like he doesn't want anyone to see him crying.

"My lord in heaven, look how thin you are!" Mom says. Then to Father Donlevy, "I know he's had more than his share of colds this year, but . . ."

"Mom, it's okay. Jewels 'n me, we've didn't want to worry you."

"It's my job to worry!" she says.

I speak up, "He got kicked in the side really hard. But that was months ago and . . ."

"My guess is he's re-broken some ribs," Father Donlevy says. "I'll get some pain pills from my first-aid kit. That'll get him through the night. Then, tomorrow, first light, we'll get him up to Coastal General."

"Rex, honey, can you walk? Father, help me get him back home, will you?" Mom says.

"No, he better stay right where he is, Alice," Father Donlevy says. "Broken ribs can be tricky. Let's not move him more than we have to."

Mom looks to me. "Jewels, you go find that old sleeping bag. Look in the rafters in our cabin. I'm sleeping right here on the floor next to him."

"Now, Alice," Mr. Kaye says, "if anyone sleeps on the floor, it's me. You take my bed. We'll both take shifts with him tonight."

It isn't until we get Rex sedated and the beds made up that Mr. Kaye's eyes land on the corpse of The Old Man. He walks over, kneels down, and picks up a lifeless limb. He looks up at me and says, "Everything, everything is my fault."

Which all of us know isn't true. Everything is *my* fault.

• • •

Father Donlevy rushes in at first light and says from the landing, "Things are a panic out there. The whole area has been put on alert!"

"Alert to what?" Mr. Kaye asks.

"You."

"Me?"

"According to Janie Johnson, the Japs have landed," he says, bringing his first-aid bag downstairs. "How's our patient?"

"He's still asleep," Mom says. "He coughed some during the night, but he's been sleeping pretty soundly."

Father Donlevy kneels next to Rex, listening to his chest through the stethoscope. He sort of nudges Rex a little. "Son, wake up."

"What's the matter?" Mom jumps in. "Won't he wake? Rex!"

"Those pills shouldn't have put him so deep. Rex?"

Slowly, Rex's eyes flutter open. Father Donlevy feels his forehead.

"Mom?" Rex says, looking around. His lips are bluish and he looks confused. My heart is pounding.

"I'm here, Rex," Mom says. "How do you feel?"

"Not so good," he says. He coughs again and this time some blood comes up with it. He grabs his sides. "It's so hot . . ."

Father Donlevy takes Rex's blood pressure. He doesn't have to say the number. I know by his glance up at Mom and Mr. Kaye that Rex is in big trouble.

We wrap him in a blanket and Father Donlevy carries him up the steps.

Mom turns on Mr. Kaye as he tries to follow. "You're staying here."

"The hell I am."

"You heard what Father Donlevy said. The whole county's looking for Japs. Careful, Father! Jewels, get the door." She holds the blackout curtain aside while Father Donlevy carries Rex outside. Mom turns back to Mr. Kaye and snaps down at him, "And in case you haven't noticed, you're a Jap!"

CHAPTER 38

Sheriff Hillary stops us before we get out of the parking lot. Father Donlevy is driving the church station wagon. I'm in the passenger seat, and Mom and Rex are in the back.

"So, just the people I've been wanting to see," the sheriff begins.

"Get out of the way, Hillary. Rex is sick. We need to get to Coastal General," Mom says.

"Just a minute. So, where have you Stokes been? I've looked everywhere for you."

"I mean it, Hillary. Rex is really sick! Father, keep driving," Mom says, leaning forward.

"I need to talk to Jewels. Why don't you leave her with me while you and the father go on to C. G.?" She opens the side door.

"Mom? I want to stay with you."

"Jewels," Sheriff Hillary says, "I'll take you up to C. G. after I've asked a few questions."

"Mom?"

"Jewels, honey, go ahead. We've got to get Rex to a doctor quick."

"She'll be fine with me," Sheriff Hillary says. "Just have to clear a little mix-up so we can get this so-called Jap invasion foofaraw settled."

And then they are gone—Father Donlevy, Mom, and Rex. And here's me, sitting in the front seat of Sheriff Hillary's squad car.

"Well? Any explanation?"

I play it dumb. "For what? Alls I know is my brother's sick."

"I mean about Janie Johnson. She said she saw you last night with a Japanese man."

"Janie Johnson? You mean all this foofaraw is over something that little brat said?"

"Yes."

"Well, Janie Johnson is a liar. Everybody knows that! Yes, I was out last night. Me and Rex were walking Hero when Janie's little rat-dog attacked us. If there was any Jap invasion last night, it was by Janie's Jap-dog."

"She said she saw a Japanese *man*. And you. Not Rex."

"Well, it was Rex. And I wisht it wasn't, because he fell trying to get the dog fight broke up and that's why he's on his way to C. G. right now. Now, will you please take me up there like you promised my mom and Father Donlevy?"

She looks at me hard. "You know, they still haven't caught that Tommy Kaye."

I return her hard look. "Well, maybe they have bigger fish to fry and that's why they haven't caught him."

"I always thought it was very interesting that he runs off and you Stokes step in pretty as you please with Kaye Enterprises."

"If it wasn't for Kaye Enterprises, there wouldn't be much of a Sea Park. Guess we wouldn't even need us a sheriff," I say.

She narrows her eyes and glares at me. "Remember who you're talking to, missy. I hope you know your little dog fight last night is at no small expense to this community. I had to call the National Guard. Things like this are not taken lightly, not in these times." She points north toward the Columbia River. "You may think this is a game, but this is war! Every Japanese sighting is taken very seriously!"

"Tell that to Janie Johnson, then. She's the one who said she saw something. Now, can you just get me out of here?"

"All right. Just one more thing."

"What?"

"Where were you, Rex, and your mother last night? I knocked on the café, I called your apartment, I went to Edna's, and I checked all the cabins. Just where do you people vanish to?"

This one I'm ready for. "Church." It's not a lie.

"Church? Didn't know you folks took church so serious."

"My brother was hurt! Guess you didn't know Father Donlevy knows a lot about medicine. Since Doc Ellis enlisted, just who else is there to help someone?" I look out the window and know I've talked myself out of the woods. She sighs, puts on her cap, and drives me the five miles to Coastal General.

"Look, Jewels," she says, as I get out, "I'm sure Rex is going to be okay. Besides, his term as Town Hood isn't up yet. You just tell him that for me, okay?" And, for the first time since before Pearl Harbor, she winks and smiles at me.

But I can't tell him even if I wanted to.

Mom tells me Rex has gone into a coma.

• • •

"What am I going to do?" she asks over and over. "Oh, Jewels. It's bad."

And we—Father Donlevy, Mom, and me—can only sit and wait.

The doctor finally comes out.

"Doctor?" Mom asks.

"It's what I thought, Mrs. Stokes. Two broken ribs. One has punctured a lung."

Mom gasps. "What do we do?"

"Well, surgery and soon as possible."

"Do I have to sign something? I can't remember, is he allergic to anything?"

"Mrs. Stokes, I can't perform this operation. Our surgery isn't nearly as sophisticated as this calls for. We just can't break open a chest here."

Did I hear that right? Break open a chest? *Break open my brother's chest?*

"Well, then where? Astoria? Tillamook? Where do I take him?" Mom asks.

"I doubt they can, either. He's needs a thoracic surgeon."

"Well, then where can I find one of those?" Mom demands.

"Portland or Seattle."

That puts Mom into the nearest chair. She begins sobbing into her hands.

I go to her side and Father Donlevy asks the doctor, "What's our time frame on this? I mean, getting him to Portland will take at least half a day—Seattle probably a whole day. That's if we can do it during daylight hours."

I see the doctor take Father Donlevy aside, but I can't hear what he's saying. But I can tell by the ever-so-slight shake of the doctor's head that this is really bad.

I need air. I go outside and look north toward Seattle, east toward Portland, and south toward Sea Park. The keys to St. Bart's station wagon are still in the ignition. And it hits me. *They* may not know what to do, but I do! I climb in the car, flip the wagon around, and drive to Sea Park, going sixty and not giving a hoot who doesn't like it.

CHAPTER 39

"And don't tell me you can't because I know you can!" I holler down at Mr. Kaye.

"Jewels, what are you talking about? How's Rex? What is going on out there?"

"Fly!"

"What?"

"We got to get Rex to the hospital in Portland fast! He's got a punctured lung! And you're going to fly him. I saw your plane. Don't tell me you can't!"

"But . . ."

"You look me in the eye and tell me you can't fly, Tommy Kaye!" I scream down at him from the landing.

He looks up at me. "I can't fly."

"I found that old photo of you and Mom in the plane!"

"Jewels, a lot has happened since then."

"I don't care! I got a dying brother, and you got an airplane! I don't care if I got to fly it myself—we're getting Rex to Portland!"

"Just let me think." Mr. Kaye looks around his room and then rushes to the strongbox. He pulls out some keys and some papers. He mutters, "Cash. We'll need cash."

From there, he goes through some of the Japanese books I'd gotten him and he fans out hundred-dollar bills that are pressed between the pages. He sees my face as the bills go drifting onto the Oriental carpet.

"I haven't trusted banks since 1932," is all he says. He grabs the bills up and says, "Get me my slicker! The green one."

He puts on his slicker and holds up a pair of sunglasses. "I've been keeping these in case I ever get out in the sun again."

I check to see if any of the beach or civilian patrols are still looking for Janie's Jap invader. Then I give him the high sign and Mr. Kaye scrambles from the stairwell to the station wagon.

I head for the airplane hangar out on Beach Berry Road, only slowing down for the stop signs.

"When did you learn how to drive?" Mr. Kaye asks.

"I don't know. When I got tired of hauling Mom home in a handcart from Edna's. Rex taught me." Silence. "When did you learn how to fly?"

He takes off his sunglasses and rubs his eyes. "My eyes aren't use to the sun."

"When did you learn how to fly?" I ask again.

"I told you, that picture you found was taken a long, long time ago."

"I know. Since back in the twenties. Barnstorming."

"You should be hearing this from your mother, not me."

"Hear what?"

He sighs. "Your mother and I have known each other a long time. Before Rex was born. We were in business together."

"What kind of business? The airplane business?"

"Stop!" He is looking dead ahead at the landing strip.

I slam on the breaks and see what Mr. Kaye is staring at. It's the McAloon twins on horseback, patrolling the landing strip.

"Get down," I say, slowly driving close to the hangar's side door. "I'll get rid of them."

I get out and run toward the McAloons, waving my arms and hollering. "Help! Help!"

They come galloping over and pull up in front of me. "What's the matter, girl?"

"Back in town! Something's up! Something big!"

"But we're guarding the landing strip," one of them says.

The other says, "What's happening in town?"

"I don't know. They just told me to get you boys back to the beach."

They look at each other. "This could be it," one says.

"Let's ride!"

And they do. I feel a brief blush of guilt. Not for lying, but for those two poor, old horses, having to run like the wind back to town. I pull the car door open. "It's safe! You can . . ."

But Mr. Kaye is inside the hangar pumping gas from huge barrels into the plane. "I'll get her ready. You go get Rex!" he hollers.

"Will this thing even fly?" I holler back.

"We'll see, won't we?"

"Thought you said you can't fly."

"I can't. Legally." And there, *at last*, is the confident Mr. Kaye smile I haven't seen in months.

CHAPTER 40

"How is he?" I ask, rushing into the waiting room.

"He's conscious, thank God," Father Donlevy says. "He's getting some blood now."

Mom looks up at me and demands, "Jewels, where have you been? As though I don't have enou—"

I cut her off. "Come on. I got the car running. We're getting Rex out of here."

"What? How?" Mom asks.

"We're flying him to Portland."

"On what, fairy wings?" Mom asks, looking up with huge tears streaming down her cheeks. "There is no way we can fly Rex anywhere."

"Yes, there is."

Father Donlevy says, "We're getting him an ambulance. It has to come from Longview, though."

"Mom, come on! Everything's ready!"

"Jewels, what are you talkin' about?" Mom asks, sounding agitated.

I look at the woman at the reception desk and pull Mom down the hall. "Mr. Kaye is waiting at the hangar," I whisper. "He's getting the plane ready. And don't give me 'Jewels, honey, what plane?' because you *know* what plane!"

"But there is no plane, and even if there was, Tommy can't fly it!"

"Yes, he can! Mom, come on."

A light above Rex's room flashes red and we can hear a buzzer ring. The doctor comes dashing down the hall and into Rex's room.

Mom follows them in, but the door closes on me.

Father Donlevy puts his arm around my shoulder.

"But everything's ready. I got Mr. Kaye and everything," I say, crying into Father Donlevy's chest.

Mom comes back out of the room. "I told the doctor to get him ready. He most likely won't last the day without surgery. Jewels, I don't know what in heaven's name you and Tommy have cooked up but, we'll do it!"

The doctors fix Rex up on a stretcher and strap him in. The blood in the bottle hanging by his head is gone and they put another bottle on a rack with something else flowing into Rex's hand. They tell Father Donlevy what to do with it and hand Mom the X-rays and file, then we're off. The doctor has called ahead to Multnomah County Hospital so a surgeon will be on call.

"Where're we going?" Rex mutters up at me in the back of the wagon.

"We're *flying* you to Portland."

"Oh," he sort of nods, then gives a little smile. "Bet we get shot down."

"Don't be stupid. No one's shooting us down. Why would they do that?"

"You never read the papers, do you?" he says, eyes closed.

"Don't let him talk! He needs to save his strength," Mom says from the front seat. "You're goin' to be fine, Rex. We are gettin' you to Portland. You just rest."

Rex gives me a slight glance. "No one's supposed to be flying now. They'll shoot us down. You wait and see. Are there parachutes in this thing?"

I know he isn't in his right mind. He thinks we're already flying. "Yes, we have parachutes. Now do like Mom says and shut up," I whisper down to him, tucking the blanket around his shoulders.

"You're getting pretty bossy in your old age, Shorty," he says, drifting off again.

Mom gasps when she sees the airplane on the landing strip. "That beautiful Twin Beech. He told me he sold her years ago to pay for Rex's knee surgery," she mutters. "But look at her—like new."

Mr. Kaye and Father Donlevy carefully pull Rex's stretcher out of the back of the station wagon once we've come to a stop. Mom grabs the bottle and walks alongside, holding the line and the bottle high.

"I cleared the cargo hatch for him. Should be plenty of room," Mr. Kaye says.

We all help to lift the stretcher up and through the plane's back door. It looks a lot smaller out here on the runway than it did in the hangar. We set Rex down and I see Mom and Mr. Kaye catch each other's eyes. There's one of those ever so brief moments of something—I don't know—some adult kind of spark maybe, that seems to zap between them.

"You up to this?" she asks him.

"Are you?"

"I'm game," Mom says.

Mr. Kaye goes to check the plane's engine. And then I notice Mom climbing into one of the pilot's seats.

When Mr. Kaye climbs back onboard, she takes his hand and says, "I'm scared. It's been so long."

"Like riding a bike. You never forget. Come on. You used to be one of the best."

"You were no slouch," she says, looking over to him.

I touch Mom's shoulder. She grabs my hand, squeezes it, and says, "Don't you worry, honey. Everything's goin' to be just fine."

"I'd like to come," Father Donlevy says up to the cockpit.

"No, we don't have a full tank," Mr. Kaye says. "We need as light a load as we can get."

Mom starts one engine first, then the other. The plane makes a huge noise and I sure hope that's normal.

"I'll pray for you," Father Donlevy says, climbing out of the plane.

"You can do more than that," Mr. Kaye says, indicating the road. Sheriff Hillary's squad car has just sped up. "You can run a little interference."

"Leave it to me," he says. Then he pulls a silver necklace over his head and hands it to me. "Here, give this to Rex."

Mr. Kaye pulls the side door closed. Father Donlevy gives us the sign of the cross as he steps away, his black robe whipping in the wind of the propellers.

I wave back as the plane bumps down the runway. Mr. Kaye gets me strapped into a seat next to Rex and he joins Mom in the cockpit. I look down at the necklace in my hand. St. Christopher Protect Us it reads. I don't care who St. Christopher is or how he can protect us, but we need all the help we can get, so I tuck it under Rex's pillow.

The plane engines are roaring and I can't hear what Mom and Mr. Kaye are saying as they point to gauges and flip switches. Probably just as well. I look down at Rex, then back out the window where Father Donlevy stands, gesturing to the McAloon boys, the mayor, and Sheriff Hillary. I see him point up to us, now over the hillside and almost gone. I figure I'm in so deep, not even St. Christopher can pull me out, let alone Mom and Mr. Kaye. But I don't care. Alls I care about is getting Rex out of the fix he's in.

I catch Mr. Kaye signaling to me. "Hang on to that IV bottle," he calls back. "This might get a bit rough." Then, to Mom, he says, "Easy, Alice! Remember that sticky rudder? Easy!"

I can tell by the way the IV bottle moves that we are pointing toward the sky. I steady it with one hand and hold on to my seat belt with the other.

I admit it. I'm scared to death. If my measly, miserable twelve years of life flashes before me right now, I will not be surprised. And I didn't even get to finish pooooo-berty!

Higher, higher. Shake! My ears pop and the plane makes a lot of noise and it seems every little creak and groan echoes back here.

I finally dare to look out the window again. She's done it! Good ol' Malice Alice! Mom! Mrs. Stokes, the good-time barfly, has flown us high into the air! And she's keeping us up here! I look down at Rex, sleeping through all this excitement. "You're going to be mad as snakes you missed this!" I whisper to him.

We have leveled off and the plane now sounds like it's purring, not growling. "Can I get out of this now?" I call up to the cockpit, tugging at my seat belt.

"Okay, but just to that bulkhead," Mr. Kaye calls back. Both he and Mom have headsets on. We're heading east and there's the Columbia River right below us. I'm still petrified, but it's sort of neat. I can see the shadow of the plane kissing the tops of the trees.

I creep up to the bulkhead and tap Mom on the shoulder. "You going to tell me about all this?" I say, pointing to the controls.

"Um, I'm a bit busy right now," Mom says, keeping her eyes straight ahead.

Mr. Kaye is fiddling with a dial.

"Is that like a ham radio or something?" I ask.

"Sort of. I'm trying to listen in, hear what they're saying."

"Who? Why?"

"Because civilian planes aren't allowed in this airspace," Mr. Kaye says.

"They found us." Mom points off in the distance. "Didn't take them long."

"Who?" I ask again, thinking, *we* are *going to get shot down!*

"Let's not panic yet," Mr. Kaye says. "Just stay on course. That plane off the left wing is probably reconnaissance. They may be just the Civilian Air Patrol."

Our plane takes a huge dive and I grab for the IV bottle.

"Alice!" Mr. Kaye barks.

"Sorry," she says. "I don't know who that idiot is, but it's like he's challenging us."

She soars way up then and I got to grab onto the bulkhead. I feel my stomach somewhere around my feet.

I look into the cockpit and cripes! There's the other airplane coming right at us! "Mom! What's happening?"

"Everyone wants to be a hero!" she shouts. "Hang on!"

We take another dive and I think I got to puke. Mr. Kaye looks back at me. "Don't worry. She knows what she's doing. Come on, Alice. Put the pedal to the metal. You can outrun that old tin can."

"Well, we could play a nice game of tag if we had a full tank of gas, but . . ." She looks around. "All right. He's in our wake. He's backing away." She catches my face. "Honey, you all right?"

"I think I'm going to puke."

She looks back at me and you know, in her leather cap and all, she could pass for Amelia Earhart. She smiles and says, "Don't you dare puke in my plane. How's Rex doing?"

"I don't know. He's asleep. The IV stuff is almost gone," I say, looking at the bottle.

Mom looks at Mr. Kaye and smiles. "Just like old times, huh?"

CHAPTER 41

"Do you think Portland Columbia is best? What about Swan Island? I can't remember where Multnomah Hospital is in Portland. It's been so long," Mom says. "Pearson Field in Vancouver might be closer?"

"Can't you just use that radio to call someone?" I ask, going from Rex's side to the cockpit bulkhead. "And won't we need an ambulance once we get there?"

Mr. Kaye and Mom look at each other. "She's right, Alice. We need help once we land. We're going to have to break radio silence to get an ambulance waiting for us."

He reaches for the handset. "Don't," Mom says. "Let's think this over. We're still about a half hour out."

"Alice, they'll need that long to get an ambulance no matter where we land."

She glances back at Rex, then at me. "God only knows who'll be waiting for us down there. That spotter reported us; you know he did. They run our numbers and you know who's going to show up."

"So we're in trouble either way. I'm calling for an ambulance."

"Uh oh, look who's back, and he's brought a few of his friends," Mom says, looking around the plane. Mr. Kaye and I plaster our faces against the windows and sure enough, now there's three planes trailing us. One on each side and one behind. "That sure didn't take long."

"That's not some civilian Great War retread," Mr. Kaye says, looking at the plane to our left. "I see they're sending in the big boys. DC-5."

"The United States Army Air Force. I'm honored," Mom says. "This is going to look great when I write my memoir. Hopefully not in some prison cell," she adds, sort of under her breath.

The radio sputters on. "Twin Beech 34211, identify yourself. Over."

Mr. Kaye reaches for the hand piece. He pulls a card out of his jacket pocket and speaks into the piece. "Twin Beech 34211 here. Requesting ambulance at Portland Columbia. Over."

"Identify. Over."

"Requesting you contact," and he reads from the card, "Special Agent Herman Boothby, FBI Portland office. Main 5 4545. Over."

"Identify yourself. Over."

Mr. Kaye looks over to Mom while he says, "Tell him Isao Kiramoto is turning himself in. Over."

"Who? Repeat. Over."

Mr. Kaye takes off his headset, cap, and sunglasses and shows his face to the pilot on our left.

A long silence, then, "Stand by. Over."

Then a click.

It's a long time before the radio comes back on. Then, "Twin Beech 34211. Hello, Mr. Kaye. Herman Boothby patched in here. How was Canada? Over."

"I have terms," Mr. Kaye says. "Alice Stokes is flying this plane. Her son is seriously ill. We need an ambulance to Multnomah County Hospital. We have surgeons on call for a punctured lung and request several units of O Negative blood. Over."

"I assume all this is in exchange for you? Over."

"Affirmative. Over."

"You know I have you anyway. Look around you. Over."

"Yes, Herman," Mr. Kaye says, sort of laughing. "You have me anyway. One more thing. Over."

"You aren't in much of a bargaining position, sir. Over."

"Mrs. Stokes and her children are held blameless. Over."

Mom and I look at each other.

"Blameless covers a lot of territory, sir. Over."

"I put them up to everything. Are we clear? Over."

Another long pause on the other end. Then some static. Finally, "We're clear. I'll arrange the ambulance. Over."

"Thank you. And thanks for the escort," Tommy says, looking around us. "Good to know I'm the only Jap up here. Over."

"Just doing my job, sir. Over. Out."

I hear a big sniff. "Mom, are you crying?" I ask, reaching for her.

"Don't be silly, Jewels. I'm flyin' a darn airplane. Be quiet and let me alone. This takes concentration. Flyin's one thing. Landin's another."

Mr. Kaye says, "Don't worry. You'd be amazed the landings your mother pulled off in her wild, unfettered youth."

"Well, that wild, unfettered youth was a long time ago," Mom mutters. "Go back and buckle yourself in, Jewels. We'll be landing in about twenty minutes."

I get into the seat and look down at Rex. His eyes are open and he's looking around. "Hi," I say. "Ol' Malice Alice is going to land this thing."

"I heard."

"I don't know if this is a dream or a nightmare," I say, looking around the plane. "It can't be real."

"It's just a dream, Jewels. Pretty soon we'll wake up and be in our cruddy old cabin, wondering how the heck we're going to pay the grocery bill."

We fly in silence for a while. Just the steady hum of the airplane. I sort of like this. Except for that dip! I feel it in my ears, then in my stomach. There's that shimmy like maybe the plane is shaking the sky from her wings. We dip down. Lower, lower, lower. I'm not breathing. I reach over and grab

Rex's hand. He grabs back. My eyes are closed and I'm hoping that St. Christopher under Rex's pillow is pulling for us.

Finally, *bump*! *Screech*! Bump a little up, bobble a bit down.

"Alice! Pull back!" Mr. Kaye hollers. "Easy on that wing!"

One more bump and squeal and I can tell our wheels are on the runway and we are slowing down. Rex and me lock eyeballs. His weak smile tells me she did it—Mom did it. I see Mr. Kaye grin at Mom as he says, "And the great Alice of the Air does it again."

"Alice of the Air?" I ask.

But I will have to wait for the answer because right now, in front of us, a man on the ground with flags is signaling Mom where to go. Our three escort planes are landing one, two, three behind us. We go toward some huge hangars. One of the doors is open and there, inside, is an ambulance. I see three policemen on motorcycles along with some other black cars parked nearby. And there, standing out larger than life, is Herman Boothby, Special Agent in Charge.

• • •

"Multnomah!" Mom shouts at the ambulance driver as Rex is loaded into the back. Mom climbs in after and off they shoot with two motorcycle policemen in front. They all leave me standing here and I don't even know where here is!

I look around for Mr. Kaye, who is being loaded into one of the big black cars. We don't even get to say goodbye or anything. Will I ever see him again?

"What about me?" I whisper.

"Need a lift?"

I whirl around and have to admit I'm glad I see a familiar face, even if it is from the FBI.

I'm scared, worried, and feel like I need to puke, but I'm determined that Agent Boothby will not see me cry.

"Come on," he says. "I'll drive you to the hospital."

He opens the car door for me and we get our own motorcycle escort. It's kind of exciting, seeing other cars having to screech on the brakes just to let us through the streets. This is the fastest I've ever gone on land. It's like my whole life has gone into super-speed in one day.

I look over at Agent Boothby and try not to grin at how funny he looks with his knees nearly to the dashboard on either side of the steering wheel.

I got to get this said before we get to the hospital, though. "Um, I got to tell you something."

"A confession?" he asks. His big face holds a big smile.

"Sort of."

"Careful, Jewels. Everything you say can and will be held against you."

"For real?"

"How old are you?"

"Twelve." I wonder what age they start sending little girls to the big girls' lock up.

"So, what's your big confession? Don't worry. It'll be off the record."

"What's that mean?"

"That means you're just a kid in the middle of something you don't know much about but with people you care for a lot. And you know what?"

"What?"

"I have kids, too. So go ahead, say what you want. I'm not taking any notes."

I look out the window and wonder where to begin. "It was all my idea."

"What was your idea?"

"Hiding Mr. Kaye. I made him do it."

"You hid him? Where?"

"In the basement of the Catholic church." I look down at my hands and mutter, "Mom, Rex, and Father Donlevy had nothing to do with it. It was just me."

"Mr. Kaye said it was all his doing," he says.

"Well, he's lying. It was me—just me thinking sanctuary."

He sort of nods his head like he's putting it all together. "Sanctuary, huh?"

"Like in that *Hunchback of Notre Dame* movie. Anyway, it was all my idea. No one else had anything to do with it. Not even Mr. Kaye, and I'll sign or say anything to help him."

He smiles, nods, and says, "Sanctuary. Clever."

"Yeah, except there's no sanctuary anymore."

"Nope, I guess not."

"Am I going to jail?"

He shakes his head, keeping a smile on his face and his eyes on the road ahead. "Here we are," he says. The siren buzzes down and we pull into a parking lot acrost from the hospital.

"What about Mr. Kaye? What's going to happen to him?"

"That's not for me to decide."

"Who's to decide?"

"The United States Attorney General." That sounds pretty darn serious—an attorney *and* a general to boot. Then Agent Boothby adds, kindly, "Come on. Let's get you inside and see how your brother is."

Mom pulls me to her for a hug the minute she sees us enter the waiting room. "Thank you for bringin' her, Mr. . . . ?"

"Boothby," I remind her. "Where's Rex?"

"They had two doctors waitin' and rushed him right in through those doors. They're goin' to operate."

"Don't worry, Mrs. Stokes," Agent Boothby says, his long fingers fiddling with the brim of his hat. "He's in good hands. Come on, let's sit down." He indicates some chairs.

"I'm just relieved there *are* any doctors left," Mom says, pulling a hankie out of her bag. "I don't mind rationing food and gasoline, but I'll be darned if I am going to ration my son's life!"

"I don't blame you for being angry. A lot has changed, hasn't it?" he says.

She sinks into a chair and starts to cry. I cannot tell

you the last time I saw Alice Stokes cry like this. I mean, head in hands, out-and-out bawl. I sit next to her and put a hand on her leg, and Agent Boothby folds himself into a chair nearby. He seems sort of awkward, being so big and in such a small chair and with Mom crying and all, but there he sits, waiting with us.

Just waiting. It's hard to be so still, so quiet, after what we've been through. Agent Boothby brings us lunch from the café acrost the street and gets Mom cigarettes. I get a comic book. He lights her cigarettes, smiles kindly at me, makes sure we have coffee. One, two, three—it's been almost four hours now.

"I don't know how we're goin' to pay for all this," Mom says to me.

I'm seeing those Japanese books stuffed with money sitting in the basement of St. Bart's, waiting for me to flap them free of cash. But Agent Boothby probably doesn't need to know that so I just squeeze Mom's hand and say, "Mr. Kaye wouldn't want you to worry, Mom."

Her head comes up. "Oh, Tommy . . ." She looks around the room like maybe she's trying to find him. Her eyes land on Agent Boothby. "What's going to happen to him?"

He gives a big sigh. "It's all going to be very complicated. We put quite a premium on a man with his, shall we say, his 'qualifications'?"

"What's that mean?" I ask, grateful at least he doesn't say anything about a jail cell and throwing away the key.

"That means Mr. Kaye is a very valuable man."

I look toward the emergency room doors where somewhere beyond my brother is on an operating table, his chest wide open.

"Yeah," I say. "I already knew that."

CHAPTER 42

Rex is still in surgery. It's been more than five hours now. Mom and Agent Boothby are down the hall, getting an update. How long can it take to fix a few ribs? A janitor comes by and pulls all the blackout curtains together and that leaves just those florescent lights overhead, making this place look even scarier and colder than it already feels.

"Well?" I ask as Mom comes back into the waiting room.

"They had to get a specialist from another hospital," she says. She's looking so tired, so worn. I wisht there was something I could do. Was it just this morning we were home in Sea Park?

Agent Boothby looks at his watch. He's looking tired, too. "I'm afraid I have to leave, Mrs. Stokes."

Mom looks up. "Of course. It's late. Your wife must be worried."

He smiles and says, fingering his hat again, "No, she's passed on. My kids, though. Well, you know about kids when left alone too long." He winks down at me.

"You've been very kind," Mom says.

"I've made arrangements for you and Jewels at the Hillside Motor Court. It's just down the road. Nothing fancy, but clean and within walking distance."

"I don't know how to thank you."

"Well," he says, "I know what it's like to sit and wait in a place like this."

He says good evening, puts on his hat, and it's like he's a giant shadow as he walks down the darkened hall and disappears around the corner.

Mom looks after him. "I guess you never know about a man until there's an emergency," she says.

"Yeah," I say. "And I thought he was going to arrest me."

She takes my hand.

• • •

"Mrs. Stokes?"

I pop awake.

"Yes?" Mom says, rising to meet the nurse, a hospital blanket dropping from her shoulders.

"Your son is in a special care unit right now."

"What's that?"

"It's very normal after surgeries like this. He's had a hard time. Don't worry. We think he's going to recover."

"Fully?" Mom asks.

"That's hard to say. But he's out of the woods now."

"When can I see him?"

"We'll come get you when we move him to his own room. Let's give it another hour."

Poor Mom is *this* close to melting into a puddle of tears. "Thank you," she says. And as soon as we lock eyes, talk about melting! It's funny, I never remember us crying together. One or the other, yes, but never both at the same time, especially while hugging. Us Stokes don't get good news very often, but when it comes, well . . .

"Come on, honey, let's get us some fresh air."

The hospital is on a hill overlooking the Willamette River. But here, in the total darkness, you'd never know there's a city as big as Portland out there somewhere.

"Kind of spooky, isn't it?" I say.

"It all is."

"Mom? Are you going to tell me?"

"About what?"

"About how it is you and Mr. Kaye, I mean, the flying and the airplane and everything?"

"Well, I was going to wait until you kids were older."

"Why?"

"Because I'm not exactly proud of some of my past."

"But being a pilot, Mom, that's something to be proud of!" I say. "I mean, a man pilot is pretty cool, but a woman pilot? You're like Amelia Earhart, only not lost."

"Back in the day, maybe I could have been like her. There's lots I could have been." She looks to the sky and sighs. "There was a lot of money to be made during Prohibition."

"What's that got to do with—"

"Well, I met your father and fell in love. I think I broke Tommy's heart. But, really, he's Japanese and I'm white and, well, you know . . . it isn't . . ."

"But what's my father got to do with Prohibition?"

"Well, for a very short period of time, the four of us—your father, Tommy Kaye, Edna Glick, and me—well, we were very successful in the trades."

"What trades?"

She looks at me and gives me her goofy smile, the one I haven't seen in ages. "The rum trades."

"You were a rum runner?"

"I'd rather you didn't sound so impressed. It was highly dangerous and even more highly illegal. We had quite an operation goin' for us. Remember that day in the Kozy Korner when the whole town was implicatin' Tommy?"

"Yes. The search light, the lookout tower, the cash," I say, adding things up. "You needed all that for—"

"Yep. But it was your father who, well, got into runnin' other things. Drugs and such. That's gettin' pretty serious. Anyway, runnin' rum is how Tommy got his money for the Stay and Play. And that's how your father got ten-to-twenty in prison and that's how Tommy and me got our flyin' tickets pulled for life. I could go to jail for flyin' that plane today. Well, just let them try to put me away! I have kids to raise and a business to run."

So, in the blink of an eye, everything I thought I knew about my mother has changed.

CHAPTER 43

"Now, I want to prepare you," the nurse says, stopping just in front of Rex's room. "He looks pretty awful."

Mom takes my hand and we walk in together. The nurse did not lie! Rex is tucked into bed with bottles of stuff running into him and tubes of stuff running out of him. He has an oxygen mask on but the nurse takes it off, saying, "I think we can dispense with this for a few minutes." She looks over to Mom and says, "You *do* know not to smoke around oxygen, don't you?"

"Yes," she says. "I know."

"Good, because after what all of us have gone through, I'd hate to have us all go ka-blooey," the nurse says, using one of my favorite words.

"How long will he be asleep?" Mom asks.

"Probably another five or six hours, which is good. We want him to rest. Now, you can curl up in that bed there," she says to Mom. Then, to me, "I can have a cot brought in for you."

"Yes, thank you," Mom says, looking down at Rex, pale in the glow of the overhead light. She pulls up a chair and sits next to him. "Jewels, you crawl into the bed. I want to stay up with him just a bit longer."

I'm so tired, I don't know if I can even fall asleep, but the bed feels cool and comfortable.

• • •

For a minute, I forget where I am. I've never woken up in a hospital room before. I rise on my elbow and look around. Mom's asleep in the cot at the foot of Rex's bed and the light's off. Then I hear some talking just outside the door. I sit up.

The door slowly edges open, throwing the light from the hallway onto Rex's bed. A man with a flashlight comes in and looks down at Rex.

The flashlight goes to Mom, then to me.

"Hi, Jewels," the man says.

"Mr. Kaye!" I cry out, springing Mom awake.

"Tommy!" We both run to him.

"I'll bet you didn't think you'd see me again, huh? How's our boy?"

Mr. Kaye goes to the bed and looks down at Rex. "Lord, what this poor kid's been through."

Mom places her hand on Rex's forehead. "They tell me he's goin' to be fine. He had a fever after the operation, but it's gone now. The fluids are goin' in and comin' out."

"Always a good sign," Mr. Kaye says.

"I don't understand," Mom says. "Didn't they arrest you after we landed?"

"Boy, did they! They even had some charges left over from . . ." He stops when his eyes land on me.

"I told her," Mom says, looking at me.

"Everything?"

"Are you crazy? No. But how did you get here? Tommy, don't tell me you escaped!"

"I know a nice church basement in a nice quiet town," I say.

He looks at me and smiles kindly. "Yes, I'm familiar with it." Then, to Mom, "Look, I have to go. My escort is waiting outside. I just came to see how Rex is and to say goodbye."

"Are they taking you to Leavenworth?" I ask, unable to speak above a whisper.

He reads the scared tone in my voice and says, "No. Not Japan, either. They're flying me to DC tomorrow."

"To the FBI office?" I ask, my eyebrows hitting my hair.

"That's all I can say," he says. "Top secret. Seems being Japanese right now, knowing how to fly, speaking the language, well, that's all I can say. I'll tell you all about it when the war is over. We'll have wonderful stories."

We share a silence. Then Mom says, "I'm sorry I called you a Jap, Tommy."

He takes a lock of her hair and places it behind her ear. "Well, it's an honest mistake."

He pulls her to him and they hold each other for a long time, even sway a little, like maybe they're having them one last dance. Then they pull me into their embrace and, like we did a million years ago, we sway to music only we can hear. When we pull apart, he kisses my mother, then takes my hand, kisses it, and holds it to his chest.

"And you, my Jewels. My one, true, good, honest, trusting, lunatic friend. How can I ever thank you?"

"By leaving out the lunatic," I say, wiping a tear off my face.

"But that's what I love the most about you. It takes a lunatic to want to save one man from a whole town." He holds both me and Mom to him again, and we're in what feels like a family embrace.

He finally breaks away. "Look at you two," he says. "Bawling like babies. That any way to send your man off to war? How about some smiles?"

We give him the best we can.

"And will you show Hero a picture of me every day so he doesn't forget what I look like?"

"Yeah," I say.

"Good." He backs away slowly.

"Don't go," I whisper, taking a step toward him. Mom pulls me to her.

"I have to. I just have to," he says. Then, I see his big, wonderful grin. "See you in the funny papers."

And like that, he's gone.

THE LAST CHAPTER

It's August 15, 1945. My birthday. Sweet sixteen.

But guess what? No one even mentions my birthday to me. Not one person. But I don't care. We're all celebrating something else today. Today the whole earth is celebrating the end of the war. Japan surrendered—another day that will live in infamy. Now maybe the world will get back to normal, whatever or wherever that is! So I don't mind sharing my birthday.

I think about my war years a lot. War is more than two men in different uniforms trying to kill each other. No, I know war is a lot more than that. It's opinions, it's rumors, it's anger, it's sorrow, it's pride—and the one thing it isn't is fair. But, I'm not in charge, and like everyone else, I just do the best I can with what I have.

Pooooo-berty and I finally parted ways. I am no Maureen O'Hara but, as my mother tells me, "You are comin' along just fine in the woman department, Jewels honey!" I have a figure. I have grown, thank heaven! I'm not going to be a fireplug like Edna Glick. Heck, even my grades have improved! This keeps up, I'll hit my junior year maybe not with honors, but with no dishonors, either. And get this: I have just been chosen Sea Park's first ever *girl* Town Hood. Now I get to watch over all the kids in Sea Park and make sure they all toe the line.

It seems like December 7, 1941, was a million years ago, and it seems like it was just yesterday, too. I can honestly say not one person in all of Sea Park is unchanged by what we now call World War Two.

Corliss Ainsley is still waiting for "her man in uniform," Arley, to come home. Bet it won't work out. She's become a lot more than a waitress helping Mom run the Stay and Play, and I'll bet Arley has become a lot more than a fry cook while serving in North Africa.

Eldon Johnson had already reported for duty by the time we got Rex out of the hospital. Poor Eldon died in Europe in 1943, and sometimes I feel bad about wishing he'd drop dead back when it was me against everyone. His mom proudly hangs a medal they sent her in their front window.

Bully Hallstrom left town and no one knows where he went or cares if he ever comes back. Let Bully bully someplace else. The rest of the SCOUTS enlisted and all survived.

Little Janie Johnson got herself a special award from the governor for collecting more scrap than any kid in the whole state of Oregon. Guess where she got a lot of her scrap? It was in June 1942, just after we were all working hard at saving each other's lives. Ft. Stevens up at the mouth of the Columbia River got shelled by—yep, you guessed it—a Japanese submarine that peeked out of the ocean long enough to take some pot shots. Alls they hit was the backstop of a baseball field, but it made for good scrap metal. I always thought that was sort of funny—the scrap metal a Japanese shell made was made back into some bullets to shoot back at the Japanese. War is just crazy sometimes!

Anyway, if Janie was tough to be around before, you should see her now! As Town Hood, I'm keeping my eye on that little con artist. Look out world when pooooo-berty hits her!

The McAloon twins had to stop their horse beach patrol when those huge blimps out of Tillamook started going up and down the coast. Every one of their beach nags pitched a fit when they saw the blimps. They were, the McAloons and the horses, getting too old for war, anyway. Leo McAloon died last winter. It was sad. They say that Siamese twins will die within a few hours of each other. They weren't attached physically, but they were just about everywhere else. Frank died within the month. I put their horses out to pasture up in the fields beyond the Feed and Seed. It was a sad day for all of us two- and four-legged friends.

You will never in a million years guess what happened to Sheriff Hillary. She got remarried to none other than Special Agent in Charge Herman Boothby. He came to Sea Park quite often after our flight to Portland to save Rex's life and we all got to know him well. At first, his visits were to do "wrap up work." But soon I figured out what—or who—it was he was wanting to wrap up: the widow Sheriff Hillary Dutton. They now live in Portland. He's still with the FBI, and she's raising his kids and probably making them take turns as Town Hood up there.

Father Donlevy turned down an offer to transfer to a bigger church in '44. He said right from the pulpit one day that folks in Sea Park are in pretty serious need of good counsel and a mean sermon now and then. That facial tick he developed during our days of sanctuary finally went away.

And how's this for irony? Someone accused Mayor George Schmidtke and his wife, Alma, of being sympathetic to the German cause. Yep! Shipped them and their hand-stuffed sausages off to Seattle and were never shipped back.

Edna Glick got appointed temporary mayor and one of these days maybe Sea Park will get around to officially electing her. It's funny about Sea Park. We just sort of do what we have to do, legal or no.

Good ol' Edna Glick. That woman hasn't changed any in all the years I've known her. She looks the same, dresses the same, acts the same. I like that about her. Turns out, she was on the receiving end of some of that rum Mom and Mr. Kaye ran during Prohibition and had to pay a lot of money in fines and stuff. Here's some more irony: Mr. Kaye loaned her the money for the fines and now we know where he got that money in the first place. Talk about robbing Uncles Peter and Paul to pay Uncle Sam!

Now to Rex. He couldn't stand at graduation because of his surgery, but he passed his exams and got his diploma. Then he enlisted. Yes, he enlisted on the very day he turned eighteen, September 13, 1942. He didn't tell anyone what he was doing except me. I remember waiting in the car outside the enlistment center in Astoria for him.

As he got into the car, I said, "I told you they wouldn't take you! Look at you! You're still ten pounds underweight from your surgery. You can barely lift a book, let alone a gun."

He handed me a piece of paper.

"What's this mean?" I asked him.

"It means I'm to report to Portland on September twenty-fifth."

"Mom's going to kill you! I can't believe you actually passed."

"There wasn't any physical, Jewels. They don't want this," he said, indicating his body. "They want *this*." He pointed to his head. "You know those college entrance essays and exams I was working so hard on?"

"Yes."

"Well, somehow Agent Boothby got wind of them. Anyway, there's some legal clerk jobs with the Army.

They're going to send me to a special school back east and everything!"

Talk about the ol' Oriental rug being pulled out from under you! I wanted to dissolve into the air. "You can't leave, Rex," I said. "Mom needs you. I need you. Who's going to teach me how to debate? And what about—"

"Jewels," he said, "I have to do this."

"No, you don't. It goes against everything you . . ." I stopped when I saw his face.

"I just have to."

I remembered Mr. Kaye saying that very same thing in the hospital room. "Don't go," I whispered to Rex, the same as I did with Mr. Kaye.

"Jewels, you see how this war has changed everything in our lives. And here we're sitting pretty in paradise! The only thing we're without is some gas and some sugar. Big deal. Imagine what this war is doing to all those millions of other people around the world. I've got to do *something*."

So, Rex went to war—only his war was sitting at a desk and helping some military lawyers get things settled with the Japanese people who were unearthed and unsettled. The last we heard, he'll be coming home around Thanksgiving. In his latest letter, he wrote that some politicians are going to offer all the servicemen a free ticket to college! I can just see Rex, in his room at the Washington, DC, YMCA, typing out more college entrance essays. Bet he'll have the pick o' the litter!

Oh, speaking of Thanksgiving, Sailor the Turkey of War is still with us. And no, we are *not* going to eat him, even to celebrate Rex's homecoming. It's like something from that first day of infamy has to live on. And since turkeys can live for up to twenty years, I'll have to take good care of him. He follows Hero just about everywhere. Tourists get a real kick out of it and are always taking photographs of them. But to be honest, I think it embarrasses Hero to have a dang turkey as a sidekick.

Good ol' Hero. You know there are still times I see him stick that nose of his in the air as though he's sniffing for a trace of Tommy Kaye.

Now about Malice Alice Stokes, even though we hardly ever call her that anymore. I think she's the one who's changed the most from this war. She stepped up once everything from Kaye Enterprises fell on her shoulders. She's even taken on caring for all the bonsai that survived, including some grafted pieces of The Old Man. She says they give her just what they gave Tommy Kay—sanity and serenity. Yes, I'm talking about the same Alice Stokes!

I'm not supposed to talk about it, but I guess now that the war is over, I can. Agent Boothby got pretty interested in Mom being an ex-pilot, pulled ticket or no. He found her old file from when her rum running all went ka-blooey. Agent Boothby told her a talent like hers was a pretty sad thing to waste. Now, she couldn't go off and join those WASPs moving planes all around, but she was called on several times to move other things around for the

FBI—prisoners, politicians, and secret papers every once in a while. Kind of like honest to goodness spy stuff! Alice Stokes, special attaché to the FBI. Doesn't that sound nifty?

You know, I never thought I'd say this, but I'm sort of proud of the old lady. It didn't come all at once, but rather in itty little bits and pieces. Sort of like a bonsai that takes its own sweet time to grow into what it's going to be. Like Mr. Kaye used to say, "Sort of balanced in a lopsided way." That describes Mom all over.

Oh yes, remember that old footlocker under her bed she called a hope chest? She finally handed me the key and said I could have everything inside. I'll never be as tall as her, so the jodhpurs, leather jacket, and boots she wore when she was Alice of the Air will never fit me. But I'm keeping them all the same. I'll put the photos and fliers and newspaper clippings and arrest warrants into a scrapbook someday. She'll get a kick out of that when she's old and gray. Okay, when she's old. Alice Stokes will *never* let her hair go gray. Not as long as there's a hair on her head and henna rinse at the corner drugstore!

So, now I come to Mr. Tommy Kaye, also known as Mr. Isao Kiramoto. I still have a hard time thinking he'll never be coming back. But I thank God he never lived to learn we put the atom bomb over Nagasaki, orphanages and all. That news alone would have killed him.

Special Agent Boothby, on one of his trips to Sea Park last spring, dropped by the café as we were closing up and gave us the news himself.

"He died a hero for his country," he said. He handed Mom Mr. Kaye's dog tags, a Purple Heart, and a Distinguished Service Cross. "A one-of-a-kind man." Agent Boothby went on to tell us that Mr. Kaye had been ushered into the Nisei Military Intelligence Service. "The first thing we did was to promote him from Issei to Nisei. Tommy called it a mere technicality."

So Mr. Kaye went to war as a Nisei in the 442nd Regimental Combat Team. Flew combat in Europe, took a few lives, saved a few lives. After the Germans surrendered, he was sent to the Pacific theater as an interpreter. He was shot in the back of the head while sitting at a table, interpreting for Admiral Halsey dockside somewhere in the South Pacific. Tommy Kaye took the bullet meant for Admiral Halsey.

Mom just sat, looking down at the medals and slowly nodding her head, tears and mascara running. Finally, she looked up.

"What's this?" she asked, looking at a folded set of papers.

"His will. Standard for military induction," Agent Boothby replied.

Mom got everything. But the will also said that there wasn't to be any funeral of any kind. Mr. Kaye said he didn't want to make hypocrites out of the whole town. I didn't understand it then, but I think I do now.

So, Tommy Kaye didn't live to see his bunkers built, either. Once more men come home from the war, Mom is going to put Rex in charge of the project, though. Turns out, The Bunkers was the name of the golf course Mr. Kaye was going to build on all his land.

When Agent Boothby returned the maps and the rest of the stuff they had confiscated from the warehouse after Pearl Harbor, he said, "Well, we had every reason to worry. After all—"

"I know. It was war," Mom said, fingering Mr. Kaye's dog tags. "Tommy loved golf. And he loved this town. Makes total sense to me. Now."

"And I'll be the first man to tee off when you get it built," he said, patting her hand.

After he left, Mom went upstairs to the ballroom at the Look-Sea Lounge. It was dark except for the huge windows spilling in a beautiful sunset. She just stood there, a champagne glass in her hand.

"Mom? You okay?" I asked as I came up behind her.

"Pour yourself a glass," she said, pointing to the bottle on the bar. I did and then joined her in front of the windows. She looked at me, her face a total wreck, but her eyes sort of calm.

"To Tommy Kaye," was all she said, lifting her glass to the horizon then taking a sip. "The best enemy anyone ever had."

I did the same, then left her alone to the rest of the bottle, and her memories.

I found Hero and gave him the sad news. Call me crazy, but I know that dog mourned.

Anyway, now that the war is officially over, there's talk of some big city newspaper man who wants to write up Tommy Kaye's story. Well, if he comes to me with questions, good luck! I'm not talking. A story like Mr. Kaye's isn't meant for newspapers. It isn't for strangers or gossips or the *Sand Dune Telegraph*. A story like his is meant to be told around a campfire, in a smoke-filled room, or late at night with the lights down low, as though the windows are all covered in black cloth. It should be told someplace quiet, someplace incommunicado, like the basement of a church. That's how quiet hero stories should get passed on. Sort of like I'm passing it on right now. Just you and me.

But enough of this. According to the *Sand Dune Telegraph*, some kids are throwing a surprise birthday party for me tomorrow at the bowling alley. Yes, me. Town Hood. The Town Clown that everyone laughed at back in '42. How's that for irony? So I'm going incommunicado myself for a few hours.

Have to go practice looking surprised.

Author's Note

It's always difficult to address the use of disrespectful slang in a work of historical fiction. One needs to be true to the times, yet sensitive to the current way of thinking. What went unnoticed—and indeed was encouraged—by the culture during a time of war is simply inappropriate today. Words to describe foreigners and especially the enemy such as Jap, Kraut, Chinaman, and even Oriental were commonly used during the World War II-era, but are considered derogatory today.

People in the 1940s used different slang than we do today, and some words in this book might not look familiar to you. To read more about the slang used throughout the book, please visit the author's website at www.plattbooks.com.

JUST WHO IS THIS RANDALL PLATT?

(Hint: Not a guy!)

Randall Platt writes fiction for adults and young adults and those who don't own up to being either. Platt, a lifelong resident of the Upper Left Hand Corner, has been a full-time writer for twenty-five years, which is certainly long enough to know better. But since Platt finds no shortage of fascinating characters and stories springing from the beautiful Pacific Northwest, the books just keep coming. This explains why nearly all of Platt's novels take place in Washington or Oregon, the exception being *Liberty's Christmas*, which takes place in Texas during the

Depression. A film, *Promise The Moon*, has been made of Platt's humorous western, *The Four Arrows Fe-As-Ko*.

Platt's novels have won several awards including twice winning the Willa Literary Award and twice winning the Will Rogers Medallion for best young adult literature. Platt has also received the Keystone State Reading Award and has been a finalist for the PEN Center USA award as well as the Washington State Book Award. Platt is a sought-after speaker and presenter at conferences, schools, and libraries, and specializes in fun and honest answers shot straight from the hip.

Several times a week, Platt puts away the words and heads for the nearest handball court or hiking trail.

More information than you ever wished to know about Platt is available at www.plattbooks.com, Facebook, and LinkedIn, as well as the usual book websites.